The Bluejay Shaman

The Bluejay Shaman

Lise McClendon

Walker and Company
New York

THANK YOU TO the many people who helped with this book, including Andy Villanueva and John Munis, Federal Bureau of Investigation; Pat Coffey, formerly of Camas Prairie, Montana; Jean Larsen Hurd; the books of Sigrid Undset; Mitch Young of the Lake County attorney's office; my Big Sky writing friends; my editor, Michael Seidman; my nonpareil boys, Evan and Nick; and my forever friend, my husband, Kipp.

First published in the United States of America in 1994 by Walker Publishing Company, Inc.

Published simultaneously in Canada by Thomas Allen & Son Canada, Limited, Markham, Ontario

Library of Congress Cataloging-in-Publication Data
McClendon, Lise.
The bluejay shaman / Lise McClendon.
    p.   cm.
ISBN 0-8027-3179-1
I. Title.
PS3573.E19595.B58   1994
813'.54—dc20   94-32769
                      CIP

Printed in the United States of America
2 4 6 8 10 9 7 5 3 1

∇

Prologue

THE TETONS SCRATCHED the summer sky, still sporting a hint of orange from the long-gone sun. Rough and hard, the mountains proved man's impermanence. Woman's too.

When I pointed my old car north, leaving behind the gallery in Jackson, the hum—the *hymn*—of the road gave me the feeling my life was going somewhere. Being on the road was like that, a trickster highway. Somewhere in the distance is happiness, satisfaction, whatever it takes to feel good. Over that rise. Just a little farther.

The mountains were quiet, sleeping. They never looked the same twice but they always sounded like peace to me. But I crossed the pass into Idaho and drove north. For a Norwegian a purity fills a northern mission, like the search for the Holy Grail. The lights shine bright in the North.

I grew up in Montana but my northern mission wouldn't bring me back my childhood. Montana had changed. The mountain ranges still sprang up from the prairies like gopher tunnels in a rich man's lawn. Cowpunchers still tried to live out their fantasies. And some of the original inhabitants, the Indians, remained.

But sure as I'd left, some other folks had moved in. The people I met in Montana were older but not necessarily wiser. That happens to a lot of us. But they should have known the wheels of time go in one direction only. You can't fight it.

Try as you might.

1

The hinges of the metal doors of the U-Haul trailer complained, the sound multiplying in the cavernous police warehouse. The darkness in the trailer cloaked unrecognizable shapes. I peered harder, willing my eyes to adjust, smelling mildew, dust, oil paints melting, and canvas rotting. The heat in the metal barn was stifling. Sweat trickled down my back as I shifted my clipboard to my other arm, stuck the pencil behind my ear, and stepped in the open jaws of the trailer.

Before I could begin examining the art objects inside, the job I was being paid to do if I ever got the chance, the sound of footsteps echoed across the space. The warehouse must have been an old airplane hangar, designed to make humans feel like ants. Whatever it was, it attracted and trapped heat like a giant Buick.

Lieutenant Malsome had just given me the pep talk, the indoctrination. Interruptions make me irritable. Make that cranky. I like to work, with order and perseverance, and most of all I like results.

The footsteps came toward me, louder, through the tangle of recovered bicycles, shelves of unclaimed tools, toys, and guns, speedboats and motorcycles, even a moon-carved wooden outhouse. I wondered briefly why an outhouse had been seized, and if it was still in use. Montana, land of my birth, was not that backward. Not anymore.

The feet belonged to a lady cop, Rita Fenimore, young and dark with chipmunk cheeks and sleek figure, a rookie no doubt. She looked at my blue business suit, heels, and purple blouse (the only concession to my true nature) as I stepped back out of the trailer.

"Miss Thorssen?"

I smoothed down the jacket of my suit, wiping dust off the skirt. This outfit had gotten me lots of places and lots of information. I had to be nice to it.

"Call me Alix."

Ms. Fenimore held her head straight on her rigid neck. There must be a class in eye contact. "The lieutenant wants me to ask you a few questions, for the files." She held a clipboard like mine.

I tried to smile at her. Ms. Fenimore needed a smile. "Can I work while you interrogate?"

Her face darkened. I climbed back into the trailer. It offered almost enough headroom to stand, but not quite. I kicked off my heels and kneeled down before the cloth-draped square on the right side of the trailer.

"The first question is your full name and address."

I pulled the drape from the painting. "Alix Skipp Thorssen. 36 North Broadway, Jackson, Wyoming. 36-24-36."

Ms. Fenimore's pencil stopped. "That's your zip code?"

"My phone number."

"Really?"

So much for Miss Know-it-all. "It's a joke, Rita."

I put my clipboard on the floor of the trailer and picked up the painting. Inching out backward, I stepped to the concrete floor to look at the painting in the light.

The large canvas was covered with the painting of a mountain landscape à la Albert Bierstadt, complete with rosy rainbow over the lake and magical mountains that looked cool yet inviting. Rita sucked in her breath.

"Like it?"

She nodded. "Much."

I looked closely at an odd patch in the upper right corner. The paint was crackled, as on many old works, but . . . I poked daintily at the spot. A tiny piece came off on my finger.

"Miss Thorssen! The lieutenant said to make sure you didn't damage any of the works."

"Did he?" I leaned the Bierstadt-imitator against the trailer and stood back. It was good, very good. "This one isn't going into any museums anyway."

Rita rounded the trailer to look at the painting. "A forgery? But it's so beautiful."

"The best ones are."

I hung the cloth back over the painting. The in-depth stuff was going to have to wait until later. I needed an idea of what I was dealing with first. I'd get in touch with the FBI office, the art forgery guys. I made a note on my clipboard to call Kenyon in Chicago and climbed back in the trailer.

"I need the name of your business and any partners, silent or general."

Ms. Fenimore was getting boring. But the treasures— potential treasures—lay waiting in the dim trailer.

"Second Sun Gallery, same address. My partner is Paolo Segundo. He isn't silent."

"A foreign national?"

I paused, lifting the lid on a box. Paolo could still give me pause though we'd been business partners, nothing more, for six months. When we came out to Jackson Hole from New York seven years before it had been different. But our relationship worked better as strictly business. We redis- covered that at least once a year.

"Naturalized. From Argentina."

Ms. Fenimore scribbled; I lifted an Indian basket wrapped in tissue paper. It was round and looked very old. It would require research to figure out where it was from. I made a note to call my friend at Sotheby's auction house in New York.

"It's says here affiliations and organizations," the policewoman said.

I gave her my credentials. "Where did they find this trailer?"

"Abandoned at a rest stop on the interstate about a

hundred miles from here," she said. "They traced it to a U-Haul dealer in Clearwater, Florida."

"Who rented it?"

"Phony name and address. They're still checking."

At noon I left the police warehouse to meet my sister Melina, my other reason—besides getting a breather from Paolo—for taking this consulting job. Melina lived in Missoula with her husband, Wade, an anthropology professor at the University of Montana. She was doing graduate work in sociology and teaching classes at the local career center.

We settled into a booth at Montana Pies, a place that looked like a vinyl-clad truck stop but smelled like your grandmother's kitchen. I noticed the circles under Melina's eyes when she rubbed them behind her glasses. We hadn't had much time to talk late last night when I arrived.

"So tell me about you and Paolo." Melina sipped her water.

"History. For good this time," I said. Her question, unlike Ms. Fenimore's, didn't catch me off-guard. "He's got a new girlfriend. Rock climber, blond. Muscular thighs, sinewy arms. Thinner too."

I expected a comment about that description, like, why do you always compare them to yourself? But Melina slipped away mentally, gazing out the window at the shimmering asphalt parking lot. I tried to read her face. Becoming a salesman had made me a student of faces, of people. To kill the boredom I tried to read each one.

But Norwegians were the worst. Melina and I had been brought up to show no pain; her face was placid, blank. But that could sometimes be a clue too.

"So what is it?" I said, cutting to the chase.

"What is what?" Melina smoothed back her frosted hair, pulled into a tight ponytail. She was shorter than me, more like our mother. I resembled Rollie, our lanky father who had died twenty years ago.

"Something's bothering you," I said.

She cast down her eyes at the tabletop. "It's nothing."

"Spill it. This is your sister."

She looked outside again. "I'm just worried about Wade. He's off doing his thing on the reservation."

"He does that every summer, doesn't he?"

"This year there are all these groups around that drive him crazy. Crystal types, you know? Easterners. I don't know."

"So?"

"Well, he hates them, to put it simply. He just hates them."

Our burgers came. There was little more to say about ol' Wade. My sister's husband had always been different from us, wearing his heart on his sleeve, ready to do battle with the forces against him and the Indians he loved. Worrying about him at this late date was like stirring the ashes of a forest fire after the trees have burned. Interesting but beside the point.

Under Ms. Fenimore's eager eye I worked through the afternoon, cataloging, measuring, sorting everything in the trailer, from pots to baskets to paintings to ancient beads and ceremonial masks. The thief, or owner, had a penchant for Indian artifacts and old western art. The Indian items would require more than a bit of work to track down since they were probably looted from public land. Some traveled in underground circles, from dealers to collectors and back, for years before surfacing at a major auction. At Second Sun Gallery we were offered not a small number of artifacts of questionable provenance. We did our homework and steered clear of most of them.

The policewoman and I wrapped up each piece and put it back in the trailer rather than risk leaving it sitting out, even in a police warehouse. The heat made my business suit a soggy rag. The artworks would be better off protected from the atmosphere. By the time I got back to Melina's I was ready for a shower.

I climbed out of the Saab Sister, my trusty '67, maroon with gray-primed rust spots, in front of Melina and Wade's house. Their bungalow on Blaine Street had a permanent look. Nothing ever changed here. I sighed, feeling the ache in my shoulders and the prospect of changing out of my suit.

At eleven o'clock the sleeping porch was still. A breeze struggled to form in the elm tree but gave up. Somewhere a dog barked rhythmically, trapped, a broken record.

Melina and I had eaten dinner outside in the purple dusk on the broken concrete patio, cold tuna sandwiches and carrot sticks and potato chips. Anything not to cook, not to heat up the house. She still looked preoccupied, distant, and I worried about her. She refused to talk about Wade. A hot summer electricity hung in the air like a live wire.

Now, after sitcoms, local news, and too many gin and tonics, I lay on top of the sheets in an old T-shirt, staring at the family pictures arranged artlessly on the cheap wood paneling of the screened porch. Photographs of past lives, including my own. That wasn't me, was it, with blond curls, grinning at my dad? Was I ever that young, that pure?

The phone rang. I heard Melina jump from bed and run to the hall. When she gasped, I sat up. She stood in the doorway, a righteous look in her eye, a trembling hand tugging her streaked hair.

"It's Wade." Her voice rose, breaking.

"What is it?" I crossed my bare legs, my stomach tightening.

"Someone has died."

I was on my feet. "Not Wade. No, Mel."

She shook her head, holding her ribs to keep the sobs inside. "He's in jail, Alix. They think he killed her."

At one o'clock, I answered the door to find a young policeman, Missoula City, standing uneasily under the porch light. He and Paolo could have been brothers. His dark eyes had trouble finding mine. Just a courtesy, he said, to let us know Wade had been charged. Melina fell apart in the kitchen, over the sink. She had been waiting for this to happen, for something to boil over, all her married life. Her first nervous breakdown, waiting in the wings, finally free. The tears were bitter, the moans pierced my heart. By four in the morning we piled into the Saab Sister and hit the road for Polson.

Even in the dead of night the hum of the road had the power to soothe me. Whatever mess Wade Fraser had gotten himself into, we would get him out. It was a mistake. He was a scientist, not a killer. He was a husband to my sister.

The road lulled Melina into a fitful sleep that provided the body, not the mind, with a semblance of rest. She needed that rest. Her cheek lay against the seat back as I kept my eyes on the white line, the edge of the headlights' glare. The road bucked like the earth was tipping off its axis, careening crazily through space, to a place I didn't know, didn't want to know.

But to get back, I had to go forward. That much I knew.

$\triangledown$

2

Sweat beaded on my upper lip. The stale, hot air in the cement-block room where my sister and I waited for Wade made me sleepy.

My eyelids closed. The long night of driving melted away. My body seemed to rise from the wooden chair until I could no longer feel the straight-railed back against my spine. The shake and rattle in my head was the river, the black satin water tickling smooth stones and fish snouts. Rising, rising, breaking the cool, clean surface, smelling of bark and pine and river muck.

Melina coughed. I opened my eyes, the weight of an anvil on my forehead. The river was gone. We sat, waiting, the closest thing to inmates, in the Lake County jail.

Melina didn't look much better than I felt. She stood up as the guard led in her husband by the arm, wrists cuffed behind him.

She looked like she might hug him but something held her back. Her hands shook. She stuffed them in her pockets. "Wade," she whispered and sat down again.

I tried to smile at Wade. No death sentence yet. I pulled out a chair for him and we both sat down at the scratched wooden table.

Several years had passed since I'd seen Wade Fraser. He was heavier now, an extra twenty pounds on his big bear frame, with graying brown hair pulled into a thin ponytail and sliding back off his forehead. His dark, brooding eyes were bloodshot. The Roman nose glowed red from a sunburn above his unkempt salt-and-pepper beard and mustache.

Melina began. "What happened?"

"Wait a minute." I held up my hand. They looked at me expectantly. "Have you seen your lawyer?"

"Hondo came up early this morning."

"Hondo?"

Melina frowned. "He's an old friend."

"A lawyer named Hondo?" I searched their grim faces for answers. "Isn't that like having a dentist named Cowboy?" There was in fact such a person trying to pull teeth with a lasso back home in Wyoming, someone I avoided like the plague.

Humor. Mark one in the Not Appreciated column. Wade turned a grizzled cheek to me. "He's my lawyer," he said, his voice flat and final.

Wade slumped in his chair and moaned. "I gotta get out of here. It smells like piss and rat turds. I need sunlight, sky, the stars. I'm going to die in here." He moaned again, hanging his whiskered chin to his chest.

Despite my sympathy for Wade's situation, his whining seemed to confirm my suspicions about my brother-in-law. Leaving my sister for weeks at a time to go off cavorting with his Indian buddies in the name of research: it seemed juvenile and self-indulgent. I felt like slapping him. *Take it like a man, Wade. Show some spine.* He obviously wasn't Scandinavian. He made no attempt to conceal his pain. My grandmother Olava, a stoic from the old country, would have wiped down the windowsills and mopped the floors twice with the same energy Wade used whimpering.

Melina reached out to put a comforting arm around her husband. A gruff voice behind me barked: "Hands to yourself, ma'am." The guard stood with an authoritative glare against the cement-block wall. Melina sat back in her chair and began to cry silent, wrenching tears.

I stared at her glistening face, tried to think of a way to comfort her. What did she know about Wade's doings? How could I help her? "Wade," I said matter-of-factly, "tell me what happened."

He turned to me, no reaction to Melina's tears visible. His face twisted, remembering. "Last night? Last night I just went to sleep in the car. At Moody's cabin. We ate some dinner, then I went out to the car." He glanced sheepishly at Melina. She stopped crying. "I had a bottle out there."

"Liquor?"

"I sipped it a little, stashed it back under the seat, and fell asleep."

"Why did you sleep in the car?" Melina asked, wiping her nose on a tissue.

"What time was this?" I asked.

"It was about nine-thirty, I guess. It had just gotten dark." He flicked his eyes to his wife. "Moody only has one cot."

"The sheriff says you argued with Shiloh. Or what's her real name? Doris?"

"Everybody called her Shiloh," Melina said. "She was kind of a spiritual counselor."

Wade sat back in the chair as best he could with his hands cuffed behind him. "Moody and I went up to talk to Tin-Tin about the vandalism." He looked at his wife. "Did you tell her about the vandalism?"

"Not yet."

"Anyway, there's all these women there. Camping at Tin-Tin's place. Tepees and tents. The old lady, Tin-Tin, she tells me these women are going up to the Medicine Wheel, the one in the Jocko Mountains. Well, that ticked me off, them going there. I've taken students up there and not found so much as an arrowhead because that place has been so picked over. It's a sacred place to the Indians. Just thinking about these white women and their crystals and mumbo-jumbo pseudospiritual crap." He shook his head angrily.

"So you told Shiloh what?"

He took a deep breath. "All I wanted to do was to see their permit from the tribes. To make sure they had permission, you know? That's all."

"Did you raise your voice?" I asked.

Wade chuckled, a hollow sound. "Yeah, I guess you could say that."

"Then what happened?"

"Then about five or six of them jumped on me and sat on me until Tin-Tin came over. Orianna, she's the leader, she couldn't let Tin-Tin see her girls doing something so violent as sit on a man."

I glanced at my sister. "They sat on you?"

"They weren't featherweights either." He chuckled again, lighter. "Couple of them I wouldn't want to meet in a dark alley."

I rubbed the back of my neck. "Why did they sit on you, Wade?"

He worked his mouth to one side, thinking. "I really don't know."

"Did you say something to them? Something that they . . . took issue with?"

"I might have said something."

"Such as?"

He looked at his gray prison-issue pants, stained and wrinkled. "I might have called them a name. I got to yelling, I guess."

Melina looked sharply at him. "What name?"

"I asked them about the permit," Wade said. "They said it was none of my damn business. Basically. Said men weren't welcome there, in their group."

"It's an all-women group?" I asked.

Melina nodded. "What's their name, Wade?"

"Manitou Matrix." He curled his lip as he said it. Anger sparked again in his brown eyes with the memory. "Manitou, that means spirit or gods. As if they had some pipeline to the gods, the Indian spirits. They're a bunch of crazy housewives from New Jersey! I called them the Manitou Matrons or Motherfuckers or something."

I glanced at Melina. "Or something?"

"It was Motherfuckers. I got mad. And I guess I called them tribades, too. Bunch of dykes—that's what they are!

Call a spade a spade, that's all. When Shiloh told them to get me and they knocked me down and sat on me I was so fucking pissed I could have . . ."

Melina and I exchanged looks in the silence. The color drained from Wade's face. He inhaled as if catching his breath and cast his eyes at the floor.

"God, Wade," Melina gasped. "How could you say that?"

"Then you did what?" I asked.

"I walked away. Moody got me out of there, and Tin-Tin, too. Moody and I took a sweat in his new sweathouse and the anger got steamed out of me." Wade shut his eyes and sighed. "Tell her, Mel." His voice pleaded. He looked at his wife. "Tell her. Have I ever hit you? Even in anger?"

"No, Wade," she whispered.

"Never! Sure I get angry but I am not a violent person. They're the ones who attacked me! People feel threatened or something, because of my size, but I am not violent, Alix. I'm a pacifist."

"I believe you, Wade," I said, thinking about the words spoken in anger, wondering what lay behind them. Wade, gentle Wade, could be a beast. "I think we better go." Melina reached out her hand to Wade but drew it back.

At the door I turned. "What about the knife?"

He shook his head. "Last time I saw it it was in the trunk of my car. Weeks ago. Maybe months."

In the morning sun the primed patches on the Saab Sister looked worse, like pockmarks from a malignant disease. The streets of the resort town of Polson, Montana, hummed with summer tourists wearing backpacks and cameras and pork-pie hats. Some of them looked very familiar, like last week's Jackson rejects. Maybe it was just the white legs.

We crossed the bridge over the Flathead River, where it runs out of the lake, a hollow sound under the tires. The lake shimmered, pale sapphire at the shallows then deepening as it stretched north for endless blue miles.

"I'm sorry, Mel." She had pulled herself back together, the

pink in her cheeks coming back as the redness around her eyes faded.

"Nothing for you to be sorry about." She straightened up in the seat, looking over the steel blue lake with whitecaps where the wind whipped the waves. "We just have to get him out of there. You will help, won't you? I need you, Alix."

She squeezed my hand as I nodded, my throat clogged with emotion. This request went over the very private line each of us drew to others in the family. But how natural it seemed that Melina would ask, and how natural, even imperative, that I would accept.

I turned my thoughts back to Wade. So far the evidence was circumstantial. But if they found the woman's blood on the knife that would cut it—no pun intended. Enough evidence to make a charge stick with an unsophisticated jury.

What kind of person was Doris, aka Shiloh? Who was she? The cruel turns of fate. Yesterday, playing Indian with her girlfriends in the forest. Today, cold and dead, her throat slit, her blood spilled onto the grass. Wade's hunting knife found at the scene, covered with blood. The gravity of it all—to Wade, to Melina, to Shiloh Merkin—was finally sinking in.

"I think we should start with Moody," Melina said. "Since he was with Wade last night." She leaned back in the seat, tucking her blue plaid shirt into her jeans. She was rallying. After all, she had put Mom and me back together after Rollie, our father, had died. No mention of the nature of Wade's outburst, the potential for violence, and the very real hatred in his voice. Like true Norsewomen, we swept the bad stuff under the rug and looked forward.

I smiled at her. "It's good to see you." Her returning smile was for an instant pure, full of the old strength, but as the edges drooped I caught a glimpse of sadness, of disappointment. There was more she kept from me; I felt it. But Wade was the priority now. Professor Wade Fraser, Indian expert, former hippie, anthropology teacher, passionate believer, gender bigot, and husband: his own worst enemy.

3

THE DAY WARMED as if full summer had come overnight. Everywhere I looked there was something better to occupy my mind than the problems of Wade Fraser, like the way the mountains are reborn by the golden rays of summer, the melting glaciers glistening. The flowers stretch their buds toward the sky and fields of grass turn green. And the highway crews come out of mothballs to start tearing up the roads.

We were stopped by what you must now call a flagperson. You can't call a black-haired girl with a vivacious smile, no more then seventeen years old, a flagman. She wore a fluorescent orange vest over a T-shirt and jeans. I rolled down the window and smelled dust and hot asphalt. We were almost to Moody's cabin and I felt like I could nap anywhere, any time. But Melina looked ragged and frail after the visit with Wade so I summoned my strength to continue.

I wasn't as young as I used to be, when I could stay up all night on caffeine and not feel like road kill in the morning. The night's coffee had crashed in on me, imploded. I ran my fingers through my almost-blond hair. I ignored the mess of it by hiding behind my dark Ray-Bans and trusty slouch hat.

"You know what they say in Wyoming, don't you?" I smiled.

"No, what do they say in Wyoming?"

"There are two seasons: winter and road construction."

Her smile faded quickly. "Moody's place is just around that hill, if I remember right."

"You know Moody?"

"He's a friend of Wade's. He moved back to the reservation about five years ago. He's got an ex-wife and some kids in Seattle. I don't think his wife was Salish."

"But he is?" Melina nodded. "Salish and Flathead are the same thing, right?"

"Yes, but don't let Wade hear you say Flathead. Remember that time he gave us that big lecture at Easter about the jerks that missed the tribe that flattened their foreheads by five hundred miles?"

The flagperson spun her Stop sign to the Slow side. I steered the car down a pavement ledge onto a new dirt roadbed, giving the Indian girl a wave as we passed.

"Wade mentioned someone named Tin-Tin," I said as we crept along the ravaged roadbed.

"Tin-Tin Quamash. Her Christian name is Mary Virginia or something. She's a Salish elder. She's had a summer camp along the Little Bitterroot River for years. In the late sixties the University sponsored it, part of the back-to-the-earth movement. Lots of Indian sentiment then. In fact someone in Wade's department was responsible for helping get the camp started."

"Ah, a Marlon Brando type? Remember when he refused his Oscar and sent that Indian woman instead?"

"And everybody booed her," she said. "That was only the beginning. The American Indian movement was big on campus then. They advocated a violent change though, to right old wrongs."

Melina licked her lips, warming to the subject. "But after the shoot-out at Wounded Knee, remember those two federal officers were killed? After that, the movement lost a lot of its support."

"So what does this have to do with the old woman?"

"While all the political turmoil is raging, this one old woman is teaching people—reteaching people—the native ways. How to tan hides, how to bead moccasins, how to cook the native plants. She kept Salish culture alive in a time when her tribe was either rejecting it or had forgotten it."

"She sounds fascinating."

"First we talk to Moody." Her voice was deliberate and determined, strong again, I noticed with relief. She looked at the highway and yelled, "We just missed it. Back up."

Atop a grassy hill dotted with flowers a small cabin squatted, a rustic, run-down place built generations ago of sturdy lodgepole pine logs with the bark left intact. Moss and lichens grew on the walls below the galvanized tin roof, dotting the cabin with lime and gray-green splotches, making it look like a living part of the forest. We had bumped down a narrow dirt road marked by a tiny sign high on a tree, then up a hill to the edge of the forest. The sign read Camas Prairie.

An Indian man waited for us in the open doorway. Bees flew by him into the cabin. The tire marks in the tall grasses gave the place a feeling of forboding. It made me feel the weight of the events that had taken place here.

We walked the last hundred yards to the cabin. The man wore a greasy Stetson with a snakeskin band and a bear claw tied to the front. His dark eyes were framed by the broad planes of his cheeks. Black hair was gathered into a single braid down his back. He wore skintight jeans on wiry, bowed legs, dusty black cowboy boots, and a dirty yellow Crow Fair T-shirt.

His smile was toothy. "Hey, company!" He laughed. "Come have a cup of coffee."

Inside the dark one-room cabin furnished with a cot, a small, boxlike refrigerator, a hot plate on a dresser, and a transistor radio, he poured us coffee from a speckled blue tin kettle. I watched the grounds flow into my chipped china cup but smiled as he handed it to me. We took up positions on stumps outside, which served as patio furniture.

"Moody Denzel, this is my sister, Alix Thorssen," Melina said, doing the honors.

He grinned at me, showing his stained but straight teeth. "Melina. It's good to see you again."

She smiled wanly. "We've just been up to Polson, to the county jail."

Moody's face fell, making him look older. I guessed his age at mid-forties.

"We want to know what happened yesterday, Moody," I said. "Start where you first saw Wade."

"Up at Tin-Tin's camp?"

"You were there?"

He nodded. "I got a ride down the road with my sister. Sometimes my mother lets me use her car but she was playing bingo yesterday." He took a sip of coffee. "I guess I got over there in the late afternoon. My watch don't work so I never know exactly."

He pointed to the watch on his arm. "People ask me what time it is 'cause I'm wearing this watch. I say, the watch says two-thirty. Then they get all excited, 'cause they're late or something. But the watch, it always says two-thirty!"

He laughed by himself, collected his thoughts, and continued. "At Tin-Tin's camp Wade was running toward me, his face all red and arms swinging. His eyes were dark like storm clouds. He was mad about something. So we get in his car—"

"The red Cadillac?"

"Right. That boat. The Big Cherry Mojo. We get in—in a big hurry. I can tell he's riled up about something but I don't ask him what and he don't say."

The sunshine warmed my back and shoulders. I took off my old hunting jacket. It was my father's, washed twenty times but with impenetrable stains from dying grouse and pheasants in the back pocket. Melina had been shocked to see me wearing it. She had checked the back pocket and shuddered. But to me it was comfortable and familiar. My faded gray T-shirt, a cast-off from Paolo, had an ugly coffee stain down the front.

"Did Wade see you last week when he was up here?" said Melina.

"He heard about the sweathouse burning down and wanted to know all about it."

"Your sweathouse burned?" I asked.

"Somebody burned it down. It was old. My grandfather and his brother built it. Had a couch and a chair under the shelter and some old antlers my uncle tacked up there. All burned."

"You didn't see it happen?"

"It sat over the hill, down by the creek. I took my sweat early that night, before the moon came up, or I might have burnt up too." Moody's eyes widened; his hand shook as he raised his cup to his lips.

"How can you be sure it was arson?" I asked.

Moody looked embarrassed at my doubt. "We know."

Melina stood up and stretched her back. "That was one part of the vandalism Wade was talking about. Another sweathouse burned too. It was too coincidental to be anything but arson."

I could buy that. "So the two of you came back here in Wade's car. Then what did you do?"

"We finished the new sweathouse. We had the willow frame done. We had to cut some cedar branches for inside, stick them in the walls, throw a couple of old bedspreads over the top, anchor them down. Then we heated up the rocks and took a sweat. You want to see it?"

"Maybe later," I said, sipping coffee and trying to place the events in order.

"Whatever was making so much anger in him seemed to go away some," Moody said. "We had supper. My brother gave me half a deer that he shot last week so I made bitterroot stew."

"Where did you eat?"

"Out here. Right where you're sitting."

"Then?"

Moody shrugged. "Then the skeeters started getting bad so I went to bed. Wade said he wanted to drink and I don't do that no more." He glanced at Melina, then back to me. "My wife, back in Seattle, that's what we broke up over. She wanted to go party every night. So I started working double shifts so I wouldn't have to tell her I didn't want to go party no more. I worked in this pancake-flour place. I always came home white as a ghost." He made a face, widening his eyes and arching his shoulders menacingly, then laughing at his own playfulness. His face clouded then. "My wife, she goes out and drinks and who-knows-what with some other guy. I know about it. I hear things. So pretty soon I'm packing a bag."

His voice was strong and animated, more like a storyteller's than someone seeking pity. "So anyway, Wade goes out to his car and I go inside to bed. Then it's night, the stars are out, the moon is bright as a lantern, and somebody's banging on my door."

"The sheriff?"

He shook his head. "Fred Lamareux. He's tribal police. We went to school with the nuns together. He tells me the sheriff's got a warrant for Wade. I look outside and see Wade is already in the back of the squad car. The doors of the Caddy are all wide open and the light's on. A couple of guys are searching around in the car."

"What happened to the car?" I asked Melina.

"They impounded it."

"Then what?" I said to the Indian.

"I pulled my boots on and tried to talk to Wade. Them cops wouldn't let me too close. They said Wade had given them a fight, said they were going to charge him with resisting arrest too. Didn't want me letting him out of that squad car. I got close enough to hear the string of curse words he let loose. Would have given the old nuns apoplexy." Moody smiled. "I even learned a few new ones."

Melina sat down again on the stump, throwing the dregs of her coffee into the grass. She covered her face with her hands for a minute. Moody turned on his stump to look down the valley, with the Mission Mountains outlined in the haze. Something about the long view, that faraway place that is still visible, calmed me. Maybe it was like believing in fairy tales, trusting that there was another world out there that you couldn't touch. A world where goodness reigned. Where the randomness of life was banished. Where every deed, every life had order and meaning. Where the good were good, and the bad wore black hats.

Here in Camas Prairie Moody had almost everything he needed. No material wants conceived by ad-men, no gourmet water, no sushi or Häagen-Dazs. A life pared down of frills. Moody's faraway eyes were dark, peaceful.

And then there was Wade, a man who embodied the peace/love/sixties generation more than anyone else I knew. He belonged here as much as Moody, didn't he? He was only protecting this place from marauders, from charlatans who came with their snake oil to sell a sip of karma to the gullible. They didn't belong here. Wade knew that. I could understand how he responded to Moody and his life, bonding to them. Even if you couldn't become one of them you could be sensitive. You could sit quietly and listen to the breathing of the land. You could respect the ancient ways of people whose culture we had pillaged. That was Wade's way. I was beginning to feel, to understand, that spirit, those bonds, myself.

4

"**H**ER SPIRIT FLIES with us!"

The voice boomed over the meadow. The meadow hugged the riverbank, with grandfather cottonwoods on one side and aspens and pines on the other. As the voice echoed away, an odd stillness hummed through the tall grass at the forest edge. Even the bees stopped their frenetic buzzing for an instant as if in homage to the murdered woman. I paid her an involuntary moment of silence even though we'd never met. Melina snapped a twig behind me and cursed.

A hundred or so women sat with their backs to us on the trampled, yellowing grass. On the far side of them, a row of twelve or fifteen conical white tepees marched in the bright sun. A woman—the one attached to the voice—paced in front of the crowd waving a brilliant purple and green scarf over her head. Her dark red skirt and black blouse framed a glittering pendant on her chest that caught the sun as she moved. She stopped and the women strained toward her. She gathered them in as if they were attached to strings.

The stillness swelled and burst. Whispers rose from the seated women. The speaker held the ends of the scarf in each hand raised above her head and shouted: "She had the power and that power does not die! It is returned and renewed by those who loved her. By you, and you, and you!"

Moody, Melina, and I tiptoed slowly along the ring of trees that surrounded the meadow. The Indian had explained that this was Tin-Tin's camp. Moody had a way of taking you under his wing. Making you feel like a treasured relative in just minutes. It seemed natural to trust him to lead us skulking through the woods, prying into a private funeral service. Even skulking felt pretty natural.

Watching the dynamic woman with the booming voice, her graying hair in neat braids above her powerful figure, I assumed she was Tin-Tin. I found myself drawn to her words, fascinated as I was by Melina's description of the old woman. I strained to feel Shiloh's presence in the crowd, flying around them, entering a new body perhaps. But all I could hear in the moment of stillness was my heartbeat in my ears. I frowned and flicked a fly off my arm. The meadow rippled with heat.

Wails undulated through the crowd. Apparently the women didn't feel reassured by the speaker's words. They were dressed in prairie skirts, suede leggings, and peasant blouses, some in black, some not. Sitting cross-legged in groups, holding each other in grief, or sitting alone with heads bowed. Never had I seen so much beadwork and frizzy hair in one place.

"Shiloh had lived before! She could feel the spirits of her ancestors as clearly as the sun shines on us today, our day of sorrow and loss." The woman stood motionless now, arms outstretched at her sides, palms up in a Christlike pose. She was not tall but an imposing presence, her long-sleeved black blouse fluttering in the breeze. I could see the pendant better now; it was mirrored, the shape of a flower hanging on a beaded rope on her full bosom. Her round face was accented by the gray braids looped in circles below her ears. "She will live again!"

Moody nudged me. "That's Orianna Gold Flicker. She's the head woman." I blinked in surprise. He looked solemnly at the women and pressed into a tree, trying to make himself less visible.

"Where is Tin-Tin?" I whispered.

Moody scanned the crowd for a minute. "Maybe in her tepee."

We listened to the eulogy for Shiloh for a few more

minutes, then moved back to approach the tepees on the other side. When Moody and I started out into the open to cross the meadow, Melina caught my arm.

"I'm going back to the car," she whispered, though we were well away from the women. "I feel very uncomfortable here."

I put my hand on her arm. "You go back. Moody and I will talk to Tin-Tin."

Melina backed away for a few steps, then turned and ran through the trees toward the car. The air was charged with emotion as Orianna Gold Flicker continued the requiem, talking of reincarnated spirits and "the good red road," mixing Native American and Hindu religions in a slick, easy way. As we trod softly toward the groups of tepees she launched into a rousing climax.

"To behold the spirit of death, open your heart into the body of life. Because life and death are one, like the river and the sea are one. Deep inside you lies your silent knowledge of the beyond. Like seeds dreaming beneath the snow, your heart dreams of spring. Trust these dreams, for in them is hidden the secrets of eternity."

She moved across the front of the group, her skirt flowing behind her.

"When you drink from the river of silence you will sing. When you reach the mountaintop," she intoned, stretching both arms toward the peaks behind us, "then you will begin to climb. And when the earth claims your limbs, then you will truly begin to dance." She paused for effect, turning suddenly to face the women. "The time has come for Shiloh to dance. Dance, Shiloh, dance!"

The women shouted Shiloh's name, standing together, hugging one another, crying. A few danced wildly in circles like dervishes. A group rushed to Orianna, her arms outstretched to embrace and comfort them. Something about her finale rang familiar to me and I made a mental note to look it up later.

Moody pulled at my sleeve. I had stopped to listen, curious about the control the woman had over her flock. Moody nodded toward a tepee ahead. Ancient designs had been painted on the old hide tepee, of buffalo and the sun and the moon. The other tepees were plain, canvas, and ordinary.

We entered a ring of rocks near the closed flap of the tepee. Moody approached the flap, cleared his throat, and scuffed his boots in the dirt. In a moment the flap flipped open from the inside. The bent frame of an old woman emerged.

She wore a gauzy lavender peasant blouse, with a yellow vest and red calico skirt that reached her ankles. Around her neck was a white beaded choker and a small leather bag on a thong. A red bandanna covered her white hair, plaited in two long braids on either side of her head. Her soft, lined face brightened at the sight of Moody.

"Little Cricket," she purred, holding his face in her hands for a moment. "My day is brighter now."

"Tin-Tin, I have someone I want you to meet." Moody turned toward me, pulling me closer. "This is Alix. She is Melina's sister."

Tin-Tin was thin and taut as a lariat. "Yes, I see some of Melina in your face." Then her face clouded. She dropped my hands, adjusting one of the bobby pins that held her hair in place. "You've come about Wade." She held up her hand. "First we eat."

With the bowl of soup and a hunk of homemade bread slathered with butter in front of me, I realized I was ravenous. Tin-Tin looked pleased with my appetite and refilled my bowl. As we finished she seemed to ready herself for telling the story.

The old woman's black eyes looked up at the blue sky dotted with white puffs of clouds. "It was a day just like this one. Only yesterday. Yet so much . . ." She shook her head, braids swinging, and stared at me intensely.

"You are here to help Wade Fraser?"

"Yes," I said.

"Then you want to know the truth."

"Yes."

She stood up and set her jaw. "I call him Buffalo Tears, for he cries for the spirits of the old ones. He made many women very angry. He called them indecent names. He acted poorly."

"He told me," I said.

"Did he? Good. Maybe he will learn to let other people live the way they want. I was ashamed to call Buffalo Tears my friend." In her voice was hurt.

I ate the soup, trying to recover from my embarrassment for my brother-in-law. It's a terrible thing to let down those who love you. Even if he was found innocent, Wade would never find relations on the reservation what they were before. "Why did he come here?"

Tin-Tin set our bowls by a kettle near her campfire. "He came here to talk to me. About the Medicine Tree. You have heard what happened to the Medicine Tree?"

I shook my head. From Tin-Tin's circle I watched the women from the memorial service file by to their tepees in twos and threes, faces flushed and streaked with tears. "What happened to it?"

The old woman sat on a rock, her back straight, the sun on her walnut-colored face. "A person—" she swung her bony fingers around as if the humanity of this being was in question—"some person removed all the prayer ribbons on it, took all the coins stuck in the bark. Then this person cut off limbs of the tree." Tin-Tin closed her eyes, the pain of saying these ugly facts on her face.

Moody stared at his boot tips.

"This tree is special to you? Sacred?" I said.

"The Medicine Tree is a big old yellow pine, about three or five or eight hundred years old," Moody said. "Nobody knows for sure. It's in the Bitterroot Valley. That's where we lived before the government sent us to the reservation. Our home."

"Home." Tin-Tin seemed to sing the word, her lips soft and wrinkled but not chapped by the sun like mine. "Have you seen the Medicine Tree, Alix?" I shook my head. "Then let me tell you why it is sacred to us."

"Long ago," she began, "a ram lived in the Bitterroot

Mountains. This ram was vicious and cruel. He wouldn't let anyone pass through his land. He ate them if they tried.

"One day Coyote tried to pass through the ram's land. 'What are you doing here?' asked the ram. 'Just traveling through,' said Coyote. 'I let no one pass,' said the ram. 'I must eat you.' "

Tin-Tin grinned, her teeth strong but yellow with age. "Now Coyote was too smart to be eaten. He thought about the ram, how proud he was of his beautiful horns, how strong and grand he thought he was. Then he said to the ram: 'I will make you a bet. I bet you can't knock down that tree. If you succeed, you can eat me. If not, you must let me pass.'

"Now the ram loved to gamble, just like Coyote. So he quickly agreed. He moved back and ran as fast as he could at the tree, butting it with his horns. It didn't budge. He tried it again. Still no luck. The third time he moved way back, got to running so fast that when his horns hit the tree they dug deep into the trunk.

"The ram was stuck. Coyote had tricked him. Coyote knew he had to free the mountain pass of the cruel ram so he cut off his head, leaving the horns embedded in the tree." Tin-Tin frowned, looking at me. "When I was a girl you could still see the horns in the trunk. But now they are gone."

"Someone took them?"

She shrugged. "They are gone."

Moody spoke up in her pause. "Our people honor the grandfather tree by making gifts to it. Ribbons on the branches that twirl in the wind, money in the bark or on the roots if they can afford it. You make a prayer there, for your family, for your tribe."

"Cutting limbs off the Medicine Tree is like cutting off the arms of your grandfather," Tin-Tin said.

I thought about the story and wondered what Wade had been doing. Why was he so intent on finding the vandals? Did he know who was behind it?

Suddenly Tin-Tin stood, shading her eyes to look down the line of tepees. A brown sheriff's car was parked at the far end. Several uniformed officers stood talking to Orianna and a cluster of women who surrounded her. The leader nodded her head, listening intently to what the officers said. Anxiety seemed to ripple through the women as they watched the policemen.

"Did you tell Wade anything about the Medicine Tree? About the vandalizing of it?" I asked, sensing our discussion would soon come to a close.

Tin-Tin shook her head sadly. "I know nothing about who did this terrible thing. Wade went off to argue with Orianna and Shiloh. The next time I saw him some women were holding him down on the ground and he was cursing. They let him up because he is my friend." She sighed, looking at the clouds again. When she spoke her voice was a whisper. "Ah, Buffalo Tears. What have you done?"

I examined the toes of my running shoes for a minute, not wanting to speculate, hoping this feeling of mine was wrong. "Did he hate Shiloh, do you think?"

"I don't know. Wade can be so loving, so generous. But I see bitterness in him too, hatred that I do not know." She looked at me. "Do you love him like a brother?"

"I do."

"Then I tell you that he did not kill her, that he could not kill a living thing. But there was bad blood between those two, somewhere, sometime." Tin-Tin's eyes darted away from mine. I shivered involuntarily. Her words were not comforting. I was glad Melina was not here to hear them. I turned as Orianna and her entourage swept into the circle.

"Tin-Tin, excuse me. The sheriff's deputies want to question everyone who was here yesterday. I hope you don't mind." The leader's demeanor was surprisingly humble. At close range her round face was freckled and lined but not unattractive. She was as tall as I was, with a mountainous chest that swelled like an opera singer's as she spoke.

Tin-Tin gave her a slim smile. "I will cooperate."

"Fine." Orianna turned to go then looked at Moody and me. "Who are you?"

"Moody Denzel. Pleased to meet you." Moody stuck out his hand. "Shiloh asked me to conduct sweats for you women. She said you wanted 'em starting day after tomorrow." Orianna just looked at his hand, then glared up at me.

"And you?"

"Alix Thorssen." I offered no hand or explanation.

Orianna waited a beat, then yielded to Tin-Tin's obvious authority. "Well. We've got work to do." She turned, her skirt swishing behind her, and led her women away.

I watched her a minute, then turned back to the old woman. "What do you know about her?"

"Orianna?" Tin-Tin asked, busying herself with getting the dish pan ready to wash the bowls. "An interesting woman. A powerful storyteller."

"Does Wade know her?"

Tin-Tin picked up a dish towel and dried her hands. "I don't know. Maybe some. He knew Shiloh from somewhere, like I said. But Orianna? She likes to keep to herself, like her power is stronger if she guards it."

Tin-Tin was the antithesis of that idea, I thought as we said good-bye and walked to the car. Her power was strengthened by giving it away, like a potlatch or giveaway ceremony. The more you give, the greater you become.

The world, in fact, could be divided into two kinds of people, those who hoard and those who give. And it wasn't the material things necessarily that a person had to give. Some of my clients, thick with the odor of money, seemed so pitiful to me. Withered by their money somehow. By the sheer energy involved in keeping every penny safe. Maybe they never gave it away.

$\triangledown$

5

IN THE WEST, time is measured by mile markers on the highway. Mile 3, mile 35, mile 135. You don't know where they start or where they stop but you drive, on and on into the sunrise.

It was morning. In the backseat of a late-model Toyota littered with gum wrappers, belonging to Hondo O'Brian, whose real first name was Taylor, I lay back and tried to make my mind work.

Yesterday afternoon, late, we had climbed the worn marble stairs in a renovated brick office building to Sachs and O'Brian, Esq. The light bulbs gave off a scorched dirt smell. Across the street sat the Missoula County Courthouse, an ornate, lordly castle built around the turn of the century.

Despite my objections to a lawyer named Hondo, the man turned out to be a skinny, red-haired garden patch of a man: a string bean with a carrot top. I had expected a Hulk Hogan and was pleasantly surprised.

We discussed Wade's case for half an hour or so, then went out to dinner, where Hondo looked serious behind his horn-rimmed glasses and Melina drank too much wine and started to get weepy. The designated driver (yours truly) got us home early, tucked in bed, where we both slept like the dead. Well, almost.

Now, three cups of coffee into the morning, we were headed to Polson for Wade's hearing. Melina and Hondo talked softly in the front seat, over the radio news.

"So the judge sets bond?" Melina said.

"Right. That's how much bail money is necessary," Hondo said. "You pay the bondsman 10 percent of the amount the judge sets."

My mind raced ahead. The money didn't concern me; it would be found, somewhere. Wade had no alibi. That bothered me. I had brought along yesterday's edition of the *Missoulian*, which blared the headline "PROF CHARGED IN FLATHEAD MURDER." There was a picture of Shiloh, the first I'd seen. She appeared to be giving a lecture, with both hands on a wooden lectern. Her hair was shoulder length and darkly wavy, pushed behind rather large ears; her nose bordered on hooked. Her earlobes sparkled with jewelry. The photographer had caught her midsentence, her mouth open, small, sharp teeth, deep-set eyes fiercely serious, eyebrows taut, nostrils flaring. I stared at the half-tone dots, trying to read her. If anything could be read into the photo it was her intensity, her sense of purpose.

I found myself looking for something to dislike, to justify Wade's quarrel with Shiloh. Had she fought with her attacker? Had she wounded him?

The article described the "grisly slaying of the local woman" in scant detail, simply that she bled to death. A knife found at the scene had allegedly been traced to the accused.

How did Wade's knife get there? Did someone hate Wade enough to frame him for murder? It all seemed farfetched to me. In investigating art forgery I rarely had to look for a motive past money, but I enjoyed probing the psyches of failed, bitter artists who got their kicks out of bilking people. Why they chose the low road—forgery—when they were often accomplished artists in their own right was sometimes a mystery.

But usually the reason hit you over the head: the game, the chase. Finding the old canvases, the old pigments, using the same techniques, the same brushes and strokes as the masters. These were parts of the puzzle constructed to show how much smarter the forger was than his prey. But subconsciously the forger wanted the recognition for his masterpiece and slipped up somewhere, put in that little imperfection like a Navajo weaver does to prove she isn't as perfect as the Great Spirit. That imperfection was the key to the puzzle you had to find.

The odds were that whoever murdered Shiloh Merkin didn't really want to be found out. There was no artistry in slashing a woman's jugular. Someone hated Shiloh. Someone wanted her dead.

Something else in the newspaper article grated on my morning grogginess. I picked up the paper again as we pulled into the parking lot at the Lake County Courthouse. Where was that sentence? I drew my finger down the printing.

"Professor Fraser had been arrested previously for assault in 1984. Charges were subsequently dropped."

The hallway outside the courtroom was jammed. Not big-city jammed, wall-to-wall without elbow room, but a western jam. That means four reporters trying to talk to the same person. We have our own perspective on these things out here.

We didn't stop to talk to them. They recognized Melina though, hurling questions at her from all compass points. "Do you know where your husband was Saturday night?" "Was Fraser having an affair with Miss Merkin?" "Can you give us a statement, Mrs. Fraser?" Hondo put his skinny arm around her shoulders, just like in the movies, and we plowed our way through the strobes.

Melina and I eased into wooden chairs behind the railing where Hondo spread his papers on a scarred, walnut-stained table. Melina had washed her hair and whipped it into a fresh concoction. She wore a white blouse and a skirt the color of the sky. I wore The Suit again, with a clean T-shirt underneath.

The courtroom was a drab twenties-era hall with wood paneling and tarnished brass fixtures, three-quarters full. Despite the air of stale banality the courtroom exuded, the people who had come to watch the hearing were colorful types: elderly men with a gleam for scandal in their eyes, solid Indian women in brightly colored dresses, nervous teenagers, and pinch-faced young women who scowled, probably in the presence of all men.

The battle of the sexes was on.

Wade shuffled in, still handcuffed, with four guards. They stood on either side of the table, hands clasped behind their backs. Just then Orianna and three of her cohorts waltzed in and found seats as far from us as possible.

Wade seemed to be losing weight. His face sagged as if under a greater gravity than normal. His clothes hung on him: khaki janitor's pants with acid holes by the knee, a faded flannel shirt. His shoes made a statement all their own: black high-top Converse basketball shoes, worn and faded to a chalkboard gray, with laces broken and tied back together.

When the judge entered and the bailiff shouted out his harangue ending with "All rise," Hondo and Wade could not have looked more opposite. The lawyer had moussed his wiry red hair into position and put on a dark blue suit that hung surprisingly well on his meatless frame. He actually looked competent. Wade had a glassy, haggard look next to him, his head down.

When his turn came, Hondo O'Brian began to speak in a booming bass, a voice of confidence and command. He had appeared relaxed and knowledgeable when we talked at his office, allaying Melina's fears. With his scarecrow physique he wasn't an imposing figure. But how many real lawyers could measure up to Raymond Burr's burly Perry Mason? His mind was what mattered, I told myself, and on that score he appeared at least adequate.

"The evidence against my client, your honor, is purely circumstantial. The prosecution has no evidence that my client was anywhere near the woods along the Little Bitterroot River last Saturday night."

He stepped around the table, a pencil wagging from his long fingers. "We have a witness to testify that Mr. Fraser spent the evening at Camas Prairie, some ten miles away.

There are no witnesses to testify that my client was near the scene at the time of the death. No blood, no witnesses, nothing found on my client or in his possession. Nothing, in short, to indicate that my client was involved in this death. The prosecution, your honor, has not a shred of evidence that my client was involved in this crime in any way."

Hondo's face had flushed, washing out his freckles above the white shirt he wore. He swung to face the crowd dramatically. "Therefore, your honor, I ask you to dismiss the charges against the defendant as arbitrary and without basis in fact."

The judge, a woman in her fifties with dyed brown hair cut at a severe blunt angle and bifocals, made a note on a pad in front of her, then looked up calmly. "Mr. Albrecht?"

The young deputy county attorney bounced to his feet. By his clean-cut looks he would have passed for twenty-five but I doubted they gave murder trials to new recruits. He was short and athletic in a squatty, body-builder way, with a full head of blond hair combed away from his face.

"Your honor, Mr. Fraser has been charged with first-degree murder. This is a serious charge, very serious. Let me tell you why the county feels Mr. Fraser should be tried for this crime.

"First of all, the murder itself. A woman, not a large, strong woman, but a woman small in frame, is dead. Murdered. She struggled, we are told, but couldn't overcome her attacker, who came at her with a long, sharp hunting knife. A knife that, consequently, has been said to belong to Mr. Fraser."

"Objection, hearsay," Hondo shouted from his chair.

"This is not a trial, Mr. O'Brian," the judge reprimanded and turned her attention back to Mr. Albrecht.

"The woman, Miss Merkin, loses the struggle. The attacker makes a clean, sharp cut across her throat." Albrecht drew his pencil across his neck slowly.

"Objection, your honor!" Hondo was on his feet.

"Mr. Albrecht, don't be dramatic. Get on with it," the judge said.

The prosecutor stepped around his table and paced in

front of the judge, waving his pencil and punctuating his phrases with stabs into the air. "Doris Shiloh Merkin falls to the ground. She tries to call out but cannot. Her throat is cut. So she lies on the ground, bleeding, and dies. The attacker panics now that he has done what he set out to do. In his rush he drops the murder weapon."

Albrecht faced Wade now, his boyish face animated. "Now we come to Mr. Fraser. By the witness of hundreds of bystanders, he argued vehemently with Miss Merkin that day. He insulted her. She told him to get out of the women's encampment on the Little Bitterroot River. When he refused, Miss Merkin ordered six women to push him to the ground, holding him there until he calmed down. She was frightened by the anger, the violent temper, of Mr. Fraser. So frightened she had some of her friends detain him until he relaxed enough to cease being a threat to her."

"Bullshit," Wade said in a loud whisper. The judge looked at him sternly.

"And Miss Merkin had cause to be frightened," Albrecht continued, addressing the audience rather than the judge, playing the crowd. "For Mr. Fraser had been charged with assault before. He attacked a coworker at the University in a vicious, uncontrollable rage. Mr. Fraser was known to be a violent man who would strike out if he didn't get what he wanted."

"Objection!" Hondo pounded his fist on the table for emphasis.

The judge looked at him like he was a pitiful child. "Please restrain yourself, Mr. O'Brian. Continue, Mr. Albrecht."

"Lastly, Mr. Fraser's whereabouts the night of the murder. He states that he was with one Moody Denzel at Camas Prairie that night. But Mr. Denzel went to bed at nightfall, about nine-thirty that night, while Mr. Fraser, oddly enough, went to his car. Why didn't he sleep in Mr. Denzel's cabin? He was offered that opportunity and refused. He wanted to sleep in his automobile."

Albrecht shook his head sadly as if sleeping in your car

was tantamount to a confession of murder. Then he turned to face the judge. "Camas Prairie is, as Defense has stated, only ten miles from the scene of the murder. An easy fifteen-minute drive under most circumstances. Easily a short drive in the dead of night, at the time of the murder, approximately eleven o'clock last Saturday night."

Everyone in the courtroom held their breath. Albrecht's heels tapped across the wood floors as he returned to his table and faced the judge. "The defendant is a danger to the community, your honor. He has an uncontrollable temper and has lashed out at others in the past. He has been charged with assault before. In front of nearly one hundred witnesses his anger got the better of him. He has a high potential for violent behavior. Therefore, your honor, we request that Wade Fraser be bound over on the charge of the first-degree murder of Doris Merkin without bond and file a motion to file direct into district court."

Melina grabbed my hand. No bond, the county attorney said. They can't do that, can they? Hondo touched his forehead with three fingers. Wade glanced at him, bushy eyebrows pinched, then resumed staring at his hands in his lap. A ripple of whispers went through the courtroom as Albrecht sat down.

The judge made more notes. Melina closed her eyes and moved her lips silently like she was praying. I squeezed her hand. I knew she wouldn't cry here. Hondo began to rustle papers and stood.

"I'd like to respond, your honor," he said, his voice still strong. I thought I detected a quaver but he continued confidently. The judge nodded to him.

"Professor Fraser is a respected university instructor, a teacher for more than fifteen years. He has ties to the community. He is married and owns his home in Missoula. He has been promoted to associate professor and given tenure based on his outstanding teaching and research in this very region."

Hondo cleared his throat. "The charges referred to by

prosecution were dropped and never pursued. They were the object of a professional disagreement that when thought through was discarded. Dr. Fraser is a scientist, your honor, a teacher, a husband. I urge you to post bond for the defendant based on his excellent record to the community and the area."

Once again the judge looked thoughtful and wrote herself some notes. I thought she would call a recess to think it over but she raised her face to Hondo and Wade and spoke softly to the bailiff.

"Defendant will rise," said the bailiff, a portly Indian.

Hondo and Wade stood up and straightened themselves before the judge. She looked out from under her neatly cut bangs and over her half-moon glasses. "Do you understand the charges against you, Mr. Fraser?"

Wade glanced at Hondo, who spoke for him. "We do, your honor."

"And how do you plead?"

"Not guilty, your honor," Hondo said in his loud baritone.

The judge nodded slightly and returned to her scribblings. The air in the courtroom took on a heaviness, making breathing difficult. Scuffles, doors opening and closing, and noses being blown made a soft cacophony behind us. Melina was white now, stabbing her glasses back on her small nose, biting her lower lip, then trying not to.

The judge looked up at Wade, waiting a beat for the room's attention. When she spoke her voice was clear, emotionless: "The Court of Lake County orders you, Wade Fraser, to stand trial in district court on the charge of first-degree murder of Doris Merkin and to be held without bond until such time."

▽

6

THE SCENE IN the conference room in the basement of the courthouse was not pretty. In this same room where I had felt so light I could float off my chair the air now hung heavy, full of dread. Wade paced across one side of the room, his wrists free of the handcuffs at last; Melina and Hondo sat in the wooden chairs, tense, drilling the table with fingertips. I stood against the opposite wall with the same burly, bald guard as before. He now gave me cold sidelong glances. His uniform smelled of cigarettes.

Wade struggled to control himself, keeping his eyes on his sneakers as they squeaked on the cement floor on each turn. O'Brian apologized for not getting him bail and pledged to do his best to get it changed.

"I can meet with the judge but I don't know, Wade," the lawyer said, shaking his head. "I'll have to get a new hearing date and dig up something. I'll try."

"Damn right, you'll try. I gotta get out of here." Wade stopped pacing and faced us, hands supplicant. "Look at me. I'm a caged animal."

Melina spoke as Wade began walking back and forth again. "He's doing his best, Wade."

"His best?!" He swung to face her, his voice rising. "Maybe his best isn't good enough. And why are you sticking up for him, Mel? What's going on when the office doors close behind you, huh? A cozy little arrangement, I must say."

"Now, just a minute, Wade," O'Brian began. Then Melina let out a little cry, her face reddening before she covered it with her hands. She jumped to her feet then, stamping her heels hard against the floor. Arms stiff at her sides, she glared at Wade and walked to the door. It refused to respond to her yanks on the knob. Melina bellowed, sobbing.

Wade melted. His face twisted with compassion and he walked up behind Melina, speaking softly to her.

"Oh, Mellie. I'm sorry, honey," he whispered. "I didn't mean it. I'm sorry. It's just this place and all. Forgive me, Mel. Honey?"

Melina turned to face him. A cry racked through her chest. Her face was puffy and red. She closed her eyes after taking an exasperated look at her husband.

Wade bent his neck, moving into position with his lips, pausing halfway there. He turned his head to the guard. "Can I kiss her? Is that all right with you?" he asked belligerently. The guard shrugged. Melina let Wade press his lips against hers. He murmured in her ear then, holding her hands in his. "It'll be all right, honey. Hondo will get me out soon. It'll be all right."

The guard made a movement toward them. Wade anticipated it and dropped Melina's hands. His face revealed that his mind had raced ahead to more serious matters. He walked back to the wall and leaned against it.

"So this is it, huh? The final reckoning, the last supper. A little more legal jockeying, then the Queen of Hearts says, Off with his head!" Wade spat out the words.

"Now, Wade, no theatrics. We'll save that for the trial." Hondo grinned at Wade, who scowled at the ceiling corner.

O'Brian glanced at me. I nodded, urging him silently to ask what we had prearranged. "We want to know what you were looking into on the reservation last week, Wade. Some vandalism?"

"Hmmm?" Wade jerked his head back to his lawyer. "Yeah. Vandalism."

"Of what?"

"Various things."

"Like the Medicine Tree?" I asked.

His head jerked up. "Yeah, the Medicine Tree. Did Tin-Tin tell you about it?"

I nodded. "What else? The sweathouse?"

"Moody's sweathouse." Wade began to pace again. "There was a bunch of things happened in one week. Seemed strange to me. And not ordinary things like spray paint on the school walls or some prank."

"Why?"

"That's what I want to know. Why all these things clustered together? Messages."

"From who?"

Wade shrugged and began to speak as the doorknob jingled behind Melina. She stepped away. The door opened. "Time," said another guard with keys in his hand. "Let's go." The two guards walked warily over to Wade, grasping his upper arms in their meaty hands.

"I've got a file. In my desk, Mel, show her," Wade called out as we walked out through the greenish, fluorescent-lit corridors and left him behind.

Two hours later I sat up to my elbows in Wade's notes. His study was an under-the-eaves, second-story bedroom just big enough for his massive old oak desk and two small bookcases. A tall black filing cabinet stood in the hall, covered with a thick coating of dust.

Melina came in before her afternoon class and tried to open the window. Fifty years of paint fought that effort, so she brought me a small fan. When it blew the stacks of papers scattered around the study, she set it in the hall.

She had to go teach a class at the Career Center: "Marriage and the Family." Her eyes still looked puffy from the scene with Wade but she smiled as she left the house. Maybe the class kept her mind off her troubles.

Wade's filing system was easy enough to figure out. It was chronological, the latest information on top of the heap. I began to read all the scribbled scraps of paper and file them into two piles: related and unrelated. I was just guessing at this point, but after several hours of reading I had a fair idea of what Wade had been doing on the reservation.

From newspaper clippings and notes to himself it appeared that four incidents of vandalism had occurred, all within a day or two of each other. Three I already knew about: the Medicine Tree, Moody's sweathouse, and the other sweathouse, equally old and located on the Jocko River, probably torched. The other piece of malicious mischief was perhaps the most disturbing. Wade had clipped an article from the Missoula newspaper.

VANDALS DESECRATE MISSION

Intruders broke into the historic St. Ignatius Mission on the Flathead Reservation last night, destroying statuary and defacing artworks. A spokesman from the Lake County Sheriff's Office estimated damage at close to $100,000.

A side entrance to the chapel appeared to have been pried open, the spokesman said. Father Julius Percy, mission priest, said a small statue was smashed that dated from the turn of the century. Two murals, painted when the mission was built in 1891, were slashed, and a third painting, not original, was also badly damaged.

On the corner of the clipping Wade had written the date of the article: 6/22, Thursday. The article on the Medicine Tree vandalism was in Friday's paper, but it apparently happened on Wednesday night. The sweathouse fires had occurred either Tuesday or Wednesday night.

Wade's old wooden chair with its threadbare cushion cradled me. I dozed off to the rattling hum of the tiny fan, staring at the piles of information on the desk. When Melina woke me for dinner I held a slip of blank paper clamped in my sweaty fist.

▽

7

Raindrops pounded the Saab Sister's roof, a kettledrum for the clouds. My hair was still damp from my shower but Melina and her friend Zena discussed newspapers, hats, and umbrellas before deciding to use their purses as a last resort to shield their heads from the downpour.

Zena Glenn sat behind me, dressed in a black chiffon skirt and a tight navy blue sweater that hugged her thin chest. Her dark hair stretched to a bun at her nape. Her ghostly white skin shone in the dim light. She looked more like a ballerina than a clerk at a bookstore, which was what she claimed to be. She was a friend of Melina's who was to help us identify people at Shiloh's memorial service.

We were parked three houses down the street from the Cosmic Lunch, an eatery near the campus where the service would be held. This service promised to be just as nontraditional as the one in the meadow.

The rain seemed to slow; I pulled the old hunting jacket tighter until I could smell musty forest smells on the collar. So much for twenty washes. I put on my hat. "Ready?"

"Ready," Zena called. She had a nasal twang like a Texan.

"Do we have to?" Melina said. She was getting cold feet. Thinking about the glory of clearing your husband's name and facing hundreds of people who think he murdered their friend were two different things. But here we sat and it was her idea. I lowered my eyebrows at her; she gave a strained smile. "All right, all right."

We dashed into the puddles and paused to shake like dogs

under the awning before pushing through the big wooden doors to the delicatessen.

Zena assumed her role almost immediately; Melina had been right to bring her. Zena had known Shiloh through working at the bookstore, a near-campus literary magnet with café attached called Freddy's Feed and Read. Although they weren't the closest of friends, Zena could reasonably come to a memorial for Shiloh.

"Sit in the back row," Zena whispered. No sooner were the words out than she saw someone she knew and went to make consoling noises. Melina and I kept our eyes down for the moment, as if in grief, settling ourselves into a row of folding chairs that leaned against the deli's tables stacked in one corner. We pulled off our wet coats and began to look around.

The building that housed the Cosmic Lunch looked like it was built as a gas station in the fifties. The old cement floor had been painted numerous times—this latest, a wild display of silver stars and neon planets outlined in black. I ran the wet toe of my clog over the worn rings of Saturn.

Two small windows faced the Clark Fork River, running high and muddy. The panes of glass were speckled with teary drops tonight. Across the river lay the university campus with the big cement *M* on the barren hillside above it.

Zena slipped into her chair. She was flushed now; the room had become warm with the flow of people. She leaned over Melina and whispered, "Everyone is here." I pulled a small notebook and pencil from my coat pocket and passed it to her.

Melina bumped my arm. "See that man across the aisle, one row up?" A small, older man with peppery hair in a crew cut sat slumped in his chair. "That's Marcus Tilden, chairman of the anthropology department."

"What's he doing here?"

Melina shrugged. I raised my eyebrows, trying to get another look at him. He turned his head away, talking to someone beside him. Zena passed the notebook.

"Elaine Farrar," the first line read. "Roommate. First row,

strawberry blond." I had a view of the back of her curly head. "Yogi Charles, third row, turban," said line two. I had already spotted the white Hindu turban. Charles appeared to be authentic, that is, a real yogi, if dress and complexion were any evidence.

"Yogi *Charles?*" I whispered, squinting my eyes in disbelief.

Zena smiled. "He's big on the local mystic scene. He came over here to go to school in the sixties, then he ran a meat market—"

"Wait a minute. As in beef?" I asked.

"A butcher. Can you believe it? Then he sort of came full circle. Now he has a group of followers who feed him, pay his bills, and listen to his teachings."

"I heard him once." Melina rolled her eyes.

A woman stood up in the front. A table draped with a white linen cloth had been strewn with fresh flowers around dozens of fat candles lit in the evening gloom. Lilacs, roses, iris, violets, and even dandelions were heaped in an orderless display that seemed to symbolize the jubilant but unorthodox life of Shiloh Merkin.

A hush fell. Just as the woman began to speak a man quietly sat down in the seat next to me. I glanced at him. Crew cut, beer belly, cowboy boots. A relative perhaps?

"We have come to remember Shiloh," the woman began. She was a statuesque woman with long gray hair pulled into an elastic band and flowing down her back. She wore a black business suit with a bright white shirt.

"And remember her we should," the woman said, beginning a short speech about why it is important to keep the memory of someone so wonderful alive. I kept waiting for the anecdotal story, something to tell me what kind of person Shiloh was, but the woman droned on philosophically without any personal tales.

Zena passed me the notebook. Mr. Beer Belly saw it all happen out of the corner of his beady brown eyes. I sat back so he couldn't see my face and held the notebook to one side of my lap.

"Sylvie Kali," Zena wrote. "Holistic counselor. Same as Shiloh."

I passed the notebook back to Zena, then whispered to Melina. "See anyone?" She shook her head. We listened to Ms. Kali some more, then a new speaker came forward. A short man, fortyish, receding brown hair, with glasses and an inappropriate palm-tree-motif Hawaiian shirt. He opened a book and began reading a poem.

The notebook came back. "Fred Borger, owns Feed and Read." Her boss, complete with loud shirt. He finished the poem and sat down, a grim look on his face.

The smell of patchouli reached me. Memories of dorm rooms, lit by candles like the ones at the front of the Cosmic Lunch, floated back. I tried to push them aside and concentrate on the motley group of mourners before me.

The task suddenly seemed comic. Imagine learning anything about a killer here! A laugh, more astonished than happy, escaped from my throat; the woman in front of me turned around and scowled. I slouched under my hat, feeling my wet coat soak through onto my back. *What the hell—! I have to get out of here. There's been a terrible mistake.* I pulled my coat closer, not realizing that my savior was approaching.

A flash of metal caught my eye. I looked up to find a sheriff's badge and the big square face of Beer Belly bent down toward mine. He smelled like onions.

"May I speak to you outside a moment?" His gravelly voice rattled in the quiet, too coarse to be called a whisper. Three women in front of us turned around. I grabbed my jacket. I felt relieved, following him out the door onto the sidewalk. The clean night air was a release. The man stepped out onto the sidewalk where a streetlight surrounded him in a circle of yellow.

"What is it?" I said, feeling the pleasure of talking aloud.

"Deputy Schaefer, Lake County sheriff's office." The man was big. Strapping, with the belly covered with a jean jacket and a western shirt.

"Was I speeding or something?" I tried to smile. I was told to always smile at policemen. That he had ordered me out of the service had only just dawned on me. I could be the poor woman's sister for all he knew.

"No, ma'am. I'm investigating the murder of Miss Doris Merkin." He short haircut didn't cover the rolls of skin over his ears. His voice was slow to the point of retarded. He waited, licking his lips like he wasn't waiting. Not retarded, just cagey. I waited him out. At last he got the words out. "I saw you passing names of people at this here funeral."

"Did you?"

"Yes, ma'am."

The door opened, swinging out. Melina and Zena stepped onto the sidewalk. They looked at me quizzically, coming to my side, staring at the deputy with contempt.

"This deputy saw us passing notes," I told them.

"Is there a law against that?" Zena asked.

The deputy blinked slowly. "No, ma'am." He shuffled his feet and put his hands in the pockets of his polyester slacks.

"Then what's the problem?" Melina said, startling me with her authority.

The deputy looked at us. "Didn't I see you up at Polson?" Melina and I looked at each other. "Aren't you relatives of the man we got charged with this woman's murder?"

"What if we are?" Melina demanded.

"Well, I'd appreciate knowing what you were doing here tonight. It didn't appear you were here to pay your respects."

Melina's shoulders sagged. I picked up the ball. "We were here paying our respects. We also don't believe Wade killed her." I stepped toward the deputy. "Why were you here if you believe Wade killed her?"

The deputy shuffled his feet again on the grainy pavement. "We're still looking for evidence, ma'am. It is against the law to withhold evidence in a capital case."

"What makes you think we have any evidence?"

His eyes bulged in his haggard face. His cowboy hat, which had been tucked under his arm, emerged and he put it on. "Nothing, nothing. But if you do you'll call me, won't you?" He pulled a business card from his jacket and scribbled on the back of the card, handing it to me. The card read, "FLATHEAD MOTORS, Quality Used Cars. For deals on wheels see Vern." On the back he had written his name— Lowell Schaefer—and a phone number.

"Nice meeting you ladies," the deputy said, half-turning to go. He straightened the gray cowboy hat on his head.

"Lowell," I called. He stopped and turned, a look of surprise at hearing his given name. "Lowell, if you get any evidence, will you call us?"

The deputy smiled, or tried to. "Well, now, I can't promise that." He tilted his head so that the yellow street light angled across his features. "I would recommend however that you ladies let the professionals take care of criminal cases. Just don't worry yourselves."

"Don't worry our little selves?" Melina blurted out. "When my husband is sitting—rotting!—in jail for a crime he didn't commit?"

The deputy took a step backward, away from us, as he could see the conversation was going nowhere he wanted it to go. "We'll do our very best, ma'am. I promise you that."

"It better be good enough!" Mel hollered. "The life of a good man is at stake!" She took two quick steps toward him, her fist raised in anger, but almost is if cheering the deputy on, putting the fear of God in him. He turned, stumbled, and walked quickly into the wet night.

We were still laughing as we climbed the porch steps on Blaine Street. At least Zena and I were; Melina fumed, too incensed to see the humor in her attack on Lowell, the lowly deputy. She put on hot water for tea as Zena and I took off our wet things. Zena wrapped herself in a wool throw. Melina's house, once the picture of Scandinavian order, was strewn with papers, books, dead flowers in vases, old popcorn on the floor.

"We didn't get to see too many people, did we?" I said, flopping onto the Indian bedspread that covered the couch. "I mean, the potential ones."

"I did," Zena said. "Who do you want to know about?"

"Well, how about Shiloh? What was she like?"

Melina came in with a blue earthenware teapot and cups on a tray. I cleared a space on the coffee table. Zena took a cup into her lap, warming her hands.

"Shiloh was different. You were curious about her, you know, just from looking at her," she said.

"What did she look like?"

"Shoulder-length curly hair, always ratty and unkempt. She dressed real plain, nothing to remember. But her face held you. Not that she was pretty. Striking maybe. A big face with a long thin nose. Her eyes were small and kind of speckled."

"Was she a big woman?"

"Average, I guess. Solid." Zena sipped the tea. Melina had settled onto the couch beside me, calming herself with the steaming beverage.

"What about her personality? What was she like?"

"Very intense. She was usually caught up in this or that movement." Zena frowned.

"Did she try to get you to join a movement?"

"Oh, sure. She'd bring in posters to put in the window every so often. And she'd make a point of asking me to come. She always made you feel like she was asking you personally, like she really wanted you to come." She shook her head. "But I also got the feeling she just wanted lots of people to come to her thing, whatever it happened to be this month, to, like, rationalize her zeal. To lay to rest any doubts she might have herself about this latest guru."

"Like if enough people came to her meeting it was the real thing?" I asked. "The guru with all the answers?"

Zena nodded, pensive. Shiloh hadn't found the answer to life's dilemma, to its meaning, to the questions of the spirit and the soul, I guessed. Dying, she still searched for it. I shivered, thinking of her cold body in the woods alone. For her sake, I hope she found whatever it was that would comfort her.

"I know it's hard right after her memorial service but I need to ask you, Zena," I said. "Did you like Shiloh?"

Zena's dark eyes grew wide in her pale face. "What do you mean? You don't think I—?" Her hand flew to her throat.

"No, no," I stammered. "I'm sorry. I just wanted a personal reaction to her. Someone who knew her."

Her tenseness eased a little as her eyes darted to my face and away. She seemed to only half-believe that I wasn't accusing her. Finally she sighed. "She was friendly. She always talked to me at the store." Her voice was reserved, cautious. She fiddled with fringe on the throw. "But underneath she seemed cold, calculating. I don't think she really liked me, she was just nice to me because there was something to be gained in being nice to me." She paused, thinking. "And anxious."

"Anxious?"

Zena knitted her eyebrows together and closed her eyes. "She was tense, high-strung. Always moving around, almost jumpy. It made me nervous to be around her for very long."

"What about Manitou Matrix, this women's group?"

She shifted in the chair, letting the wool throw fall from her thin shoulders. "I don't know much about them. They had a meeting last summer up on the reservation. I think they're from back East somewhere."

"Is there someone you know that might know more about them? Someone you could ask?"

Zena set her empty cup on the table, nudging aside the popcorn bowl. "I could ask Sylvie. She's the one who was giving the talk tonight. With the gray hair."

"The counselor?"

"Right."

"Would you do that for me, Zena?" She nodded, shrugging her shoulders. "What is a holistic counselor anyway?"

"Oh, they counsel people with problems—emotional, family, relationship problems. Just like a psychologist, I guess, but they aren't maybe as well trained. Sylvie is, but I'm not sure Shiloh really had any formal training."

Melina cleared her throat. "She was an anthropology student." We jerked our heads toward her; she had been so quiet we had almost forgotten she was there.

"She was?" I asked. Melina nodded, staring at her tea. She was slumped on the sofa, her glasses spotted by the rain. Was that the connection between Shiloh and Wade? I turned back to Zena. "So how does a holistic counselor differ from a psychologist then?"

Zena looked a little sheepish and leaned forward. "To tell you the truth I think they're quacks. But don't say I said so at the bookstore!" She laughed nervously. "People down there are into dreams and astrology and numerology and parapsychology and crystals, all sorts of stuff. Whatever the latest trend is, you know? Of course we sell all sorts of books and have all kinds of customers. But still there's that image."

The phone rang; Melina went to answer it. She called me to the kitchen, handing me the receiver. She looked mortally tired.

"Go to bed, Mel," I said, my hand over the mouthpiece. She nodded and rejoined Zena in the living room. "This is Alix," I said into the phone.

"Hi." It was Paolo. His sensual voice sent a surge of pleasure through me that I tried to ignore.

"Hi, yourself. What's up?"

"Not too much. The gallery's still standing. No fires or earthquakes." He was making fun of the long list of instructions I had left him with: insurance agent's name and number, police, fire, plumber, electrician. I guess I was a little nervous leaving him on his own. Hearing his confident Spanish drawl made me feel silly about all that.

"Good. Sell anything today?" This was our standard greeting, worn into familiarity over the years. It was more a way of connecting than caring about what sold.

"Um, let's see. The print of the girl in the Cadillac. That's all."

"I'm sorry to see that one leave. It was one of my favorites."

"As soon as you left I called up this fellow I know who wanted it. I told him it was safe to come in now and buy it." He laughed. "So here's why I called. This woman came in today, a tourist. She wants you to look into a painting she wants to buy."

"What is it?"

"Ah, let me look at my note. Jackson Pollock."

"Pollock?" I assumed all Pollocks were in museums and big collections. He was too big for even the wealthy tourists.

"She said this guy in Florida wants to sell it. From 1952. Isn't that the drippy stuff?"

"Uh-huh. Listen, Paolo, do you think you could handle this for me? I've got my hands full up here." I paused. "Did you hear about Wade?"

"It was in the paper. I was pretty sure that was your sister's Wade." He paused. "Listen, I'll do the research. But you got to call her. She wants you. She was really specific about that." He paused, then let out a little chuckle. "She says she heard you are the best. You never let an old biddy make a fool of herself."

"She didn't say that." I heard the door open and close in the other room; Melina came to the door of the kitchen, leaning against the frame wearily. I smiled at her, trying to cheer her up. "What's this woman's name then?"

"Charlotte Vardis. She gave me a phone number too." He rattled off a Jackson number. "I'll do some digging and call you back tomorrow."

"Look above my desk there. And call Wanda Gilley at the Museum of Modern Art. Her number's in my Rolodex." Melina looked pale suddenly and stood up straight, her mouth trembling. "I've got to call the FBI anyway so I'll handle that. I've got to go, Paolo."

"One more thing."

"What?"

"It's Valkyrie," he said. Valkyrie was my pet horse, a high-spirited mare I pastured out in Wilson. I called her my pet horse because I rarely rode her except bareback a few times each summer. Tack—saddles, bridles—was too expensive.

"What about her?"

"She's missing. J.J. called this morning."

"She broke out?" Sometimes I felt like a jailer, keeping my wild horse in barbed wire.

"Seems to be. J.J. called the sheriff so he's keeping an eye out for her."

"Okay, let me know when they find her." I sighed.

"Okay, kiddo. Mañana."

"Adios."

Melina's eyes were round as she stared at me.

"What is it, Mel? Are you sick?" I took a step toward her, expecting her to faint or throw up. "What is it?"

"Tilden," she whispered.

"What?"

"Dr. Tilden." She cleared her throat and grabbed my arm, her fingers digging into my skin. "Shiloh was his student."

8

GRAVEL CRUNCHED UNDER the Saab Sister's bald tires. The sun crept over the mountains, shining now on the old brick church, the St. Ignatius Mission. I parked by a chain link fence that surrounded the church and stepped into the morning air. The road had calmed me again with its curative powers. I gulped the crispness of the mountain air and climbed the steep concrete steps to the door.

The mission looked like a Gothic miniature, straight and proud, rising high above the valley floor, struggling to compete with the proud peaks behind. The brick church was dedicated to Ignatius Loyola, founder of the Jesuits.

I pushed open the heavy wooden doors, stepping through a lobby into the chapel. Sun streamed through the solid squares of colored glass into the high, arched room painted a robin's egg blue. In the front of the chapel intricate carved wood frames embellished Gothic-arched paintings above a white marble altar. The straight wooden pews sat empty and solemn; I instinctively tiptoed to preserve the peace.

The air smelled still but not unclean. This was a working church where people knelt and prayed and received guidance and blessings. Tall frescoed murals, painted directly into the plaster, lined the side walls and the front of the church. I walked a side aisle, staring at the murals of saints, Biblical characters, and miracles, until I reached a mural near the front corner that was covered with a drape.

I stood for a moment in front of the altar rail, a short white fence. The painting above the altar was pleasant to the eye but typical. Saints on puffy, billowing clouds, Mary and the infant Jesus on puffy, billowing clouds, Jesus with the cross on puffy, billowing clouds. God, it was tough being an art dealer. It was enough to make you billow.

The trimwork curled, intensely ornate, with fancy cutout leaves and grapevines and doodads of all sorts, gilded of course, as only the Gothic style can muster. The effect was overpowering. But it worked in the sense that this type of art belonged in this kind of church. It fit. The way a frilly pinafore, lace anklets, ribbons, and ruffled organza only look right on a little girl.

Quiet descended. Too early for tourists; too late for the pious. I wondered where the priests hung out. I sank onto a pew, calmed by the place.

When I got up at six this morning Melina had already made coffee and was almost out the door. The sound of chirping birds in the backyard trees punctuated the early morning quiet. The circles under Melina's eyes deepened daily. She had a briefcase in one hand and a stack of files in the other. The same blue skirt now looked wrinkled and messy on her, especially with oxfords and anklets.

"Did you sleep?" I had asked, cradling a coffee mug in my hands.

"Yes," she sighed but I didn't believe her. "I have a class at nine and papers to grade before then. I haven't gotten anything done."

"I'm sure they understand."

Melina straightened defensively, her shoulders twitching into alignment. "I don't want them to understand."

We hadn't discussed her strange reaction to remembering Shiloh's connection with Dr. Tilden. Last night she told me Shiloh had studied anthropology as a graduate student a few years back. Melina wasn't sure when. Tilden had been her advisor.

Melina told me this with trembling fingers squeezing my forearm, her lips pale and nervous. It unnerved me to see her so shook up, so different from the solid person I knew. She was my idol, the perfect sister. It had been that way for so long that I felt something slipping away from me, something important, something precious. I felt like crying when she went to bed.

Now in the church I tried to pray for Melina. She wanted me to help Wade but it was her I worried most about.

The heavy door behind me opened. Recognizing the black suit and Roman collar, I stood in the aisle. The priest took some holy water from a font, bowed his head, made the sign of the cross.

His hair was slate gray turning to white. His face held the wrinkles of a man who has heard too much. I glanced at his ears as he strode up. Yes, his ears were small. They had shrunk in protest. Overuse, I thought wickedly.

"You're here for confession?" The priest stopped a few paces away and looked at me curiously. He had a kind face but his blue eyes were all business. He waved his hand toward the booths in the back in the church.

"No." I shook my head, smiling. "I'm a friend of Wade Fraser's. Alix Thorssen."

The priest changed his stance, facing me squarely, his hands behind his back. His eyes, graying now as he cooled toward me, bored through me. Only a priest could give you so much selfless eye contact. The rest of us have too much to hide.

"I heard about Wade's . . . problems," he said. "What can I do?"

He introduced himself to me as Father Percy. He had talked to Wade about the vandalism and appeared to have some affection for the old hippie. I was grateful. Such people seemed in small supply. We sat down on a long wooden pew.

"Did you and Wade come up with a possible motive for the slashing of the mural?" I asked, glancing at the draped wall.

"No. The police tell me vandalism is random hostility. It's not pointed toward anything really. But aimed away from the self, the bad-feeling self."

I nodded, impressed by his analysis. "Did Wade agree?"

Father Percy shook his head. "He thought someone held a grudge against the church. That they'd been let down or felt betrayed." The priest followed my gaze to the drape. "Would you like to see it?"

He pulled back the faded yellow cloth. The painting revealed a holy woman, Mary perhaps. I had been conscientiously forgetting my religious education ever since that first, only, horrible year at St. Olaf's. The mural was framed in another ornate Gothic arch, stenciled and carved and trimmed ad nauseam as if the priest who painted it (he doubled as the mission's cook) hadn't known when to quit. It was his life's work. He kept at it until he died, finished or not.

Mary stood on puffy, billowing clouds, naturally, with her feet on a set of golden horns and a nasty-looking snake who was about to take a bite out of an apple. (Hmmm. Maybe it was Eve.)

The vandals had done a number on the poor woman. With some pointed object they had scraped lines in the plaster. Slashes reached across the entire width of the mural, about six or eight feet. The cuts were high over my head. The culprits must have climbed onto the marble piece that stood against the wall under the mural.

The hostility of the vandal was palpable, sneering at the congregation and the priests. The painting could be repaired, restored. But it would never be the same.

"Such a pity," Father Percy said, letting the drape fall back across the mural. "Useless, really. A waste of energy. These are priceless treasures."

"This was the only thing damaged?"

"Oh, no. The Kateri statue was smashed to bits. And one of the newer paintings was badly damaged. I took it down and put it in my office."

Father Percy's office sat in a walled-off back corner of the chapel, opposite the confessionals. Flimsy plywood walls contrasted with the sturdiness of the old building's thick brick wall, which formed one side of the office. A small, high window shed a pale light into the space. An old wooden desk faced closets and three nicked school chairs. A small metal cross hung on the wall.

Father Percy flicked on a metal gooseneck lamp. "Here." He picked up a large stretched canvas with a too-small wooden frame. The oil painting portrayed an Indian man with strong features. A stereotypical Indian chief with a wise, beatific look and an ornate Plains Indian headdress. A bright glow in the dark sky gave him an ethereal air.

I stared at the rich new colors and the contemporary style, intrigued by the difference between this painting and the frescoes in the chapel.

"Who is he?"

"Shining Shirt," Father Percy said. "Before the white man came he had a vision that men in black skirts would come. And he had a cross." The priest pointed at a spot repeatedly smashed by the vandal. "See, here?" He frowned. "Well, he was wearing it around his neck."

"A cross?"

"The legend goes that it came to him with the vision." He set the painting back on the floor against the wall. "His vision was the reason several delegations of Indians were sent to St. Louis to ask us—the Jesuit priests—to come."

"The black skirts."

"That's what they called the priests." We both gazed at the destroyed painting, still beautiful despite its wounds. Someone had a deep dislike of old Shining Shirt. The cuts crisscrossed the canvas to the point that several triangles of fabric hung tenuously by threads.

"It'll be hard to repair," I commented. "It may be easier to commission a new one."

Father Percy nodded. Sadness overcame his face. "We can do that. The artist is local. That won't be possible with Kateri, though."

I sat down in the chair opposite the desk. "Do you have a picture of that one?"

The priest began opening drawers and leafing through brochures. He stopped, staring at an upper corner of the office, squinting his eyes in concentration. "I can't think of—wait." He went out the door. While he was gone I picked up a glass figurine of Christ and dusted it on my shirttail.

Father Percy returned with a small photograph. "Kateri Tekakwitha," Father Percy said. "We celebrate her feast day in mid-June. Just a week ago."

The snapshot showed an Indian woman with braided hair in a buckskin dress, one fist clenched against her breast. A cape covered her shoulders. "And she was who?"

"Kateri? Well, if there had been monks among Indian women in the 1600s, Kateri would have been one. She converted to Catholicism and became greatly revered by her people. Some years back she was sainted. She represents the kind of pure, spiritual life that is possible within the church for a Native American." He leaned back in his chair, looking saddened by the vandalism but somewhat smug, I thought, as if he, too, led the pure, spiritual life. My prejudices were working overtime.

"Why can't another of these statues be made?"

"The sculptor passed away," he said. "He made a hundred and fifty of those statues for missions, then broke the mold."

I pulled a spiral notebook from my backpack and made a few notes about Shining Shirt and Kateri. Did it relate to Shiloh's murder? Had Wade found out too much?

"May I use your phone, Father?" He motioned to the ancient black telephone on his desk. I found Dr. Tilden's office number in the notebook. The secretary said he wasn't in so I left a message for him to call me at Melina's and hung up.

We walked into the sunshine warming the front steps. The priest's forehead was knitted with worry. "So how is Fraser doing?"

"Not so good," I conceded. "Jail doesn't agree with him."

"I always liked Fraser. Some of the university people aren't so friendly, you know."

I watched his face. "Did you ever meet the woman, Shiloh Merkin?"

He jerked his bushy eyebrows up as if I'd interrupted his musings. "I don't think so." I began down the cement steps worn by a hundred years of footfalls. A group of elderly tourists poured from a huge motor home. As I reached the bottom something clicked.

"What people?" I called up the steps to the priest.

Father Percy stood staring at his shoes. "Pardon?"

"What university people weren't friendly?"

"Oh." The priest twisted his neck over the stiff collar and looked embarrassed. "No one in particular."

"No, Father," I said, reaching his side again. "You heard me ask for Dr. Tilden on the phone. Has he been here?"

Father Percy's blue eyes flicked away. So much for selfless eye contact. His mouth opened and closed again.

"When was he here, Father?"

"Several weeks ago."

"Just once?"

"Couple times."

"What did he do?"

The priest shuffled his feet. "Do? Just like anybody else. Look at the mission. Talk."

"What did he talk about?"

"I can't really say."

"Please, Father. This is important." I put my hand on his sleeve, tugging it slightly. He looked at my fingers and sighed.

"Dr. Tilden is a disagreeable man." He pulled away. His eyes were all business again. "That's all I can say."

The tourists, white-haired grandmothers and grandfathers in knit slack sets and baggy khakis, walked around us. The priest smiled at them, opening the door to the chapel and following them into the darkness.

$\triangledown$

9

ZENA HAD ALREADY called her friend, the holistic counselor, and gotten the information when I reached her at noon. The women's group was founded by Orianna Gold Flicker, in upstate New York. They have a conclave every summer. This year and last it had been held on the Flathead Indian Reservation because of its wealth of sacred sites and tribal willingness to admit whites to them. Tin-Tin Quamash's participation had also been a big plus.

According to the counselor, Shiloh Merkin had been the group's local contact. She had helped Orianna set up crystal workshops in Missoula in the spring, which spurred local interest in the conclave. Participants, Zena had heard, paid upward of $2,500 for the two-week session.

When Melina came home from teaching her classes in late afternoon I finally got around to asking her about something that had been on my mind since the hearing: Wade's "professional disagreement" that had ended in an assault charge. My sister was weary from her day. She remembered little of the event, she said, because it had happened eight or nine years ago.

She did, however, remember who the fight was with. Her reaction was the same as last night. Pale, nervous, she spit out his name. A name that was coming up with regularity.

Marcus Tilden.

"What is it with Tilden, Mel?"

She was putting away her books and suddenly began

cleaning up the living room, whose greasy popcorn bowl and beer bottles had become fixtures.

"What do you mean?" She pushed back her hair, stiff with hair spray, carrying an armload of dishes to the kitchen. "I can't believe what a mess this place is."

"Melina." I followed her into the kitchen. She ran hot water in the sink and squirted dish soap into the stream. Bubbles began to erupt from the water. "Why do you get so bent out of shape when you talk about Tilden?"

Her hazel eyes hid behind her glasses. She busied herself with dishwashing. "Do I? I suppose it's because I don't like him. That's all."

"That's all?"

She rubbed a wet cloth over the popcorn bowl. "He pressed charges against Wade back then. I've never forgiven him for that." I took the bowl from her, drying it. "I do remember what it was about, their fight. Wade wrote something that made Marcus look bad. I guess it really embarrassed Marcus so he came after Wade. It wasn't Wade's fault."

I watched my sister. Her memory was a funny thing. Sometimes it worked and sometimes it didn't. In my experience we don't forget things that make us want to tear hair out. She took the popcorn bowl from me. Before I could say anything, she had washed it all over again.

After dinner I decided the time had come to pay a call on Elaine Farrar, Shiloh's roommate. The evening light fell orange on the street, lighting up Lolo Peak south of town. Shiloh and Elaine lived six blocks away, down a tree-lined street with cracked sidewalks and petunias nodding in gardens. The sweet flower smells hung heavy in the air.

The house was a bungalow like Melina's, low and tidy, painted peach with white trim. The treeless front yard gave the house a neglected look echoed by sunburnt grass. An unpaved driveway filled with weeds led to a small one-car garage with old fashioned swinging doors.

The bowed screen door was all that covered the entrance. The inside door hung open, revealing a small living room, decorated with overstuffed chairs and lace doilies under glass-lantern lamps. Nine or ten women sat around the room, on the floor and in the chairs, as I knocked.

The woman who came to answer my knock had long brown hair past her waist and was painfully thin. Her skin looked blue in the harsh light from the single bulb under the porch roof.

As I stood just inside the door, the conversation and laughter ground to a halt. The women stared at me. I smiled, unsure of which one was Elaine. I'd only seen her from the back at the service. I turned to the thin woman. "You aren't Elaine, are you?"

Her eyebrows twitched together. "No. I don't believe we've met." Her voice had turned cold.

"No, we haven't," I replied, trying to be agreeable. The silence was penetrating. "Alix Thorssen. I'd like to talk to Elaine."

She looked at me hard. "Elaine's out here."

Under green fluorescent light a woman dressed in a purple sweat suit struggled with a large jug of wine. She grunted, stretching the tight fabric across her back, trying to loosen the cap, as we entered.

"Someone to see you." The thin woman evaporated.

"Good. You can help me open this." Elaine handed me the heavy bottle of wine. I jostled it in surprise, then set it on a counter, took a solid grip, and ripped through the perforated metal on the cap. She watched, her hands on her hips. "Great. Thanks."

As she poured the wine into glasses lined up on the old linoleum countertop I got my first good look at Elaine Farrar. Her hair was short and blond, permed into tight curls around her face. She projected an air of efficiency pouring the wine that belied her small, round stature.

"So, you must have been a friend of Shiloh's," Elaine said,

flashing me a smile with pink-lipsticked lips. A ridge of freckles crossed her nose.

"Actually, I didn't know her."

Elaine put the jug down, replacing the cap. "Oh, I just assumed." A frown clouded her face. "What did you say your name was?"

On the way over I had wrestled with the nature of my visit. It would be easier to say I had been a friend of Shiloh's from long ago, here for the funeral. But I knew so little about her. And I hated to play games. Sucking in a breath, I faced the skeptical Elaine, repeating my name.

She frowned, confused. It was time to state my case: "I'm looking into Shiloh's murder. Privately."

"Privately?"

I nodded, hoping that would fly without mentioning my notorious brother-in-law. "I want to know more about Shiloh. What was she doing the last couple weeks. Anything different. Things like that."

Picking up two wine glasses, Elaine turned toward the door. "I've already told those deputies and the Indian cops all that. They think it was Wade Fraser."

"I don't."

She looked at me, perplexed. I couldn't tell if she thought Wade was guilty or not, but my statement must have nudged some doubt. "Well, if it helps find out who killed her. But not now." She walked to the door with the glasses.

"Can I call you tomorrow?"

"Sure." Elaine lifted a glass to her lips. "This is my group, you see. They've come to help me work through this—" Her voice broke. She took a sip of wine. "You understand."

"Of course," I said. "Shall I bring the wine out for you?"

"Oh, no, no. That's sweet of you." Elaine smiled at last, a victory for me. "You know, it just might help to talk to a stranger about Shiloh. Just woman to woman. Those policemen are so cold. Like this is just one more murder to them. More paperwork."

I twisted my mouth to one side in sympathy. I could play Mother Confessor, especially after a day with a priest. Ah, shoot. Would the Lutherans please quit rolling over in their graves?

The room Melina had given me was really a second-story sleeping porch, with paper-thin walls and leaky aluminum windows that stretched the length of it. I had them all open, relishing the breezes that rattled the leaves in the trees. A squirrel chattered as he ran up and down the trunk, scolding Melina's cat.

On the wall above the twin Hollywood bed hung the family pictures. Time, the main player in these photographs, seemed cruel and hateful to me. There was Una, my mother, slender, with skin like moonlight. She was eighteen, a bride, with the debonair lingerie salesman at her side.

Rollie (real name Rudolf) slouched like James Dean at her side, older, wiser, and infinitely cooler. His greased blond hair was combed back but a forelock escaped to hang over one eyebrow. His smile was both happy and smirking at the whole wedding thing.

Birds squabbled in the trees, waking me early. The phone rang insistently in the hall. Melina must have left already. My watch said seven forty-five. I leapt out of bed, hoping Elaine was so eager to talk she was calling me.

The voice on the line was husky. "Alix Thorssen."

"Speaking."

"Marcus Tilden. You called me."

"Yes," I said, gulping for air, flustered at hearing this voice at last. I reflexively pulled down my wrinkled T-shirt over my underpants. "I-I'd like to talk to you. Today, if possible. About Wade Fraser's arrest."

"Wade," he muttered. Papers rustled in the background, as if he didn't really have his mind on the conversation. "Thorssen. You must be Melina's little sister."

"Uh, yes."

"Come by my office about nine. We can talk then."

I tried to say that was fine and good-bye but he had already hung up. I replaced the receiver in a laundry heap around the phone. Suddenly the day's agenda came into focus. Within minutes I had the FBI Art Forgery Unit in Chicago on the line, an agent and old buddy, Kenyon Tiernan. I explained to him about the Jackson Pollock painting the woman had wanted me to investigate. I told him I doubted the authenticity of the painting.

"I'm looking into it myself," I said, "but I wanted to double-check to see if you'd had any reports of forgeries."

"Right," Tiernan said. "God, what I wouldn't give to be out there in the mountains with you."

"The mountains give you nosebleeds, Ken, remember?"

"Well, yeah, but it's so blasted hot here in Big Shoulders."

"Ken, something else. I'm doing a job for the Missoula cops here. It may be something you guys want to take over. They don't have clue one about art theft here."

"Interstate?"

I gave him the rundown on the contents of the trailer, its Florida rental joint, all the rest. I raced through it, hoping he could speed-write.

"Jesus, Alix, where's the fire?"

I took a breath. In business I tried to always protect my sources, coddle them, which is why I ended up with an FBI agent as a house guest now and again. "Sorry. Have you got all that?" He grunted. Another thought. "Just out of curiosity, would you run another name through your computer? Charlotte Vardis, no address."

Tilden's office was in the social science building, an inelegant brick box facing a green lawn and a crisscrossing of student walkways. It had a comfortable, useful feel, like hundreds of other college buildings. On the first floor "Instructional Materials Center" was painted diagonally across the wall in huge emerald and yellow letters.

Anthropology shared a secretary with geography on the second floor. The narrow hallway was deserted. The secretary's door stood ajar, a typewriter running, empty. I stepped down the hall until I found the black plastic nameplate that read MARCUS TILDEN. I knocked. "Dr. Tilden?"

"Enter," a voice called out. I pushed the door and slipped in.

The office was tiny, maybe eight by eight feet, but very organized. Bookshelves lined three walls, stacked to the ceiling. A gleaming mahogany desk, small in size but big in class, dominated the room. Behind it sat the gray-haired man I had seen at the memorial service.

"And you must be Alix," he said, leaning back to appraise me. His face gave the impression of a smile, an odd look, as if practiced in the mirror.

His handshake was bony and strong. "Thank you for meeting me today."

"So Wade is in jail." He shook his head, fingers linked on the desktop. "Poor Wade. I suppose this means I'll have to be looking for a replacement." His eyes were black, almost fiery, and bulged from their sockets.

"I wouldn't rush into anything," I said, smiling. A terrible way to start. "I mean, I don't know what will happen. He may get off."

Tilden tried to squint but his eyes were too big. "Doesn't look good. His knife found at the scene. I heard they found her blood on it." He tapped his index fingers together to a silent beat.

"Did you? I haven't heard that." I opened my notebook to show I wasn't here on a social call. "I'm trying to find out more about the vandalism Wade was looking into on the reservation. Do you know anything about that?"

Tilden pursed his lips. "No." I waited for him to elaborate. He didn't.

"Nothing?"

"Wade and I didn't discuss his activities." He seemed irritated suddenly.

"You weren't on speaking terms?"

Tilden seemed to flinch, shifting his legs and arms in a

jerking motion, then replacing them at another angle. "Quite the contrary. We spoke often. But I hadn't spoken to him since the term ended. I went to Seattle for a conference and only just returned."

"And when was that? If you don't mind me asking."

"Not at all. The police have already been here and asked me the same thing. I came in on a flight two days ago."

I made a note in my notebook. He watched me writing with a smirking twist on his lips.

"Playing detective?" he asked, batting his long eyelashes over his protruding eyes.

My stomach began to churn. If I replied our conversation would be over, so I bit my tongue. "Why were the police here?"

Tilden shrugged. "Ask them yourself."

"Shiloh was a student of yours, wasn't she?"

"For a couple of years. She dropped out."

"Why was that?"

"I don't know. There was some talk about her and Wade not getting along. I think she took a research course from him." Tilden fingered the files on his desk, sitting forward as if the talk was over.

"What do you know about the group she was involved in? Manitou Matrix."

He watched me, a professorial look taking over. "Very little. I see their posters up around town. Shiloh was interested in what we call—" he made an authoritative grimace to apologize for sermonizing—"pathways of knowledge. She was what you might call a seeker. Always looking for answers, for the true faith." His eyes shot to the rows of periodicals on the shelves. "I think I saw something about that group in one of those throwaway journals they send out."

He thumbed through several stacks until he found the one he was looking for. "Here. This is called—" he paused and looked at the cover—"*Nature Song.*" He leafed through the pages and folded them back, handing me the magazine.

The article was titled "The Good Red Road to Wisdom." Under the banner headline was a large photograph of Orianna, the leader of Manitou Matrix, looking much younger, sitting on a rock playing a handmade flute. "Search for Inner Beauty and Wisdom Drawn from Native Religions," read the bold quote attributed to her.

"May I keep this?"

He waved his hand. "It's a throwaway."

"Thanks." He was warming so I plowed on. "What did Shiloh do after she quit graduate school?"

"Not much as far as I know." His big eyes darted toward me and away. "Of course, I didn't know her that well. She seemed rather confused."

"In what way?"

"She didn't know what to do with her life. She didn't have the dedication to go into academics. That was obvious. She got good enough grades and was progressing with her research." He squirmed in his big chair as if possessed. "Shiloh was looking for the true way."

"True way of what?"

He peered at me as if I were a dim bulb. "Of knowledge. Of truth. Some eternal truth. I don't think she ever found what she was looking for." He looked out the window for a moment, his voice dropping to a whisper. I looked at his pale complexion with heavy black stubble, staring at him until he turned his head back. He stood suddenly. "I have another appointment, Miss Thorssen."

The spring in western Montana had been wet this year, the rainfall some 200 percent of normal. Now that the rains were done and the heat arrived, the hillsides exploded with wildflowers and nodding heads of grasses gone to seed. The foothills north of Missoula were ablaze in yellow sweet clover. Everywhere on the quiet campus the feeling of lazy summer held fast.

I walked slowly past tennis courts where the whap, whap of a slow game had an easy familiarity. Past the old indoor swimming pool with its swollen rusting dome. Toward the river, couples lay on a grassy expanse on blankets. At midmorning it was already 85 degrees. At the Clark Fork River I crossed the footbridge, an old iron-girdered railroad trestle fitted with wooden planks to link the campus with the old town to the north. The graffiti caught my eye: "Mike, where is your hair?" and "In memory of Frank, Victim of Society." Despite the visit with Tilden and my sister's problems, for a moment this trip to Missoula was a simple vacation, full of relaxation and ease, the sun on my shoulders melting away worries. Only for a moment.

Circling back via the Madison Street Bridge, I called Elaine from Melina's. No one answered. I cursed as I replaced the receiver on the hook. I struck out for the campus on foot to retrieve my car. The walk had been good for me. It helped me to work out a plan of attack. Moody, Elaine, Wade. Again.

My feet were beginning to burn in my clogs as I rounded the business administration building. The heat distracted me so much I didn't realize that the Saab wasn't where I left it. I stood on the curb gaping at the empty spot. The parking lot was completely empty, the asphalt shimmering. What the hell—?

My car had been towed. I had parked it under a conspicuous Permit Parking Only—Faculty and Staff sign, accompanied by the graphic for a tow truck. Damn. Even in the summer vigilantes were everywhere, bringing down the rebels.

After numerous wrong turns and not a few curses I found campus security tucked away under a towering cottonwood tree as far as humanly possible from my parking place. I pushed through the glass door, shocked for a moment by the wall of air-conditioned air.

Moments later I stumbled back out into the midday sun, confused by the heat, the cool, the turn of events. The campus police had not towed my car. In fact they did no towing between terms. Summer school did not start for a week. The Saab, they suggested, had been stolen; they referred me to the Missoula Police Department.

Lieutenant Malsome's office wasn't as cool as I had hoped but cool enough. I waited, collecting my melted parts, until he entered, closing the door behind him. Malsome wasn't a big man but he carried himself like one, his uniform trim and exact.

"I was wondering when you'd be back." He sat behind his desk, setting down a file. He had a business face, square, accentuated by a short, flat, brown haircut.

I blinked. "Oh, right. The, ah, trailer. I'm working on the research. No sense tying up your phone lines."

"You'll bill us for the calls, I'm sure."

Malsome had a sly way about him that I liked. I sensed, however, that he wasn't going to like my bill. No matter how small. He ran his fingertips through the short hair over his ears.

"Lieutenant, I have a problem." I set my backpack on the floor, leaning against his desk. "Someone stole my car."

Within seconds Malsome had buzzed for someone to take me off his hands. He opened the door, letting in a young cop. As I picked up my pack and straightened, I recognized the Paolo lookalike who had come to Melina's with the bad news.

"Officer Mendez will take your statement," Malsome said, shooing us out. The cop led me silently to his desk and motioned at a chair.

"You're sure one of your friends didn't borrow it?" Mendez had Paolo's singsong voice with only a trace of Spanish accent, more a lilt than anything else. The resemblance wasn't quite as strong as I first thought. Striking though.

"I don't have friends here. I'm visiting my sister."

"Maybe she borrowed it." He looked at me again. "You a friend of the lieutenant's?"

"I'm working for him." A twinge of disappointment stung—he didn't remember me from Melina's porch. I slipped off my clogs to feel the cool tile floor.

Officer Mendez sat and typed, asking questions around a pencil held between his teeth.

"All right, Miss Thorssen," he said, removing the pencil and ripping the form from his typewriter with a sound that made me jump. "We'll put out the description of your car. Maybe it will show up." He made it sound like a needle in a haystack. He looked over his desk at my bare feet, a smile creeping onto his lips. "Don't I know you from somewhere?"

I stood up, sliding into the shoes. Not a chance, copper.

"Do you need a ride somewhere?" he asked as I walked off, too beat to answer. My back and shoulders hurt like hell. I could think of only one thing, a cool bath.

"Miss Thorssen?" Officer Mendez (Carl Mendez, his name tag said) caught me as I opened the outer door. "I'm going on break now. I can give you a ride."

Riding unexpectedly in a police cruiser with the radio dispatcher chattering stunned me. I sat in silence, listening to ten-fours and rogers and five-oh-threes. I had no idea what they were talking about. Officer Mendez picked up the radio and told the dispatcher he was ten-seven-oh-dee. OD? Overdose? What had he said. Taking a break. Off Duty.

She came back on and told him he was assigned to ten-fourteen-eff at three o'clock. He mumbled a quick reply and set the radio back on its hook between us.

"What's that?" I asked finally when the radio was silent.

"What?"

"Ten-fourteen-eff."

"Funeral escort."

Funeral. This time they would be burying Shiloh, not praising her. Mendez drove expertly through downtown Missoula, past historic houses and cheap motels, past apartment buildings and burger joints, across the Madison Street Bridge and the high, muddy river to Melina's house. He said nothing until he pulled up to the curb.

"I'll let you know if your car shows up." He leaned toward the passenger window to see me on the sidewalk. Even with

the aviator sunglasses, he looked like my business partner.
"Thanks for the ride, Mendez," I said, letting his name
slip off my tongue before I realized what I'd done. I stepped
back, flipping my hair off my face, trying to pretend I'd meant
to say it. His smile broadened as he pulled the cruiser back
into the traffic.

$\triangledown$

10

STANDING WITH A towel draped around my pale, tan-resistant body, I dripped on the bathroom floor as the phone rang. The cool bath had revived me. Late-afternoon sun filtered through the branches into the room, orange shapes playing over the old claw-foot tub. The water gurgled, making obscene sucking noises as gravity tugged it down the drain.

On the third ring I found the phone in the pile of laundry. The adolescent voice of Kenyon Tiernan from the FBI barked on the line. I made him wait while I grabbed a robe and my notebook and pen.

"Okay, shoot." I sat on the dark wood floor.

"Jackson Pollock." The agent sneezed loudly into the phone. "Sorry. Raging summer cold. They blow in off the lake."

"Sorry." I was trying to be nice. Out of the bath now, revived, my impatience rose dangerously. "What do you have on the Pollock?"

"Nothing in the last five years. No known forgeries or thefts. There was a minor fracas, a botched theft at a museum in Texas, in '84. Nothing else. Wilsall seemed to think he was pretty well buttoned up."

"That's what I thought too. It seemed pretty odd to have a private collector out soliciting buyers."

Tiernan blew his nose. Loudly. "Better give me the details on that guy. The seller. Just in case."

I gave him the man's name and number. "Anything else?"

"I'm still working on that laundry list from the trailer.

Boss wants to check out jurisdiction. We might take it off your hands."

"Damn. I need the money."

Tiernan laughed, nasally. "Otherwise we drew a blank, like I said. Oh, wait." Papers rustled. "You asked me to run your customer through—Vardis? I came up with something. She made an inquiry about a year ago."

"About what?"

"Some Indian artifact."

I waited. "And?"

"We didn't have anything on it."

My heart began to pound. Why was everyone so interested in Indians all of a sudden? "What artifact?"

"She called it, ah, the bluejay pictograph. Some kind of stone carving or painting," he said. A dry chuckle. "I don't think we ever had any pictographs reported. They'd be too big to sell."

I frowned. "Unless it was small. Chain-sawed off a rock wall."

"Oh, well, right," the agent said. "Sure, unless it was small."

"Was it stolen?"

"Uh, not that it says so in the file. Looks like she just wanted to check up on it. Maybe she's the owner."

When Melina got home about six I had made us a dinner of sausages and salad. It wasn't much, I admitted to her, but she didn't have much in the refrigerator. She was tired and therefore grateful. I was glad to see she ate dinner, at least.

I told her about my car disappearing and reporting it to the police. She seemed distracted. My old car was the least of her worries. Shoot, her husband might never come home. Who cares about a rusty heap of a car?

"Mail's on the counter in here," I called over my shoulder, taking our plates to the kitchen. "I'll make some coffee."

Melina brought more dishes in, rifling through the mail. She stared at a white business envelope before ripping it open.

"It's from Mom." She stood in the middle of the kitchen floor reading the long handwritten letter on large sheets of white paper. Two photographs fell to the floor. She stooped, handing them to me. "They're from Syttende Mai last month."

Syttende Mai, "Seventeenth of May," is Norwegian Independence Day, celebrated much like the Fourth of July. It also serves as a spring festival after the long winter months. Lots of food and dancing and wearing costumes from the old country.

"I didn't know Una still belonged to the Sons of Norway. I mean since Rollie died," I said. The snapshots showed our svelte, young-looking mother in a red weskit and white puffed-sleeve blouse dancing with her new husband, Hank Helgeson, at the Billings Elks Club. "Hank looks like he's a good dancer." Hank was shorter than Una but they looked good together.

"Not as good as Rollie, I bet." Melina put the letter on the counter. "You can read it if you want." Her voice sounded angry suddenly. Her defense of Rollie was both touching and out of proportion to Hank's crime.

"I like Hank," I said, turning back to the dishes while Melina poured herself some coffee. "Mom seems happy."

"I'm sure she is," Melina said, cradling the steaming cup in her hands. "I like Hank too. It's just that—" Her voice trailed off.

"What?"

"Oh, God, Alix. I still miss Daddy." She choked on her words then laughed at herself, a harsh sound. "Look at me. This is so stupid." She resumed blowing on her coffee.

I turned to her. "I miss him too, Mel. I guess we always will."

She looked me in the eye. "You were always so strong. So together. Independent. And you're the one who suffered the most. I had Daddy all my growing-up years. He saw me get married. He gave me away at the wedding."

The tears welled up and spilled over; I set the towel down

to go to her. But she waved me away. "It's more than missing him, you know." She took a deep breath, staring at the ceiling with red-rimmed eyes. When she spoke her voice was a whisper: "He was the same age as I am now. When he died."

Her pale skin was splotched with red now, making her look worse. I felt paralyzed. I wasn't good at this. My heart went out to her but I had my own heartbreak to contend with. I loved him too. I missed his rough hands and his mischief-making smile too. When he drowned in Flathead Lake, his body never found, a piece of me always felt it was unfinished business. But business I kept in a hard, hard box. To take it out, to take on both of our heartbreaks, would sink me.

"Mel," I whispered. My words stuck in my throat.

She took a sip of coffee. "I'm sorry. I'm really a wreck with all this—all this about Wade." She turned, taking her cup into the other room. I finished the dishes, feeling her pain grow in me. She may think I'm strong but I'm only a better actor. I don't show it. It doesn't mean I don't feel the losses, the sorrow. I do, I do.

In the living room the doorbell rang. In a moment Melina's footsteps hurried toward the kitchen. She didn't even pause to give me her message: "You answer the door." She headed out the door that led to the stairs, leaving me with little choice.

I flipped on the porch light in the dusk. The familiar outline momentarily stopped me from pulling on the handle.

"Dr. Tilden. What a surprise." The bulb on the porch slanted harsh light over his features, the shadow from his nose slashing across his cheek like a scar.

"May I come in?" he asked, pulling the screen door from me. I backed away to let him pass, leaving the inner door ajar.

Tilden wore the same khakis and short-sleeved plaid shirt, now with half-moons of sweat under his arms. His lined forehead was sticky. He stuck his hands in his pockets and looked around the living room with curiosity. "Is Melina here?"

"Ah, she's not feeling too well. All the stress with Wade, you know."

He nodded, frowning. What a repertoire of expressions the man had. "I was thinking about our talk today, Alix." He turned and faced me, staring at me in a way that was too familiar. "Did you know I brought Wade here to Missoula? We were both from Arkansas."

"No, I didn't know that." I decided to humor him.

"It's true." He sank into a chair without ceremony, a faraway look in his big black eyes. "I was his professor there. Hogback U. Wade came here for graduate school. Oh, we had some good times then. We used to go up on the reservation and stay all summer. Camp in tepees. Have bonfires, ceremonies with the Salish, the Kootenai. Sing and drum. Oh, how we'd sing."

The clock ticked on the mantle. I hooked my thumbs over the waistband of my sweatpants. Was this the man I had thought a crusader for Indian rights? Some Marlon Brando he'd make. His jaw continued to move as if he was talking to himself. He was lost in the past. He looked spent suddenly and I pitied him.

"Do you still go up on the reservation?"

He jerked his head toward me. "Hmmm? Oh, yes, sometimes. But not so much as . . . then."

I thought about what Father Percy had said. Tilden sat like a statue, immobile, staring. How could I bring up the mission? Say, Father Percy thinks you have an attitude problem? What gives? Then, without explanation, a chill went up my spine. Tilden was strange, *off*, somehow.

Out of his reverie Tilden smiled. Suddenly he was banal and harmless, reminiscing about times gone by. Then just as quickly he turned to me, his eyes flashing. "Would you like to see my sweathouse?"

The night breathed cool velvet air, apologizing for the day's heat. I rolled down the window on my side of Tilden's old Dodge, letting the air whistle by my ears. His house was on the other side of the campus, an older, nicer neighborhood. We walked up the dark driveway to his garage.

Crickets sang to the moon, hanging like a silver dollar in the dark sky. Tilden grabbed the handle of the garage door. The rumble of the door going up sent another shiver up my spine. I wondered, not for the first time, if this was a safe thing to do. The Victorian windows of the house were lit, and a figure passed by in the light. Someone else was close by, just in case.

I shrugged off my fear. Okay, he was a little different. He was an academic, a brain. I'd always cut Wade a little slack for that. Besides, I wouldn't stay long.

He turned on an overhead light. "This is it." A large domed structure filled most of the two-car garage. It looked like a warm-weather igloo. The bent-willow structure, some four feet tall, was strewn with quilts, throw rugs, and blankets. On the left side of the room a wood-burning stove sat against the wall, a pile of rocks on it and a smokestack through the garage roof.

"I'm heating up rocks right now. That's why it's hot in here," he explained, rounding the sweathouse and smiling brightly. "You want to go in?"

He pushed back a quilt that served as an entry flap and bent down to go in. "Take off your shoes. And metal jewelry," he instructed. "And move from left to right around the circle." I did as I was told, slipping off a bracelet and dropping it into my clog. The dome had evergreen branches stuck in between the quilts and the frame.

"This is where we put the rocks when they're hot," he said, sitting cross-legged on the blankets spread for a floor. He pointed to a hollowed-out bowl in the floor close to the entrance. I stood awkwardly bent over. "Sit."

I sat. To me, fully dressed, the small space was hot enough. The garage must have been an oven today. I couldn't imagine staying in here with steam heat and the flap closed. I was ready to tell him I was claustrophobic (not far from the truth) when he began to sing.

He closed his eyes, tilting his head back with the rhythmic song, keeping the beat with his palms on his knees. The

words, if that's what they were, meant nothing to me. The
song had a familiar chant to it, a cadence of the wild, an
untamed rhythm. I began to bob my head, keeping time with
his music, loosening.

My eyes grew accustomed to the dark. Even so Tilden was
a bare outline, his white teeth flashing with moonlight that
came through the open flap. I couldn't see the house
windows but their reflective glow covered the backyard.
What a strange man, I thought, listening to him sing. So
didn't enjoying it make me weird?

But his chanting calmed me, as if the rhythm nurtured
something primal in me. I nodded along, trying to feel
instead of think. But as soon as I got a little comfortable the
absurdity of all this would hit me. And try as I might, I didn't
trust the man.

I shifted on the hard floor, my hip bones beginning to ache.
Sweat ran down my back. My throat felt parched and dry.

"Dr. Tilden," I whispered. He continued, eyes shut,
Adam's apple bobbing with the throaty chant. "Dr. Tilden,"
I repeated, louder. He stopped abruptly. "Can I get a glass of
water?"

"Of course." He blinked at me as if he'd forgotten I was
there. "This is not a ceremony." He closed his eyes again. I
rose awkwardly in the low dome and shuffled out. The chant
began again. Stretching my back, I was relieved to be out of
the tiny structure. I slid on my bracelet and clogs and
wandered into the cool backyard to find a faucet.

The stars shone now, pinholes in the sky's mantle,
twinkling their little hearts out next to the shimmering
moon, not quite full. The backyard of Tilden's house looked
white in its glow, neat but sterile, just a rectangle of lawn
surrounded by a chain link fence. A hose hung by the back
steps. I turned the faucet on for a drink.

I gulped, spilling the water down my chin and neck. Up
the back stairs a door opened. In the darkness a woman
stepped from the house, lit by the moon. "Who's there?" she
barked.

I cranked the faucet off quickly. "Uh. My name is Alix Thorssen. Dr. Tilden was showing me his sweathouse and I got thirsty. I'm sorry if I bothered you."

"Oh." Her voice softened. She turned her face toward the garage. "Well, you better go now." She stepped back inside before I could say he had driven me over.

In the garage Tilden still sang, his voice as strong as ever. The blisters from this afternoon screamed on my feet; I had my share of walking today. I had no intention of asking the professor for a ride home; he was otherwise engaged. Let him have his little chanting session. Reluctantly I mounted the back steps and knocked.

The woman was shorter than she looked from the bottom of the wooden steps. She opened the door again, silver hair cascading past her shoulders. She wore a flowing cotton skirt in a batik print. Her features could have graced a Greek statue. Even with annoyance masking her natural expression, I thought I had seen her before.

"Sorry to bother you again." I smiled and tried to look nonthreatening. "I need to use your phone to get a ride home."

"The phone's there." Her kitchen was old but spotless. Neat rows of wine glasses sparkled on homemade shelves. A throw rug with an apple design on it lay below the sink. I moved to a white telephone on a side counter.

"Melina?" I said when my sister answered. "Could you come get me at Tilden's?"

"What are you doing there?"

I looked behind me. Mrs. Tilden stood sentry at the door, lips pinched. "Yes, that would be great," I said, ignoring her question. "In a few minutes. Thanks, Mel."

I hung up. Mrs. Tilden threw back her hair. "Melina Fraser?"

"My sister," I said. "I'm here from out of town to—to visit." She didn't want to hear our family troubles. Every family has them. Then I recognized her. "Didn't I see you at Shiloh's service?"

She glanced away, smoothing her hair. "I spoke there. She was a friend, a colleague."

I stuck out my hand. "I guess we didn't get introduced properly, Mrs. Tilden."

She took my hand in a weak shake. "My name is Sylvie Kali."

"Alix Thorssen." I put my hands in the back of my waistband. Sweat had dampened the fabric. "Shiloh was a colleague?"

She licked her lips. "We were in the same field. Holistic counseling. Family therapy, dream work." She frowned as if irritated with herself. "It doesn't matter. Anyway, some of her friends asked me to speak at the memorial." She paused. "And I was glad to."

I tried to think of more questions for her. A sadness clung to her. She too mourned the loss. Shiloh had a lot of friends. We listened through the door to Tilden's rhythmic singing. It seemed to float on the night air, magical, otherwordly. "He's really very good," I said.

"Yes. He is."

"Melina will be here in a minute," I said, heading toward the door. "Thanks for the phone." The singing grew louder as I stepped into the night. Sylvie closed the door behind me without a word.

The old orange Volkswagen sedan pulled up to the curb. My sister waited for me to climb in, smiling as she pulled out.

"Let's go get something to eat," she said.

I assumed she would question me about what was going on at the Tildens'; her calm smile confused me. Wasn't she just irritated a moment ago? Or was it crying? I couldn't keep up. She turned the wheezing car around dark corners, over the bridge, parking in front of Montana Pies.

After ordering pie (she: cherry; me: pecan with whipped cream) and coffee, Melina laid her hands on the table. "Paolo called just as I was going out the door to get you."

"Yeah?"

"He said to tell you he couldn't find anything about any Jackson Pollock paintings from the 'dreepee' period being for sale or in small collections."

I smiled at her imitation of Paolo's accent. "Thanks."

"And you're supposed to call the woman. The client." Melina took a sip of coffee. "He's so sweet, Alix."

I readied my defenses and took a bite of pie. "Don't start."

"Such a shame. I guess some men never quit fooling around. Just not cut out for monogamy." She stared out the window that reflected the bright lights and nauseous pastels of the restaurant.

Straight from the Marriage and the Family text. But I agreed. "Paolo, for one."

"He said your horse was spotted near Nora's Fish Creek Restaurant," she said after a swig of coffee. "Eating out of the dumpster."

"Valkyrie always did like pancakes." Only I didn't need a renegade horse right now.

Melina looked me in the eye. "We have to go see Wade tomorrow. Hondo called. I want to be able to tell him we're making progress." Her face pleaded with me for some crumb of reassurance. I ate pie. "What did Tilden want?" she asked.

"He wanted to show me his sweathouse." I leaned forward. "Do you know his wife? Sylvie?"

"No," Melina said. "He's always been secretive about her. She never came to departmental functions, parties, or whatever. When I was going."

"You don't go anymore?"

"I got sick of it. Wade didn't care one way or the other." She twisted her fork on her crumb-strewn plate. "Alix, I have to tell you something." She straightened up, closing her eyes as she sighed. "It's about me and Wade."

I opened my mouth to protest. I didn't want to hear this. What was between her and Wade should stay there. But she held up her hand to stop me.

"Just let me say it. I love Wade. But you know he can be pigheaded too. I've been applying to doctorate programs." I raised my eyebrows; I didn't know she was going for her Ph.D. "Yeah, it happens when you pass forty. Now or never." She smiled, like the prospect excited her. She twisted a lock of her hair around her finger as she talked.

She took a deep breath. "I got accepted to a program at Brown. Back East, Rhode Island. I was so excited." Then she frowned. "But Wade doesn't want to go. And he told me in no uncertain terms that if I go without him not to come back."

I looked at her downcast face, her smeared glasses over her fair cheeks. "He didn't mean it, Mel."

"I think he did." Her voice was small. "Of course that was before . . . all this."

A group of blue-uniformed officers rose from a booth across the room just then, talking among themselves as they came down the aisle past our table toward the door. Policemen are always taking coffee breaks. The last one in the bunch seemed to hang back. I glanced up to see Officer Mendez give me a furtive smile before he rejoined the others.

Melina watched me return a weak smile. She pinched her eyebrows together. I ignored her and grumbled: "Let's get out of here."

▽

11

"BROUGHT YOU SOMETHING, WADE."

He snapped his head up at the sound of Melina's voice. He looked at her, then the sack. "Cookies," she said softly.

A spider inched up the cement-block wall in the small, hot room in the bowels of the Lake County Courthouse. Had Melina said progress? Well, physically we were backsliding. The dark circles under Melina's eyes were darker. Her glasses were smeared from a teary episode in the car on the way up. A wad of tissue hung in her jacket pocket like a bundle of contraband. As for me, the heat, a stolen car, blisters, and zero leads made me cranky.

Only Hondo looked no worse for wear. But he was no closer to springing our troubled anthropologist. He told us in the car that Shiloh's blood had been matched to the blood on the knife, as Tilden had somehow learned. This made the state's case even stronger. No fingerprints but, well, that didn't matter. Nothing new to use to petition for another bond hearing.

Melina's chewed nails caressed the paper bag's fold until it was as limp as worn leather in her hands. She'd been up until two baking the cookies. I stood against the wall again, trying to dredge up a hopeful expression.

Wade sat in a heap on the hard chair, the worst example of physical deterioration. His hair hung in greasy threads; the unkempt beard stuck out in all directions, dotted with who-knows-what, his complexion sallow. He hung his head, a beaten man.

His handcuffs were off. One guard locked the door from the outside while another stepped back by me against the wall. Melina smiled at Wade, or tried, pushing the bag of cookies across the table.

The guard stepped forward and dumped the cookies onto the table. They broke into pieces, spilling crumbs everywhere. Wade moaned and rocked his head.

"What'd you have to do that for, Leroy? Shit." Wade glared at the guard. His anger gave me hope, a spark maybe we could fan into a blaze again. Leroy didn't reply but swept the cookie parts back in the sack. "Thanks, man. Thanks a heap."

"It's all right, Wade," Melina said. "They'll still taste the same." She frowned at him. "Have you been having trouble sleeping? You're not getting that night itching again, are you?"

Wade slumped in reply, his hands limp on his knees. Hondo cleared his throat to speak. "They found her blood on the knife, buddy."

Wade looked up, out the tiny barred window high in one wall. "I heard."

"Is there anything you can remember about that night? Anything you haven't told us?" The lawyer asked.

"You mean like a confession? No way, man," Wade growled. "I didn't do it. I didn't kill her. There's nothing to tell. I went to sleep, goddammit. That's it."

Melina's hand patted the table. "He didn't mean that, Wade. He just thought you might have remembered something that would prove you were at Moody's."

"There you go again—" Wade clipped his sentence, shutting his mouth with a click of his teeth, as if he didn't have the energy now to harangue his wife. We all knew what he began to say, another suggestion of infidelity. Hondo fiddled with a jacket button, his head down. Tension lay thick in the air.

"I've got some questions, Wade," I said. "If you two are done."

Hondo stood up, the scratching of his chair on the cement floor cutting through the silence. I sat down. "I've been following up on the vandalism you were looking into. Melina and I went to see Moody. Then I talked to Father Percy about the artworks at the mission. He's worried about you."

Wade wagged his head. "He's a good man."

"Tilden's been up there."

Wade looked at me, twitched his curly eyebrows, and frowned. "I didn't think he went up on the Rez much anymore."

"Father Percy wouldn't tell me why. He just said Tilden was a disagreeable man," I said. "That's all."

"Hmmm. No shit."

"The paintings that were vandalized?" I ticked them off on my fingers. "The woman, the fresco on the wall. The other was an Indian named Shining Shirt. Father Percy told me the legend about him seeing the vision of the black skirts. Is there any more to it, Wade?"

"Just his vision. And him getting that silver cross out of nowhere. That's the story."

"How about that statue—Kateri? Do you know anything about it?"

"Never saw it."

"Why do you suppose that statue was broken? When there are some older ones, bigger ones, like the big one at St. Ignatius, or the angels?"

Wade squinted his eyes. "Maybe random. That's what the cops said."

I didn't believe it. These vandals seemed pretty damn particular. "I have to know about the fight you and Dr. Tilden had eight years ago. The one they brought up in court?"

Wade flicked his eyes to his wife. I strained to hear his answer: "That was nothing, Alix."

"I have to know everything if I can even hope to find out what happened."

He sighed and spoke in a low voice, hurrying. "All right. Dr. Tilden wrote a paper. I disagreed with it and wrote a rebuttal. He got mad and we . . . struggled."

"What was the paper about?"

"Um. It was about Shining Shirt." Wade's eyes widened. "Do you think Tilden slashed that painting at the mission?"

"It would be hard to prove."

"Wait a minute," Melina said. "What if he did? I mean, what if Tilden did go around vandalizing things? That is not our problem. Wade has to get out of jail. Proving Tilden hates Catholics isn't going to do that."

"True. But Wade was looking into the vandalism."

Hondo sat on the edge of the table behind me. "Then why didn't Tilden come after Wade? What did Shiloh have to do with it?"

"I don't know," I admitted, shaking my head. I hated this jumbled feeling, pieces alive, there, but without meaning. Wade stared at me. "Tell me about those papers."

Wade looked alert again, eyes bright. "Tilden's theory was that Shining Shirt was a sham. That the legend was a bunch of hokum dredged up by the priests to justify their place in the tribe. He said the priests must have thought the vision alone wouldn't fly so they made up the bit about the silver cross that Shining Shirt wore. Said the priests had given it to him."

Wade licked his lips, the color back in his cheeks. "I wrote a letter to the editor. I said that it wasn't our place to meddle in tribal culture. We are anthropologists. We study cultures, we don't manipulate them. In fact, we try to make the impact of our research as minimal as possible. We shouldn't be telling the Salish or anybody else what they should or shouldn't believe. Self-determination, you know."

"What did Tilden do?"

"Blew a gasket. He came over to the house."

"And you struggled?"

"More or less. I guess I pushed him down the porch stairs because he wouldn't leave." Wade drew his hand over the corners of his mouth.

"There's more to it, Alix." Melina's voice was odd, hard.

Wade jerked his head toward her. "Mel." He whispered. "Don't."

"I have to tell her, Wade," she said. "And Hondo's a lawyer, he can't tell."

Wade seemed to shrink. Melina turned to me. "Dr. Tilden told Wade that he—Marcus—and I were—having an affair. That was when Wade threw Marcus off the porch."

The pen slipped from my hand, clattering to the cement floor. It bounced there for a moment, then settled into a roll that ended at the guard's feet. He stooped, picking it up.

"And—and were you?" I stammered at last.

"No." My sister looked me in the eye, her face never more serious. Then her composure cracked. "We did have—a—a flirtation."

Wade snorted through his nose, breaking the tension. Hurt shone in his eyes as he looked at the tiny window. Hondo shifted on the table edge beside me; I dared not look at his face.

Melina sat back, stroking her hair with a shaky hand. I took a breath, trying to quash a rising tide of emotion. I felt my sister's pain, rising, rising. No. I cleared my throat. "Which means what?"

My sister's hazel eyes shot to Wade's face. Her jaw tightened. "We talked on the phone. We were friends."

I expected Wade to snort again but he was silent. I had run out of things to say, my mind in a whirlpool of feelings I didn't know what to do with, where to bury.

"You have to understand about Marcus and me," Wade said in a low voice. "Ever since I came up here from Fayetteville he's been my mentor. Or so he likes to think. Eight years ago, when all this took place, he was already washed up. He knew it. That's why he raked up all this crap about Shining Shirt." He ran his fingers through his greasy hair. "It was so ludicrous it was funny. Only it wasn't."

Melina said, "He was just trying to get back at Wade through me. I should have seen it. Wade got tenure the first year he taught. And published a paper on Salish and Kootenai religious practices that he was asked to present at the national meeting."

"Marcus's field too," Wade said.

"A rivalry," I said.

"Exactly." Wade fingered his beard in thought. "I should have seen it coming. But I never thought—Do you know what the students call him? Mad Dog. Mad Dog Tilden."

"He showed me his sweathouse last night."

"In the garage? He's had that for years." He shook his head. "You know, I feel sorry for him. He really did help me in graduate school."

"That was a long time ago," Melina said.

We stood up to go. I felt a little dizzy. Wade sat stroking his beard. He smelled like leftover salami, I thought, as I passed him.

"Wade," I turned back to him. "Have you heard of something called a bluejay pictograph?"

His eyebrows twitched. "Bluejay?"

"Pictograph. Possibly small?"

"Doesn't ring any bells. What tribe?"

"I don't know." Melina and Hondo waited in the hallway. "Think about it."

12

"THIS IS ALIX THORSSEN from Second Sun Gallery. I've looked into that Jackson Pollock you were interested in."

In the Penthouse, as I began to call Wade's under-the-eaves office, the desktop was finally clear. I had stacked extraneous stuff, monographs, files, tests, handouts, and odds and ends in the far corner, making room for only the information related to the case. The cleanup had taken all afternoon. Attend to business. Focus. Concentrate. What I needed was a Zen master at my side, prodding me.

Charlotte Vardis squealed with delight on the line. Apparently she thought this was good news.

I frowned. "The man's name you gave my partner doesn't show up as a registered owner or dealer. All the Pollocks from that period are accounted for in museums or private collections. There is a slight possibility that it is an undocumented work. But I wouldn't recommend taking that chance."

"I see. Oh, I don't throw my money away," she said. She didn't sound particularly disappointed. When faced with the truth most art collectors prefer to believe what they want to believe. They covet a painting so much they can't believe it's not authentic. "I can't thank you enough for saving me the money—and the aggravation."

"If you like the piece you could buy it based on its artistic merit," I said. "But don't pay what you would pay for an authentic Pollock."

"Hmmm. I don't think I'll do that. There was something

magical about it being a Jackson Pollock. If it's not, well, it's just another splatter thing."

Yes, and Pollock was the King of Splatter. I considered him a media phenomenon, an eccentric coddled by the press more than a great artist. But what I liked didn't have to hang on her walls either.

As I hung up the heavy black receiver the thought came to me that Charlotte Vardis wasn't dealing with me straight. Something about her demeanor was off-key. Maybe she was just a rich flake. She sounded intelligent. But what about the bluejay pictograph she was looking for? Where could I find something about that?

The phone rang almost immediately. It was Lieutenant Malsome.

"Haven't seen you down here, Ms. Thorssen. How's the work going?"

"Good. Real good." I searched the desktop frantically for my notes on my real business in Missoula. It seemed far from important now.

"Got any leads?"

"Um. I was hoping you might have tracked down the renter."

"Still working on it. An obvious bunko."

"Probably stolen then. Any reported?"

The policeman cleared his throat. "We haven't seen your report of the items so we can't reference them to the hot sheet. Can we?"

Shit. "I'll get it to you tomorrow, Lieutenant."

If I can find it. There was too much going down. I found my backpack, pulled out the notebook, and furiously typed up on Wade's old Royal what little information I had. The list would give them a start against the hot sheet. I sealed it into an envelope and walked it three blocks to the mailbox at a neighborhood grocery store. I didn't want to see Malsome, sit and talk about things I wasn't giving attention to.

On the way home I detoured onto Bickford Street where Elaine lived. The front door was open. I knocked on the screen door several times until at last Elaine came to the door.

Eyes puffy and red, she blinked at me. "Yes?"

I reminded her of who I was. "Do you have a few minutes to talk about Shiloh?" I said gently.

Not gently enough. Elaine burst into tears, sobbing into the wet tissue. "Can't you see I miss her?"

My heart sank; what a heel I was. Her blond curls hung around her smeared face. As usual, no words came to mind for comfort.

She stepped away, her hand on the doorknob. "You don't know how much . . . how much I loved her." Elaine slammed the door then, in my face. I flinched at the abrupt sound. Then she opened it a crack. "Sorry about that," she said, pushing the door shut carefully.

The peach house sat still, forlorn, the grass still dead despite the thunderstorm. I stood on the sidewalk for a minute, thinking about the two women, then doubled back through the alley, counting the houses until there, in the deepening gloom of a summer's night, I saw the bungalow's glow.

The old single-stall garage had a definite list to the south. It hugged the alley. No one had bothered to spruce up its paint, so it peeled in a dreary gray, flaking around the edges into the raw dirt like dandruff. I walked around to the far side, which clung to a straggly row of lilacs. Pushing the branches aside, I found a window and pulled out my small flashlight.

The dirt on the window was thick and greasy. Cupping my hands around my eyes and holding the flashlight to my temple, I squinted into the building.

After several seconds the outline of a car came into focus. I blinked, waiting longer for my eyes to adjust, moving the flashlight back and forth down the bulky object. I shone it on one end, then was sweeping it back the other way when it caught the corner of something. Lettering.

The flashlight turned back, down. A box there, with lettering. I moved the light up. Covered by a black tarp or blanket, not a car, boxes. I squinted, trying to read through the glare of the glass and the grime of generations. Green letters; y-f-l-o-w-e-r. Something missing at the beginning. Blank-y-flower. Mayflower.

Moving boxes. Quickly I scanned the rest of the object, with its pointed corners and square sides. A score of large cardboard boxes, neatly stacked and covered with a black tarp. In the cracked cement corners and cobwebbed ceiling, the flashlight revealed no more.

Melina sat on the porch with coffee when I returned. I had missed supper. She heated me a plate of meatballs that I told her tasted just like Mom's. The barking of a dog echoed down the alley. I settled onto the railing, sipping coffee.

"Mel, you said you knew Shiloh?" She looked surprised at the topic; she'd been thinking of something else.

"A little," she said through the steam of her coffee. "I saw her around."

"How did she dress?"

"I never really noticed. Well, hippie, you know. Dumpy hippie."

I shifted on the rail, trying to figure out a way to approach the subject that had been nagging at me since visiting Elaine. "Did you hear it said—um—did it ever occur to you that Shiloh might be more interested in women than men?"

Melina blinked. "Possibly. I mean, now that you mention it."

"It occurred to you?"

"Possibly," she repeated, trying to conceal her embarrassment.

"I was just thinking about that women's group. And tonight when I went to Elaine's. She said I had no idea how much she loved Shiloh."

Melina took a sip of coffee, slitted her eyes. "Well, that doesn't mean anything. Not everybody's Norwegian. They were friends. They might have loved each other as friends."

"Do you have any friends you would bawl over like that? Tell strangers how much you loved them?"

Melina cocked her head. "I'm not Elaine."

At Rollie's funeral none of us had cried. Mom seemed to be made of stone. The entire Lutheran church was filled with people he knew, or Mom knew, or Melina or I knew, or just knew the family. Some folks came up from Belfry, relatives and friends from Mom's youth. There were a few weepers but most of us stood and sang "I Come to the Garden Alone" dry-eyed, trying hard not to hear the words.

In the jail though, Melina had wept. It bothered me how much I'd seen her cry. More than I did in all the years of growing up. Of course, around Mom a person learned to buck up, not to show the pain. I still was like that, like Mom, and people accused me of being cold. But that's who I am. It doesn't mean I don't care as much as the next person. I just don't fall apart.

"A crime of passion, you think?" she asked, avoiding my question.

"It's a primary motive for murder."

Dark descended on Blaine Street. A string of children flew by, some on bicycles, others racing on foot like the wind. The air was still, breathless. The streets were jabbed with light from porches and living rooms. I tried to concoct a reason for the boxes. Somebody was moving, that was simple. But who? Elaine moving out on Shiloh? Shiloh moving out on Elaine? Somehow Elaine seemed too genuinely broken up to be the one moving out. Had she stopped Shiloh from moving out the only sure way? I shivered, though the night was balmy.

13

"ALIX? I DIDN'T know who else to call." The voice was familiar. My mind struggled to clear. My watch said six-thirty.

"Father Percy?"

"There's been another intruder," he gasped. "Another statue was smashed and—" His voice trailed off, overcome.

"What did they do, Father?"

"They were in my office. They've taken all my vestments."

"Just leave everything. Don't touch a thing," I said. "I'll be there in less than an hour."

He sighed. "Bless you."

"Father," I added. "Wait about half an hour, then call the sheriff." As I spun to get dressed the phone rang again. I grabbed for it, thinking he must have forgotten something.

The voice was different. "Miss Thorssen? Officer Mendez, Missoula Police Department. We've had a report of your car on the Flathead Indian Reservation."

That stopped me. I had almost forgotten I didn't have transportation; I would have to borrow Melina's beat-up VW to get up to the mission. I didn't know what to say. I blurted out: "Good."

The policeman made a noise in his throat. "You can do one of two things, Miss Thorssen." I was getting tired of his addressing me that way. It made me feel like a little white-haired schoolteacher. "You can wait a day or two for the local police to make a positive identification and bring the car in. Or you can travel to the location yourself and make the identification."

"I see. And what condition is the car in? Did they say?"

"I believe it is drivable," he said. "There may have been some damage, but it appears to be minor."

My mind tangled with logistics: driving Melina's car up there and having two cars to drive back. Melina driving me up, Hondo driving me up, hitchhiking.

"Miss Thorssen?" Mendez cleared his throat. "I've got the day off—I'm on evening today—if you need a ride up."

His voice had lost its gruff officiousness. My stomach turned over—with hunger, I told myself. So, the furtive smiles were leading to something. Still, I needed a ride and I needed my car back. "Are you sure?"

He was sure. I told him quickly about the vandalism at St. Ignatius Mission. He promised to pick me up in fifteen minutes.

Mendez and I reached the mission late, but it was only eight. The sun had reached the top of the granite-crowned Mission Mountains, promising another hot day. As I stepped into the parking lot gravel I tried to keep my mind on the vandalism, on Wade and Melina, on finding a killer. I had found my eyes wandering once too often to the back of Mendez's strong neck, or his left hand on the steering wheel, tanned and free of jewelry.

I didn't need the distraction, that much I was sure of. But perhaps he could help with the investigation. God knows I needed help. I felt like I was rowing against the current, getting further from the shoreline rather than closer.

The priest waited at the top of the stairs for us, wringing his hands. "Thank you for coming, Alix, thank you." He shook my hand, then looked at Mendez.

"This is Carl Mendez," I said. They shook hands. "He's taking me to find my car that was stolen. He's Missoula Police."

The priest nodded, looking at him warily. "The sheriff's due any minute."

I explained that Mendez was here unofficially but could help if Father Percy wanted him to. Mendez gave me a piercing look with his hot brown eyes: We hadn't actually discussed this. I smiled back. As long as he was here he could work. We stepped inside the chapel, following the priest to the front altar.

The pedestal where the statue of St. Ignatius had stood was empty. On the floor below it lay a mound of white shards. Father Percy shook his head sadly, lacing his fingers in front of him.

Carl wore jeans with a chamois shirt the color of the sunrise and black cowboy boots with a good-sized heel. He stooped, sifting gently through the debris. Fingerprints were out of the question. He held up a piece of the saint's hand holding a staff.

"Not much to go on. Sorry, Father."

The priest pinched his lips together and looked away from the empty pedestal where the statue had stood. "Come take a look at my office—I didn't go in there, just saw—" His voice trailed off.

The intrusion felt different in here, personal and vicious. All the drawers of the desk hung open, papers strewn everywhere. The desk top had been cleaned as if by the sweep of an angry arm. The priest's robes and vestments were all gone. A lonely wire hanger rattled in an empty closet.

"This is the place to be careful not to touch anything, Father," Carl said, standing in the doorway behind me. I was reluctant to go in. The air felt tense with hatred. Carl's breath was hot on my shoulder. "Especially on those closets. There may be fingerprints here."

He took my upper arms in his hands suddenly, making me flinch. "Let me go in. You wait with Father," he whispered, drawing me back, then slipping through the door.

He moved expertly, light as a cat in the cowboy boots, through papers and bookends and broken objects, looking at the desk, under it, in the open closets. Father Percy paced nervously, trailing his hand on the back pew. I leaned against the door frame feeling useless.

"Who would do such a thing, Father?" I asked.

He stopped and shook his head. "I don't know. It's crazy. Crazy!" He began pacing again, his rubber-soled shoes silent except for the squeak when he pivoted.

"Alix, come here." Mendez's voice was low, and so serious I chose not to react to him finally quitting calling me Miss Thorssen. I walked carefully into the small room, placing my feet as lightly as possible so as not to disturb things before the sheriff arrived. "Don't touch anything."

Mendez stood behind the desk, where the chair would have been if it hadn't been overturned and sitting in the corner. He stared up at the wall that partitioned off the office from the chapel. "Look."

I turned slowly. On the wall, in red spray paint that dripped like blood down the paneling, was a message. Plain and clear, aimed at Father Percy.

In two-foot-tall letters was written, "PAPISTS MUST DIE."

The phone rang on the other end of the line. I waited, huddled between the restrooms in the café where Mendez wanted to eat breakfast. I had ordered but was only able to nibble. The scene at the mission had shaken me almost as much as it had Father Percy. When we had shown Father the graffiti he had turned white and had had to sit down on a pew and pray.

Fortunately, the sheriff's deputies picked this moment for their arrival. Mendez and I left the priest in their care. He looked grateful to have someone to tell the whole scenario to again, getting back some of his color.

My sister's office phone rang on and on. She had to be in class. Mendez sat hunched over his plate, wiping a piece of toast around on his plate. He didn't look as much like Paolo as I had first thought. His looks were less exotic, more practical. Maybe it was their jobs.

Jamming the receiver against the chrome hook, I dialed Melina's home number. An old Indian man gimped past me into the men's room. The sagging door let a draft of fragrant odors through the crack. The sound of a racehorse stream hitting the porcelain echoed off the tile.

Carl seemed calmer than Paolo, more smooth and solid. It occurred to me that I was making these calls to avoid making small talk with him. It wasn't as if he pressed me. He was quiet himself, thoughtful, distressed about the vandalism. We discussed it briefly but it was just speculation. And neither of us seemed like the speculating type.

Melina answered. "I just couldn't go to work today, Alix. I've been trying so hard to keep up appearances, to make like everything is normal. And I just can't do it. Not today."

I was relieved she was only depressed, not crying. I couldn't take it if she cried much more. "They understand, Mel," I said.

"I guess. Wade called." Mel gave a low chuckle. "He sounded better. More up. Wouldn't you know it? He's up, I'm down. Saga of a Marriage."

She sounded bitter. I couldn't think of anything to say. Carl was staring at me over his coffee cup. I turned away.

"He wanted to talk to you," Melina said. "Something about what you asked him about? Bluejay something? Let me get my note," she said, dropping the phone. "Here. Bluejay pictograph. You asked him about it?"

"Right."

"He says he doesn't know of a pictograph but in Salish culture there used to be a dance for the bluejay shaman each winter. The shamans are still around. And the winter gatherings. But the ritual dance seems to have died out. He said to look it up in his files, or maybe the library, to find out more about it."

My heart began to beat in my ears. "Great." I had been

scribbling notes on a paper towel from the floor.
"What's all this about? Does this have to do with Wade?"
"I don't know, Mel."
Every little piece, I told myself.

The morning turned cloudy as Carl pointed his spotless El
Dorado with its worn elegance up the highway toward where
Tin-Tin camped on the Little Bitterroot. He kept glancing
at me scribbling notes to myself, the ones from the paper
towel, into my small spiral notebook.
  At last I closed it.
  "What's going on?" His tone was light, as if to say if I felt
he was prying to forget the whole question.
  I considered whether I had the time or energy to explain.
Yet he could help. And he had been kind enough to drive me
up here and look through the mission debris. I could
probably use the mind of a policeman.
  It still ticked me off that he hadn't connected me with
Wade. He had seen me at the house. I couldn't ask for his
help. If I told him everything the weariness of obligation
would cross his face, regret for having asked, pity for the
trials and tribulations of my family. I couldn't stand to see
that. He was just being polite. That was all.
  "Just some notes," I answered, looking out the side
window at a herd of buffalo fenced into the National Bison
Range. They looked puny in the distance. I tried—and
failed—to imagine their immense numbers and power a
century and a half ago.
  Mendez didn't ask again. I relaxed, glad I had not told him
everything. He had gotten directions from the sheriff's
department to the car. Putting the scrap of a map on the
steering wheel, he stared at it and the landmarks. He turned
onto a weedy dirt road that led into a grove of trees some
hundred yards off the highway.
  With the El Dorado parked in an open stretch off the sandy
ruts, we got out and scouted the bushes, looking for the Saab
Sister. The undergrowth was thick, tangled with berry

bushes and wild strawberries. Mossy rocks sat in the damp shade of the aspens and junipers.

"Over here!" His voice was muffled by the forest. I followed it, across the narrow rutted road, into a thicket of willows that shone like golden arrows in the sun.

"Where are you?" I called, having lost my bearings.

"Here!" His voice was closer. I turned right and pushed aside a large aspen branch, moving toward the sound. In a moment the undergrowth cleared. There, in a sun-splashed puddle surrounded by tall grass and the contents of the trunk, sat my Saab.

One tire was flat. I frowned at it but knew it was fixable. The old Saab Sister, its maroon face faded like lipstick on a matinee idol. Its gray-primed liver spots. Never enough money for a full paint job. But the salt on the roads, the gravel from the road construction, the tar, the oil? It never seemed worth it.

I cocked my head, feeling like I should have loved my car more. Like a mother loves a child. Surges of guilt rippled to my fingertips. I should have protected it from this. I opened my mouth to sigh but a strange feeling came over me. Both doors of the Saab gaped open, almost sprung, as if welcoming us to climb aboard.

But there was nothing friendly about it. I could see right through the car, from the weeds on one side to the tall wildflowers with blue tops on the other. A strong sense of violation swept over me. I was a private person. But someone had searched my car and by extension me, strip-searched me, checked my deepest recesses, plundered my secrets.

For a moment I stared at the Saab, unable to move. We had traveled many roads together, she and I. Then another car came to mind, also gaping open, doors like wings, flying. My father's car, the white Impala with its wing fins.

I blinked. That was a dream. But the image was clear. The Impala flying through the air, landing softly on the lake's calm blue waters.

But it hadn't happened that way. Rollie's Impala, weighted down with hardware samples (he'd given up lingerie for more manly items), had flown off the highway all right. But it didn't land softly. It sank like a rock, after a forty-foot dive off a cliff into the cold, dark depths of Flathead Lake. Not more than sixty miles from here. A lifetime ago.

"Alix." Carl shook my arm.

I blinked. He dropped his hand.

"Let's clean this stuff up," he said.

After fifteen minutes we had located everything but the jack handle and the radio. The handle was probably somewhere in the weeds but the radio (ancient, original equipment with only an AM band) would probably turn up in a pawn shop somewhere. The backseat gave us a little trouble. The car thief had pried up the seat bottom, bending the metal frame badly in the process. Carl tried to bend it back so it would fit again into the base and was only partially successful. Finally we both stood, hanging over the backs of the front seats. We positioned the wayward cushion just so, then sat down in unison, as hard as we could throw ourselves. Still it popped up on one side and probably always would.

Mendez was grinning. "Let's do that again. Maybe we can get it to work."

"If we do it twenty times maybe," I said, pushing down on the sprung corner. It made a metallic, scratchy *booiinnng.* "I can see us out here jumping up and down all day on it." I put my knees up on the back of the driver's seat and slouched back, folding my arms across my chest. At least they hadn't slashed the old brown upholstery.

Carl leaned forward and put his elbow on the back of the front seat. He smiled back at me, disarmingly, as I realized with a start that we were getting comfortable in the backseat of my car. I sat up and reached under the front seat.

"Did you look under here?" I asked, sweeping my hand across the floor.

He did the same under the other seat. "Got something."

He pulled out the small canister and handed it to me. I took it, frowning, trying to recall having a can of spray paint in the car. Then I saw the color dripping down the sides of the canister.

"Red."

Mendez frowned at me. Under my thumb the drips felt dry to the touch but gave slightly, as if they were fresh.

"Yours?"

I shook my head. He told me to wait while he got his long-sleeved shirt from the hood. As the day had heated up he had stripped to a white undershirt. He held out his shirt, I placed the canister carefully in it, and he wrapped it up, stashing it under his arm.

"I'll take it in to the sheriff for fingerprints."

I frowned. "Will you tell them you found it in my car?"

"Have to. But don't worry. You reported it stolen." I nodded. I didn't like it but had no other choice. I certainly wasn't going to withhold evidence, was I?

"Do you think you can drive this home?" he asked, helping me shut the doors at last. He had already changed the tire, using his own jack.

"I think so. There's still gas in it," I said. His face was beaded with sweat now. In the thin T-shirt he looked muscular and strong. "Thanks for all your help. I couldn't have done it without you." I stuck out my hand, trying to think of some safe way to show him I really was grateful. He looked at it, surprised, his black eyebrows bobbing up. Then he smiled as he shook it gently.

"Just doing my duty." He lowered his head, looking toward his own vehicle. He had done much more, we both knew. I appreciated a little humility. But it did surprise me. Paolo didn't have a humble bone in his body. *There I go again. Comparing Mendez to Paolo.*

"Let me drive it out to the highway for you. In case there's some problem," he offered, moving toward the Saab. "You have the keys?"

"No, Mendez, you've done enough." I put my hand on his

forearm to stop him from getting in the car. It was warm and moist. "I've driven this car for fifteen years. I guess I can handle it."

He looked at my fingers on his arm. I dropped them, turning away quickly to get behind the steering wheel. Putting the key in the ignition I choked it and turned the key. With a few pumps of the gas pedal it turned over. I gave Mendez an I-told-you-so smile as I passed his El Dorado.

The Mayflower Transfer and Storage franchise was housed under the interstate in an old section of town. The office was small and dusty; most customers never saw it. They were interested in the trucks, two of which were parked outside, shining with fresh yellow and green paint in the summer sun.

A young woman with a poor complexion sat behind the desk chewing gum. Her complexion was her only unattractive feature, which made it all the more glaring. Her dark hair had been permed into cascades of waves and teased to stand about three inches off her forehead.

She looked up, bored. "Can I help you?" She reached over and turned off her typewriter, even though she hadn't been typing.

"Yes. I'm checking up on a move you had scheduled on Bickford Street?" I said, trying to look in her eyes nonchalantly. "For Doris Merkin?"

"Hmm," she muttered, looking me over. I realized my shirt was soaked with sweat and probably reeked. I pulled my shoulders back to command a little presence that obviously was lacking in my appearance.

"Bickford Street," I repeated, urging her to her files.

"I don't recall anything over there," the girl said, turning toward a stack of contracts that lay in an untidy heap in a wire basket. "Let me see."

She licked her fingertip, which ended in a dagger of red nail. Sighing, she leafed through the thin crackly papers until she reached the bottom.

"No record of any moves on Bickford Street." Her eyelids half closed again as she delivered the information. I thought she might fall asleep.

"I'm sorry," I smiled at her. "I didn't say that just right. The move was scheduled but didn't actually take place."

"You mean it was canceled?" she said. I smiled, delighted with her newfound genius. Could have been canceled anyway, I wanted to say. God, I hate to lie. "Why didn't you say so?" she chided me.

In a minute she dug a contract from a file drawer and tapped it with her long nail. "Supposed to be last Saturday. She paid extra for a weekend pickup and everything. I remember now. I told her—15-percent surcharge. And then she canceled it." She grimaced her disapproval.

I looked embarrassed, as if perhaps I was "she." Or at the least a relative or friend. "I know. Something came up." Definite understatement there. I poured on the charm. "What time did she call?"

I leaned out to try to read the dimly printed carbon copy of the moving contract but the girl snatched it away, slipping it back in the file. "What do you mean? Who are you?" Her heavily lined eyes squinted at me. "Just who do you think you are?" she said as I backed away, grabbing for the door. "Do you think I give out information to just anybody? Hey, come back here! I'm calling the cops right now!"

I shut the dusty door, sending a cloud of dirt over my feet as I jumped into my trusty beast of burden. Let her call the cops. They're friends of mine.

14

Stretching the phone cord into the dining room, I pulled my robe around my damp legs. The Saab had sputtered and stalled on my way home from Mayflower. I spent thirty minutes standing on egg-frying asphalt, waiting for it to calm down enough to turn over.

At last it had. Five minutes in a cool shower, trying to wash away the day's entanglements, then I went to the phone. My notebook before me, I dialed the first number.

"Tilden here," the voice barked into the phone.

"Dr. Tilden." I introduced myself. "Do you have a minute to let me pick your brain?"

"Not today."

I pressed on. "Have you heard of a bluejay pictograph?" I said. "In your dealings with the Salish perhaps?"

No immediate answer. Rustlings and a thud of a book dropping to the floor. Finally Tilden said, "Busy today," and hung up.

"Same to you, Mad Dog." I sat in the dining room. The place smelled different when I got back. Looking around now I could see Melina had spent her day off cleaning. The smell was the Murphy's Oil Soap she used to wipe down her furniture. I smiled. It reminded me of my days at home. You can't change the world, you can't make right what's done. But you can keep your house clean, my mother would say, wiping her baseboards or scrubbing the kitchen floor.

A small measure of control, in a world out of control. I'd

been known to have an outbreak of it myself from time to time, usually when things were going badly in my personal life. Burn off that anger and get a clean house to boot.

Now Melina took a nap upstairs. All that cleaning must have worn her out. Probably not sleeping too well either. I picked up the phone again and dialed half a number, then ran upstairs to get dressed. In a moment I was out the door trying to start the Saab again.

When I stepped back out the door of the University library, a huge square brick building facing the old University Hall with its peaked dome roof, the air felt cool. Two hours in the library made the scent of flowers planted in the Hall's courtyard sharp as it rose in the aftermath of the day's heat. I stood for a moment, discouraged, on the steps.

Even the reference librarian had thought it odd. She got downright hysterical. Several old journals were missing from their collection, journals that contained articles about the Salish religious rites or the bluejay shaman. Even the microfilm records had disappeared. Eventually the entire periodical and reference staff was in an uproar over the disappearances. It wasn't like one book being stolen. These were old academic journals from the twenties, a small number published to begin with, even fewer surviving. Like Kateri, they were irreplaceable.

I didn't get hysterical. But I was just as disappointed with the disorderly state of the world. Even in libraries where order reigns, chaos had made inroads.

The Missoula Police Department is housed in City Hall, a three-story precast concrete building behind the fire department and their practice tower covered with radio transmitters. From where I sat across the street I could almost see the side door where the officers climbed into white-and-blue cruisers. The view wasn't great, especially under mercury lights at 11 P.M.

My conversation with Elaine rattled through my head. I had called her just an hour ago, hoping to get her to consent to talk again. But she was if anything more blunt this time. The answer was no.

"What about the boxes in the garage, Elaine?" I had asked in a curious tone, as if I were an intimate friend of the deceased. "Was Shiloh moving out?"

Elaine gasped. If she wouldn't talk to me at least I could get a reaction from her. It was all I expected at this point. "What gives you the right to snoop around—"

I ignored the question. "You weren't getting along so she was moving out."

"No! No!" Her voice broke, becoming softer. "You don't understand. Those boxes have been there for months. They're just her collections. She had so much stuff she was going to put some of it in storage."

Her breathing was short. "She wasn't moving out?" I asked again.

"I told you!" She moaned then and the spell that allowed her to reveal these facts was broken. She hung up without another word. I figured that was the end of the Elaine road; I'd get no more from her.

I got out of the car, leaning against its cool metal door as the policemen began to come out of City Hall. They laughed and waved to each other, getting into police vehicles or their own cars. I strained to see in the darkness. The lot for personal cars was beyond the squad cards; I couldn't see the faces of the officers that went that way. I waited longer, until no more policemen emerged. Then, with a sigh, I climbed back into the Saab, pushing the bottle wrapped in a paper bag to one side.

Elaine was hiding something. That much I was sure of. Maybe it didn't relate to the murder. Maybe it did. Maybe she loved Shiloh but Shiloh didn't return her affections. Is that a motive? She seemed so ready to talk just a couple days ago. What had changed?

I banged my open palms against the steering wheel,

frustrated. Nothing seemed to be going my way. Then I heard his voice.

"What's up?" The car had crept silently up beside me. I jerked my head and smiled. Mendez leaned toward the side door of his car, his badge glinting off the headlight of a passing car.

The Saab chugged to a stop against the curb, behind the dark green El Dorado. In a moment we were sitting on Carl's front step, drinking the wine I'd brought from paper cups. The small house, on the north side of the Clark Fork River in an old neighborhood, boasted a lawn that even at night I could tell was thick, green, and mowed on the diagonal. Very classy.

The wine was pink and cheap and too sweet. It stung my nose as I sipped it, trying to think of a way to ask for help.

"I wanted to thank you for today," I said. He started to say something but I ran ahead. "Now, wait. I have another favor to ask."

When Mendez had gone in for the paper cups he had taken off his short-sleeved uniform shirt and holster. His day fighting crime seemed to have little effect on his demeanor; he was mellow, especially now with a glass of wine in him. He sat back, his elbows on the step above, stretching his legs out in front of him, smiling with bright teeth glowing in the dim light.

"Shoot."

"I want you to run someone's name through your computer. I don't know much about her, just her name."

He looked at me from the corner of his eye. "Does this have to do with the vandalism?"

I wagged my head and tried not to answer. "There's a lot going on. I'm not sure where she fits in." He waited for me to explain. I sipped my wine.

"Are you going to tell me about it?" he said at last.

The sky was bright with stars. The Milky Way shone like a freckled ribbon, glittering. Mendez hadn't turned his porch

light on so the stars seemed closer. The neighborhood was
quiet, sleeping. I took another sip of wine.

"Do I have to?" I asked, smiling at him, trying to use some
of that old Norwegian charm. By his frown I could see I had
failed.

"No." He got up then and went in the house. I sat, unsure
if that was it. Had he said good night? I felt foolish and
ungrateful. I owed him an explanation. Of course I did. But
it hurt, these family problems. We had always kept them to
ourselves, never breathing a word of Cousin Larry's stealing
a car or Uncle Sven's drinking habits. Even in the family we
didn't talk about them, keeping them inside, safe, where
they couldn't escape to embarrass us. Never let it be said we
spilled a family secret. Even to get help.

A click. Music floated out the screen door. Old, sad Texas
music. Bob Wills on the fiddle. Mendez came back out, his
jaw still tight, and sat down on the step above me. He had
a cigarette now, the tip glowing in the darkness, and exhaled
it slowly into the night air.

"Carl," I began. I looked at him, felt that wall inside me,
and turned away. "Shit." I shifted, looking at the sky again.
I owed it to him, I told myself, my arms stiff against the old
wood steps. "Listen, it's not that big a thing. This woman
is interested in something that may have something to do
with the problems my brother-in-law is having." I took a
deep breath. I could hear him suck in on the cigarette and
blow the smoke out.

"Who's your brother-in-law?" His voice was low, without
emotion.

"Wade Fraser."

He took a draw on his cigarette. "That's where I saw you.
I've been racking my brain."

"I should have told you. I'm working that trailer full of
artworks down at the warehouse too."

"You are?"

I glanced back at him. "I'm an art dealer."

"No shit. I heard about that trailer. Some of the guys like

that antique stuff." We looked at the stars. "But the trailer and your—"

"Brother-in-law. Not related. That I know of."

I followed the Milky Way from one horizon obscured by trees to the other. An owl hooted softly, far away.

"Murder, huh?" he said.

"Yeah. This woman may be involved somehow. I have to know."

"What's her name?"

"Charlotte Vardis," I spit out, then spelled it. "Thank you, Carl." I jumped to my feet, leaving the empty paper cup on the step. I wanted to shake his hand or something but he sat stretched on the steps, cigarette in one hand and cup in the other. "Call me, okay?" I called, running down the walk to my car.

I didn't know how, but Charlotte Vardis was thick with this. She was too phony, too weird. I rolled her name over and over in my mind on the way home. Mendez had to come up with something.

In the light of the porch lamp Melina had left on for me I found a parking place in front of the neighbor's; somebody seemed to be having a party on Blaine Street. I drifted off to sleep, trying to place Vardis in the puzzle, trying the pieces without her, with equal success. My brain clouded with confusion and sleep.

Melina left early, refreshed by her housekeeping vacation, eager to disappear into the problems of her students. Her files were full of graded papers, her gradebook caught up. She actually looked somewhat happy, sipping her coffee in a clean skirt—pressed, no less.

After she left I threw all my clothes in the washing machine and scrounged a baggy pair of shorts and a tank top from her drawer. I moved to the window seat to drink my coffee in the sunshine and read the paper.

A trial date had been set for Wade, I read on the front page.

Not until late September, it said, giving both sides ample time to prepare their cases. And for the judge to take a vacation.

Poor Wade. He was going to miss at least the start of the fall quarter after all. Tilden had been right. Why didn't they let him out on bail? He was a gentle giant, nothing more. But maybe they wouldn't let a professor accused of murder teach a class anyway. I set my cup down. I had to organize my thoughts today.

Notebook in hand, I reviewed my list of questions that needed answers. Tin-Tin and Marcus Tilden had both mentioned some bad feelings, "bad blood" between Wade and Shiloh. I tried to remember if that had come out at the preliminary hearing. I made a note to ask Wade and Melina about it. A question Mendez might be able to help me with: Why had the cops come to Tilden that first morning? Was there something at the scene that implicated him? If so, why was it being kept back?

From the bay window I glanced up as a boy on a bicycle pedaled by. My coffee needed a warmer-upper. I got up to go to the kitchen and looked down the driveway to the Saab Sister. I hadn't parked too well last night, kind of at a weird angle. A strange car was parked in front of the house, like a party guest who wouldn't go home. I got a good look at it now: a brown Mercedes with tinted windows.

I poured more coffee into my cup and headed out the kitchen door for a stroll down the driveway toward the vehicles. The flower beds had dried up from neglect. I thought of watering them, then realized it was hopeless.

I rounded the Saab between the two cars, trying to see through the tinted glass of the Mercedes. The license plate, spattered with grime, read Oklahoma. The entire car was dirty, covered with mud. It wasn't often you saw a Mercedes that had that much dirt on it. Benz owners, at least the ones I knew in Jackson, were meticulous about their precious German wheels.

I opened the door to my car, making like I was getting

something. My bare feet hurt on the asphalt pavement. I closed the door again, walking lightly toward the Mercedes. I walked on the street side, lifting the handle of first the back door, then the front.

The back door latch flipped up and back. Locked. I kept walking. I expected the same for the front and was surprised to feel the resistance that meant it was unlocked. Stepping back, I checked the traffic and neighbors up and down the street. I eased up the handle, my heart beating loudly.

The latch made a quality clunk. I stepped right, to the side of the crack that the open door made, slipping my fingers against the metal edge. I drew the door wider, its solid weight heavy in my hand.

Something was resting against the door. I pulled it wider. A shoulder.

I slammed the door shut. The thumping in my ears took over as my breath grew short and light. There was someone in the car. Leaning against the door. Leaning like someone who was . . . I stepped back, taking a quick breath, trying to think what to do.

I stepped up to the car again, opening the latch quickly this time, firmly. My hand slipped into the crack, pushing the shoulder back from the door so it wouldn't tumble to the pavement. The door swung open. I took a deep breath and smelled the sour, tainted odor of death.

▽

15

By THE TIME the police arrived I had gotten a good look at her. Too good. It was the kind of thing you had nightmares about. A bullet hole in the temple, as if some astral void had sucked the life out of her with a straw. Her bluish complexion, dark, lifeless hair, features contorted in agony, mouth agape, teeth dry, eyes wide with . . . fear.

Her face was not familiar. This, at least, was a relief. I scanned my memory of women from Manitou Matrix, trying to place her, thankful that I could not. An older woman, in her fifties maybe. A cap of sienna hair and blue eyes. Those eyes.

I called Melina, told her not to come home but did she know anyone with a brown Mercedes with Oklahoma plates? She did not. Just the news of the murder, though, shook her.

My hand trembled so badly as I tried to punch out 911 that I had to hang up and take a deep breath before trying again. I didn't remember ever shaking that bad. The coffee spilled as I tried to pour it. I set down the pot and sank to the floor beside the puddle, pulling up my knees, dropping my forehead against them.

The proximity to death: quick, uncontrollable, final. The fear, the screams rang in my ears, unheard screams but very real. She—whoever she was—didn't want to die. Someone else had made that decision for her.

The woman in the Mercedes was dressed in expensive woolen slacks, an odd choice for the torrid summer days we were experiencing. The light blue blouse was long-sleeved. Her bare feet lay against the car's mat. I stared at her too long.

A detective named Knox asked me questions. I told him I saw the car—I thought—last night when I came home at about midnight. Then this morning. He said they would ask neighbors about it.

We sat in the living room. I felt thankful Melina had cleaned her house, with all these strangers walking through. I made more coffee and talked to Knox, who was heavyset, in his fifties. He was kind while being official, a trait I greatly admired. As I drank coffee another policeman came to the door. They conferred, and Knox turned back to me.

"We don't know if this is her or not. It'll be a bit before we get a positive ID," he said, glancing down at a small spiral notebook similar to my own. "But the registration on the vehicle is to a Charlotte Vardis, Stillwater, Oklahoma."

An asphalt ribbon draped over the hillsides, the road spun beneath the car. If I stared at the center line long enough it seemed to go backward while the car stood still. A tread-mill spinning round and round, the earth turning, the sun with its yo-yo planet on a string. Round-the-world, round-the-sun.

My father, the slouching Norsky salesman, told me about roads. They were his companion. He said the reason the road has so many curves is because somebody made it too long. To get it to fit in the space they had crimped it, making curves and turns over hills, down through valleys, around mountains, over bridges. I loved that, the gray ribbon that had been cut too long. I hoped someday they would get their measurements right and the road would become straight, smooth, and perfect, a line as unbending as the graphite lead in my third-grade pencil tracing the edge of the old wooden ruler.

The road had been too long for Rollie. For years he had traveled up and down Montana selling girdles and brassieres, then hammers and wingnuts, sometimes into western Washington, northern Wyoming, and Idaho. Coeur d'Alene was his destination the day he died. He traveled this road that day, I thought, my mind preoccupied by death. This very road.

He had wound his dirty white Impala through the rolling hills of the Flathead Indian Reservation, past tourist traps and verdant meadows, past ponds where chunks of ice the size of a house had broken off Ice Age glaciers and melted. Past ducks swimming, oblivious to their proximity to disaster, paddling orange feet below the crystal green waters.

His Impala was not so fleet of foot as its namesake but serviceable, Rollie liked to say, practical to the end. They crossed the Jocko River over the high bridge at Ravelli, named after yet another Jesuit priest who came to save the Flathead nation. The Impala probably strained on the hill to Camas Prairie, feeling the road wave with the giant ripples from prehistoric times, the bed of an ancient torrential stream that drained through here into the Flathead River.

He may have smiled, as I did, at Chief Cliff in the distance. He would pass it going up to the lake, rounding the western side, his favorite part of the lake, the part without all the people. I turned off into the Big Draw before I reached Chief Cliff, an Indian-head promontory, searching for the strange and mysterious ladies of the Manitou Matrix.

The nervous restlessness that plagued me in Missoula after the discovery of the body of the woman had been calmed a little by the hum of the tires. Yes, their rubber sang, your life is going somewhere. There are answers to your questions. When I strained to hear the song, it played in a minor key, all sorrow and finality and dread.

After the shakes had subsided and the policeman had made me calm myself to answer his questions, I wanted nothing more than to get out of there. I told Knox of speaking to her on the telephone two days ago. She had been a client. No, I'd never met her face-to-face.

Knox seemed to believe me. He wrote it all down. The

detective told me they might have more questions but he didn't say anything about leaving town. I paced the floor for a good fifteen minutes before grabbing my backpack and lighting out for the hills.

The wind had been blowing through the Little Bitterroot River site of Tin-Tin's camp when I arrived, caressing the drying grass, making it crackle and dance. Her tepee was gone now, I was surprised to see; I had questions. I moved on, asking at a gas station at Niarda where the women were camped, then turning back for a few miles to look for a sign nailed to a tree.

The conclave had moved to an old ranch nestled against the high walls of rock that cradled the Big Draw. Spreading below it, vast prairies of gold and green pasture were dotted with cattle and horses in the distance. A barbed wire fence ran along the dirt road leading to a field crowded with vehicles.

Behind the weathered board-and-batten ranch house, in a pasture, the tepees sat. They had been set up in two large circles, about eight or twelve to a ring. I looked for Tin-Tin's gaily painted tepee, but couldn't see it from the parking area.

Rows of picnic tables filled the lawn in front of the house. Behind the outbuildings a rocky slope arched up in buff-colored sandstone dotted with junipers and pines until it flattened out some 150 feet above the valley floor.

I found Tin-Tin in the second circle of tepees, holding court in front of her painted tent. A cluster of ten or twelve women gathered around her as she demonstrated a beading technique on a scrap of leather. She speared a tiny bead with a needle, then stabbed the leather, showing the women how to keep the spacing tight to make a better design.

Waiting, I watched the women, recognizing a few from the last time. I still wondered about them; I couldn't help myself. Would I travel across the continent to spend my vacation sleeping in a cramped tent without mosquito netting, eating on the ground?

The women of Manitou Matrix appeared to be enjoying

themselves. They smiled, nudged each other, giggled, looked intense, gazed reverently at Tin-Tin, leaning toward her low, clipped monotone. The sun was hot and there was no shade. On the way back to my car I saw Moody emerge from the ranch house with two women. I heard their voices before reaching the gate.

One was yelling. "You know Orianna won't stand for it." Moody moved hesitantly down the walk in front of the women. He had changed to a different T-shirt but wore the same dirty Stetson and worn jeans. As they approached I realized the women were identical twins; both wore out- rageously fake glossy black wigs with fat braids hanging past their shoulders. Both were built like bruisers. One wore leather leggings; the other, a tight green T-shirt that stretched across her lumpy torso, proclaiming "Grateful Dead, Dead on the Rocks, 1986."

"I never passed any notes." Moody turned toward them. He acknowledged me quickly with his eyes, then shifted his attention back to the twins.

"You pass them out every afternoon," the twin with leggings said. "We saw you yesterday."

"The sage bundles? Those are for the sweathouse. I give them out so we have the right number for the sweat."

"I don't care what you call them," the Dead fan said. "Orianna says you're undermining her authority. Saying things about her. Saying things about Shiloh."

Moody stopped, his jaw slack. The twins moved around him, then called back, "Don't forget: seven o'clock in Orianna's office." We stared at their backs as they headed toward the tepee rings.

Moody roused himself to walk toward me at the end of the wooden boardwalk. His eyes were clouded, his face stunned.

"Who are they?"

"Coupla wannabes," he said bitterly. Then a chuckle. "Can you believe it? Twins?" He shook his head as I raised my eyebrows in wonder. "Call themselves Silver Bear and Thunder Woman. Sometimes I call them Silverware and Wonder Woman just to watch them get mad."

At least he had a sense of humor about it. The women were lost now in the milling groups in the tepee circles.

"What's their problem?"

His face darkened again; a cheek twitched. "All I been getting is a hard time." He started walking around the tepees, toward the cliffs that ringed the valley. I fell into step beside him. "They asked me to conduct sweats. There is a proper and respectful way to do it. They don't want to do it that way. They want to make money conducting sweats." He shook his head angrily.

We walked a ways parallel to the sandstone rimrock, coming to a tiny creek and following along it. He continued, "Now they get mad about sage bundles. They think I'm passing notes about them. These women are loco." We stepped across the creek on a rock, walking down the opposite bank. "I'm doing this sweat tonight, then that's it."

"Going home?"

"I'm calling my brother soon as I get the fire started." We came to a clearing where the creek bent sharply, deepening at the bend and creating a small pool two or three feet deep. An igloo-shaped sweathouse sat on the far side, covered with quilts and bedspreads like Tilden's but newer and tidier. The dirt around it was compressed with footprints.

I sat on the bank to look for fish in the little pool while Moody stirred the ashes of yesterday's blaze and carefully constructed the new fire.

The cool grass of the prairie, gnawed low to the ground by cattle, soothed me. Being in the backwoods, away from civilization, always did. Then, without warning, the woman in the Mercedes flashed before me again. She haunted me. Charlotte Vardis. I shivered, turning my thoughts to the reason I had come.

"I came to ask Tin-Tin about the bluejay shaman," I

blurted out. At once, from the cautiously pained look on Moody's face, I realized this was not the thing to say. Or the way to say it.

"So ask her," he said, uncharacteristically blunt. But my statement was also blunt.

I swung my feet away from the creek bank and faced the fire beginning to smoke and flame under the logs. "Another woman was killed," I said shortly.

Moody jerked his head up, questioning me with his dark eyes. "When?"

"Yesterday." I told him how I had found her in the car in front of my house. "Have you ever heard of her—Charlotte Vardis?"

Moody sat back in the dirt, poking his fire with a stick. "I don't think so. Who was she?"

"Some rich lady. From Oklahoma, I guess. I talked to her on the phone a couple of days ago about a painting she wanted to buy. I thought she was in Jackson. Now she turns up dead on my doorstep."

Moody frowned. "You didn't know her then?" I shook my head. I wished Paolo had been in the gallery when I called before taking off this morning. I wanted to find out what he knew about her. He would get my message and call. A murder was not something to announce to a machine.

Moody set his rocks in the center of the fire to let them heat up as the logs burned down into coals. He led me back to his tepee where we ate a spare lunch of elk jerky and apples. He scowled through the meal, lowering his eyes if any of the women came by. After lunch he went to call his brother to fetch him home.

Across the tepee ring, Tin-Tin washed her bowl in a pan of soapy water. As I approached she looked up and smiled at me, tired, I thought.

"Melina's sister. Alix, is it?" She stood, wiping her hands then grasping mine. The fatigue in her eyes was confirmed as she sagged onto the log seat. How old did Wade say she was? Late seventies, I thought.

"How are you, Tin-Tin?" I found a grassy spot to sit on, cross-legged.

"Good, good," she murmured, wiping out her bowl with her apron. "And how is Buffalo Tears?"

"Still in jail." She nodded, distracted. "I've come to ask you about something. It's important to Wade." She set down her clean bowl on a towel in the grass and turned toward me, a spark of concern in her old eyes. "It has to do with something called a bluejay pictograph. Do you know a rock carving or painting called that?"

The old woman paused, running her fingers down the pencil-thin gray braids that hung from the purple kerchief on her head. Her lips moved, as if in preparation to speak. Then at last she did: "Bluejay, I know. Pictograph, no." I waited for her to elaborate, hoping I wasn't treading on sensitive ground. This was serious business for Wade, for Charlotte Vardis, and for whoever killed Shiloh.

"The bluejay shaman is what the whites call a medicine man. He is a holy man to the Salish," she said, pausing to look at me. "But I do not know of a rock drawing called bluejay."

"Do you remember anyone else asking about a bluejay pictograph?"

Tin-Tin rose, brushing off her apron. She searched the sky, watching three ducks fly overhead, quacking their travel song. Her dark eyes flickered. "I am so tired."

I rose, knowing I shouldn't push her. But as she paused before entering her tepee I gave it one more shot. "Has anyone mentioned a bluejay drawing, a rock drawing or carving, to you before? Orianna? Anyone?"

The sun baked down. I could feel my nose start to burn. She reached down for the flap. "Not Orianna," she said. "Little Cricket."

▽

16

THE CANVAS FLAP fell behind her. It floated in the breeze of Tin-Tin's passing into the tepee. *Little Cricket? Who in God's name . . . ?*

The tepee ring was quiet. A few women sat on rocks, working on needlework in their laps. They must have been sweltering in the afternoon heat, in their long skirts and leathers, but they seemed quite serene, talking low and plying their needles.

I wiped my sweaty palms on Melina's shorts, feeling out of place suddenly. The terrible morning. Now the heat. Who was Little Cricket? *Think, girl, think.*

The earth hardened under the summer sun. The grasses turned to straw. I wandered, trying to get my mind to remember where I had heard the name. At the ranch house I stopped, spun on my heel, and began to run toward the creek.

The dry stalks cut my bare legs; I was glad I had put on tennis shoes. My breath came hot, hotter than this scorching day. I reached the creek, turning my ankle in a hole, catching myself, and running on.

The clearing was empty. The fire had burned low, the coals gray now and barely smoking. The rocks Moody had placed there were gone. The sweathouse sat on its haunches by the willows, silent. I felt desperate suddenly: Where was he? He who was called Little Cricket. I put my hand on my damp forehead and moaned.

He came through the brush by the creek with a beat-up

aluminum saucepan in his hand. When he saw me he started, sloshing the water. His eyes rounded for an instant, then he composed himself, walked to the sweathouse.

"Come back for a sweat?" Moody bent down, pulled back the flap, and poured the water over the rocks inside. They sizzled and hissed as the steam began to pour out the door. He lowered the flap and stood with his empty pan.

"This day is hot enough."

He looked solemn, troubled. His run-in with the twins had taken its toll. I couldn't help feeling he was naive to come to an all-women's conclave and expect to be revered for his special knowledge. Women could be as cruel as men. Whatever back-biting they might do against each other, they would take their frustrations out doubly on the only male present. Especially a male who held secrets they wished for themselves.

Secrets. I dabbed my damp cheek on my bare shoulder. "Can I talk to you a minute? Let's go sit in the shade."

He set his pan down by the fire, following me to the creek, a spot of shade near willow bushes. The grass was cool there.

I splashed some water on my arms, rubbing up and down. Moody sat down, staring at the sandstone bluffs that radiated heat. "The woman who was killed?" I said. He glanced at me, then picked a blade of grass and examined it. "I told you her name was Charlotte Vardis."

He nodded.

"She was looking for something called a bluejay pictograph." I watched his reaction: a blink, a tightening, that was all. "You asked Tin-Tin about it for her, didn't you?"

He looked at me, hurt at the accusation. "No! I never heard of her, I told you."

"Then why did you ask Tin-Tin about a bluejay pictograph?"

His jaw tensed. He looked away, toward the tepees that we could see the tops of in the distance. He murmured something.

"What?"

He fiddled with the grass. "For somebody else." I waited

for him to tell me. My arms had dried; I was hot again.
At last he spoke: "For Shiloh."
I blinked. "Shiloh?" Moody didn't move. "When?"
"Couple months ago. Didn't do no good though. Tin-Tin
didn't know nothing about it." Moody tossed the grass into
the little creek.
"You *knew* Shiloh?" Then I remembered he had told
Orianna that the first day. Shiloh had asked him to do the
sweats.
"I went to a workshop about crystals, the powers, healing
crystals. In the back of a bar in Missoula. In the spring.
Orianna was giving it. That was when I met Shiloh." He
sighed. "She was nice to me then."
I looked at his smooth brown face in profile. "Did that
change?"
"After I told her I'd do the sweats she asked me about that
bluejay thing. A painting on a rock, she said. So I asked
Tin-Tin. But she never heard of it. And Shiloh never was
very nice after that."
He sighed, his heavy eyelids turning toward the sandstone
cliffs again. Waves of heat distorted the blueness of the sky
above them.
"Moody, what did you think about Shiloh?" I asked.
He laughed, a sudden, half-hearted sound. "I wanted to
like her. She had some goodness in her heart. Or so I thought
at first. I am looking for pathways. So was Shiloh. Ways to
live. The right road. But it come to me that Shiloh was more
interested in ol' number one. You know what I mean?"
I nodded.
"I saw her playing these different women off each other.
Flattering one in front of the other. Telling one that Orianna
thought she could be a leader. Then she would turn around
and tell the other that the first one had the brains of a cow."
"Did she have a particular friend in the group?"
"A friend? Orianna, I guess. But not really. Maybe those
twins, Silverware and Wonder Woman."
"I mean a particular friend. A lover."

He jerked his head toward me, searching my face with his dark eyes. "Shiloh?" I let him think. "I don't know. There's lots of that going on here. But I never think of it, you know. I'm just . . . I just don't think of that."

Think about it. Keep your eyes and ears open. As I left Moody with this admonition, I knew it was too late. Shiloh had been dead a week already. Her trail was getting cold. Whoever had loved her would have been at the memorial service. Many had cried for her. I turned over my image of Elaine again and heard her words: "You don't know how much I loved her."

It seemed obvious that they were lovers. They lived together. And yet they seemed so dissimilar. Elaine, soft and weepy. Shiloh, tough and calculating, climbing her way to the top of the metaphysical heap. Shiloh might have used Elaine, but did she love her?

The hills had turned even more gold since my morning drive onto the reservation. I drove the Saab toward the confluence of the two rivers, toward Missoula. The gaping hole that had held the radio made me sad. I wondered if I would ever know who had stolen my car.

So many questions without answers. And now another murder. I hoped Mendez had run Charlotte Vardis through the computer. I would call him when I got back. I had to find out what the bluejay pictograph was. Calls to some of my museum and gallery buddies were in order.

It was late afternoon. The leaves on the cottonwood trees fluttered in the white sunshine. I pulled onto Blaine Street feeling the exhaustion the heat had brought on. A hot wind blew into the car windows. I drove slowly down the block, a headache growing in the back of my skull.

Two squad cars sat in front of the blue bungalow with the burnt grass. The Mercedes was gone. I didn't feel like talking to the cops now. My head hurt. I'd told them everything. After I parked, I pulled a hose from the bushes and stretched it to the middle of the lawn, set down the sprinkler end, and went to turn on the faucet by the porch.

It squealed against my hand as the water rushed through, making an arc of silver spray in the dry air. It would take a flood to get this grass looking green again. I stood there for a moment, half in the bushes, with my hand on the cool faucet."

"Alix!" The voice, a hoarse whisper, came from the porch. "Come up here."

Melina gripped the porch railing. She frowned at me, tipping her head toward the steps. I trudged up, expecting her to tell me to forget about watering the lawn, that they couldn't afford the water now.

"The police are here," she whispered, glancing toward the door. "They want to talk to you."

I frowned. She didn't need to get so overwrought about this. She had bigger worries. Let her worry about Wade. "I already told them everything. I don't see—"

The front door opened. Knox stepped out, moving rather quickly for a man his size. His raw face was serious, pinched. He cleared his throat. "Can we talk to you inside, please, Miss Thorssen?"

This was not a question but a command. Melina looked at me, her face draining of its color.

Inside Hondo slumped against the door frame in the living room. He straightened as we walked in. I wondered why he was here, then stopped in the entry to the room. On the sofa sat two policemen in uniform. They looked up; one was Carl Mendez, sitting with his hands flat on his thighs. He regarded me coldly. The other policeman I didn't know, nor did I recognize the plainclothes cop who sat in the easy chair by the window.

"Get up, Frederickson," Knox said to the plainclothes cop. He rose, nodding to me as he passed to stand next to Hondo. "Have a seat, Miss Thorssen," the detective said.

Perching on the chair, I regarded them all. "What's going on?"

The lawyer opened his mouth to say something but the detective broke in. "We want to ask you some more questions, Miss Thorssen. Your sister called Mr. O'Brian. We thought it would be a good idea."

I swallowed, my throat parched. "About the woman?" Mendez didn't have the guts to look up from his hands.

"Officer Mendez tells us you asked him to run her name through the computer the night before she was killed. Is that true?"

I glared at Mendez. "No. It was the night she was killed."

"Alix," Hondo broke in. "You don't need to answer any questions."

"It's all right. I have nothing to hide."

"Why did you ask Officer Mendez to do that?" Knox said.

"I told you she was a client of mine. I had called the FBI to find out about a painting she wanted to buy. To see if it was stolen or forged. That's what I do." I shifted in the chair uneasily but looked the detective in the eye. "When the FBI agent called me back he told me she had asked about something else, something that I thought might have significance in Wade's case."

"You called the FBI in Butte?"

"No. The Art Forgery Unit in Chicago." I gave him Kenyon's name. "About three days ago." The days were blending together. "He called me back the next day."

The detective made some notes in his spiral notebook, then looked at Frederickson. The policeman reached to the floor for a paper sack. He pulled out a large plastic bag with a lump of something inside and handed it to Knox. The detective turned it over in his hands and passed it to me.

Inside the plastic was a wad of cloth, blue and faded, that felt heavy in my hand. "What's this?" I asked.

"Do you recognize it?" Knox said. I frowned at it. I looked at Melina, who held her hands clenched at her sides. Hondo's red eyebrows were jammed together. I couldn't look at Mendez.

"No."

Knox took it back. Pulling open the Ziploc top he extracted the fabric from the bag and held it on the corners. A knit T-shirt fell, wrinkled, from his fingers. An ugly splotch of something black dried on the lower corner. In faded white-and-black lettering it read: "Grand Tetons."

My jaw dropped. "Oh."

"You recognize it?" the detective asked, peeking around it.

"It's mine." I had bought it the first year I lived in Jackson. It was a tourist souvenir that embarrassed me now. I hadn't worn it in years.

Knox lowered the shirt to his lap carefully. "It was found in the Mercedes, next to the deceased. The blood on it matches hers."

Melina covered her mouth. My headache throbbed behind my eyes. What did he say? I looked at Frederickson, at the other uniformed cop, at Mendez, and back to Knox. "What?"

"Alix," O'Brian said, clearing his throat. "I would advise you to say no more at this time."

The detective ignored him. "I ask you again, Miss Thorssen. Did you know the deceased? Did you meet her the night of her death?"

"You don't have to answer, Alix," Hondo repeated.

I shook my head. "No. No." I looked at Mendez. "My car was stolen. Tell them! I haven't worn that shirt for years. I kept it in my car but . . . It must have been taken when they went through my car!"

"They?"

"Whoever stole my car!" My voice rose. I didn't seem to be able to control it. "Tell them, Carl."

Mendez straightened. "She reported the car stolen on Wednesday. It was recovered two days later, yesterday, on the Flathead Reservation. Her belongings were . . . scattered around the area." His voice was flat and official.

"Somebody took the shirt," I said. "Whoever stole the car."

The detective looked thoughtful as he put the shirt back in the bag. "Was the car dusted, Mendez?"

Carl blinked, jerking his neck involuntarily. "Uh, no sir."

I stood up. "I-I was just so grateful to get it back. I didn't think—"

Knox stood too. "That was Mendez's job, Miss Thorssen." The other policeman got up. "We'll have more questions for you. Don't leave the area." At that the cops filed out, leaving the three of us stunned and silent.

That night sleep did not come. I lay in the enclosed sleeping porch praying for a breeze. Drenched in sweat, I rose, dressed, and grabbed my car keys.

Mendez's house was not dark though it was two-thirty in the morning. I took a small comfort in his insomnia. Parking the Saab, I thought of confronting him with my anger, my sense of betrayal. But he was just doing his job. He owed me nothing. The look on Knox's face when he asked if the car had been dusted for fingerprints was deadly.

The night air seemed cooler here near the river. If I listened hard I could hear the water rushing. The wild river, wondering what had happened to its berry-tangled banks, its twists and turns cut by summer floods. What were these square hulks, buildings and bridges, cement embankments impeding its evolution? Who were these fair-skinned inhabitants that plied its waters with noisy boats and stole its scaly friends? The meanderings of a river, still free.

Thinking of the river calmed me. I relaxed and dozed in the seat. The Saab Sister, so recently violated, now seemed like the only safe place for me, the only place that belonged to me.

▽

17

A HARD SHIVER racked my body. I jolted in the seat, bumping my knee on the steering wheel. My breath had fogged the windows; I ran my palm over the glass to see who had knocked. A hazy figure stood in the dawn twilight.

Bird sounds filled the rarefied air, its grayness tinged with rose, blowing in chilled and fresh through the crack. I rolled the window down to see the face.

"What're you doing in there?" Mendez bent his face down to the window. His forehead was covered with beads of sweat. He wore a soaked shirt and jogging shorts. He was breathing hard from his run, hands on his hips.

My brain still felt like the inside of the glass: foggy, opaque. I cleared my throat to give myself some time to think, then jerked the door handle. It was locked. I fumbled to unlock it and open the door. The morning coolness hit me as I stood on the pavement, my mind functioning at last.

"I wanted to talk to you," I said. I contained the hurt from yesterday, the anger. I would not let petty emotions take control. If my Norwegian upbringing trained me for anything, this was it.

Mendez cocked his head, looking at me from under dripping brows. His dark skin glistened with moisture.

"Come in for a minute." He turned his back and started up the walk to his house. His invitation fell short of convivial. No doubt he felt I had compromised his position as a law officer. I shouldn't have asked him to run the woman's name through the computer. And he shouldn't have taken me to pick up the Saab.

Did that mean he considered taking me up on the Little Bitterroot, helping me with the mission's vandalism, unprofessional? Then it was personal. But now his tone was brusque, polite without the concern that he had shown before.

He left me standing awkwardly in his living room, a neat but shabby arrangement of secondhand furniture that seemed to fit a bachelor policeman. I sank onto a faded green couch that smelled like cigarette smoke. A black and white cat jumped up to greet me. The feel of the cat's fur made me think of Valkyrie, my wandering pony. She could be halfway to Colorado. God, Paolo hadn't called back.

Mendez came back with a towel around his neck and two cups of coffee. He handed me one and perched on the edge of a blue chair. I warmed my hands around the mug as the cat jumped off the couch and went over to rub against Carl's shins.

"Listen, Mendez, I want to apologize for putting—"

"You met Gato?"

I frowned: Why wouldn't he let me say I was sorry? He rubbed the cat's back.

"Let me just say it: I'm sorry." I spit it out and shut my mouth. Let him have it his way. I still needed his help. He said nothing, watching the cat arch her back and purr against his legs. I set down my coffee cup and rubbed my forehead, trying to get the words to flow. "I need to know. Were there any fingerprints on the paint canister? The one in my car?"

He sat back in the chair. "Two sets. One of them was mine."

"And the other?" He stared at me for a long minute, then took a sip of coffee. "Mine?"

"Probably. Yours weren't on file."

I drank the coffee, feeling it charge through my veins. A

sick, dizzy feeling hit me, like things were crashing in. I took another sip of coffee and sat up straighter to fend it off. "Thanks for the coffee."

Carl watched me walk to the door in silence. Then, as my hand went to the knob, he stood up. "Just a minute." He disappeared into a back room. I watched the sun warm the precision-mowed yard through the screen door. In a moment he returned and shoved some papers into my hand.

He stood close to me. I could smell his sweat. He wiped his face with the towel again, over the dark beard he hadn't shaved yet. "What's this?" I asked.

Two sheets of computer paper linked at one end and folded. Opening them I saw her name: VARDIS. I tried to smile at him. "Thanks." His jaw had gone stiff again, jutting as it tensed. He looked at me, pursed his lips.

"Damage is already done. My ass is in a sling about the car anyway."

Through the door, across the small porch, down the steps, I clutched the paper as though it was my saving grace. There were so many questions, unknowns, and I had much work to do. But this was something to hold onto, to grasp, even if it was a straw.

I had hit the sidewalk when he called from the porch, looking up and down the street. A nervousness in his eyes stopped me as he approached. He whispered hoarsely: "What are you going to do?"

I blinked at him, trying to concoct a reasonable reply. I had no idea, no plan. So I said, "I have a plan." My voice was only a whisper as I elaborated. "I'm going to find out who killed Shiloh Merkin and who killed Charlotte Vardis. The murders, they must be related."

"Why?"

"They were both looking for this thing called a bluejay pictograph. Some sort of Indian painting. I think they were both killed trying to get their hands on it. If I find it, I'll find the murderer." I sucked in a little air, surprised at my theory as much as he appeared to be.

Carl looked at the toes of his running shoes and then into my eyes. "This isn't a game. Somebody is killing people. You could be next."

I met his gaze. "I know that." I swallowed hard. "Somebody is trying to frame me for Charlotte Vardis's murder. You can see that. I'm poking my nose into somebody's business. They don't like it. That means I'm getting close."

He examined my face with his dark eyes. We stood three feet apart, faced off. I had already asked him for too much; this had to be good-bye.

"Meet me for lunch. One o'clock. Montana Pies." He turned on his last word and jogged back up the walk to his house, bounding up the stairs two at a time without looking back.

"Paolo. At last." I sank back in Wade's old office chair, running my hand across the front of the desk. A smile of satisfaction crossed my lips as I regarded the desk's orderly surface: a neat stack of related files on one corner, clean notebook paper for doodling with theories on another, five sharpened pencils lined up next to the paper. The wood top was dusted and lemon-oiled, the glass shade on the lamp wiped clean. Even the telephone, stretched in from the hall, had been exactingly dusted. It was 9:00 A.M..

"Ah, have you been trying to reach me?" Paolo said, a blithe cheerfulness in his voice that annoyed me. "We had the opening last night for Geneva Betz. I had a little too much wine, I think. You know I used to be able to drink all night, then get up and swill espresso in the morning and never have this brick on my forehead feeling." He chuckled and I imagined he was rubbing his eyes.

I had forgotten completely about the opening. Paolo had probably been crazy all day with last-minute preparations. I usually hung the shows. I had planned on being back for Geneva's; she was a friend and local artist whose work had been improving rapidly over the last few years. She was ready for the big time, in my opinion. And here I had forgotten her opening.

"Oh, God, I'm sorry, Paolo. I meant to be back. But, well, you heard what happened?"

"Hang on while I get a cup of coffee, will you?" he said, setting the receiver down without waiting for my reply. I ground my teeth, waiting for him, imagining the mess my desk had taken on in my absence and Paolo's feet resting on it as he spoke to me. He returned at last. "Oh, hey. The sheriff called about your horse. Yesterday morning she was prancing around the square in the very early morning time. I heard some tourists were taking pictures of her. Kind of some excitement. Maybe they thought Valkyrie was a moose, eh?"

I had to smile. "In the square. That show-off horse. Where did she go then?"

"Sheriff tried to catch her but she was too wild. She run off down the street toward the Elk Refuge."

"That's where she went last time." I pictured her browsing through the field the elk had vacated for the summer, turning up bits of leftover alfalfa pellets and hay. She'd be fine there.

"So what's been going on up in Montana?"

"You heard what happened here, didn't you?" I repeated.

"Hmm, what?" The slurp of coffee being sipped.

"Charlotte Vardis. The murder. Wasn't it in the paper there?"

"I didn't read the paper yesterday," he said. "But anyway, you know the paper here." He made a disparaging noise and sipped more coffee. "What happened? You mean that customer? That Charlotte Vardis?"

"Yes, that one." I filled him in on the details until he sounded alert and awake. I told him about the police finding my shirt in her car, stained with her blood. "Now you've got to tell me about her."

"She only came in one time. Then I talk to her on the telephone once." He paused to think. "You know, I thought she was a little strange to be buying a Jackson Pollock masterpiece."

"Didn't she look rich?"

"Oh, she look plenty rich. Expensive leather coat that she did not really need in the summer. But I guess she did come in during the late afternoon. Kinda coolish that day. Lots of makeup. Rich-lady tan, like she worked on it in the winter in the south of France."

I knew customers that fit that description, dripping with earrings and necklaces, fingers heavy with precious metal and gems. They wore jeans with exotic skins sewed into them, or fine imported sweaters of mohair, or ski outfits trimmed with mink, or exquisite Italian boots on their tiny, wealthy feet. Every hair on their heads would be coiffed just so, every wrinkle painted over.

Nothing he had said so far seemed out of the ordinary. "So what was it about her that seemed strange?"

"She wasn't interested in the art. Oh, I know, lots of rich peoples don't really like the art. They just like to buy it and say they have it. Show how much of the culture they have. But we had that wonderful show in here, lots of color and big canvases, and she had to wait for me because I am with another customer."

He paused to catch his breath. "So I tell her there's a rest room in the back when she asks. And when I am finally done with the customer I find Charlotte sitting in your desk chair. She could have been looking at the paintings. But no, she wanted to stare at your ugly little office." He chuckled to reassure me that it was only a joke. An irritable twinge at his humor passed quickly.

But wait. "She was sitting in my desk chair?" Now I *was* irritated.

"Yeah. She didn't touch anything, I don't think. Just sat there with her little blue gloves on, wrapped around her Gucci bag, and asked about you."

"What about me?"

"About you finding out about the Jackson Pollock. Said all kinds of things about how great you were. She knew all about you. She wanted to know when were you coming back because she needed to know right now. How she wanted you to find out absolutely everything you could about this painting because it was *so* important to her."

"She didn't sound very disappointed when I told her it was probably a fake," I told him.

"Hmmm. Well, she was pretty weird, like I'm telling you. Real, what you say, animated."

A picture of her behind the wheel of her Mercedes came back: She was no longer animated, no. Whatever energy she had expended trying to charm the Argentine had evaporated into the cosmos. But then every day's energy evaporated, didn't it? Expended, vaporized, used up: one day at a time. It was just that Charlotte Vardis's storehouse of energy, her breathing, living self, weird or not, had been raided. Cleaned out.

I hung up the phone and began scribbling down what Paolo had said about Charlotte Vardis: animated, not interested in art, interested in me, wanted to know when I was coming back, needed to find out about Pollock right now.

The computer printout Mendez had given me lay next to the paper. I unfolded it again and reread it. Vardis had a criminal record but not a significant one. Her ex-husband had apparently filed a complaint of assault against her after they had divorced. She had been fined and paroled. This had all taken place in Oklahoma over two years ago.

Apparently her ex hadn't left her destitute. Her address was still in Oklahoma so she had a second home in Jackson, or at least was well-heeled enough to rent long-term. In Jackson it took a lot of money to rent anything, let alone buy. My little apartment over the gallery, though small and drafty, was worth a small fortune now.

I sat back again. What good was this information? Unless I did a thorough background check on Vardis (which the police were probably already doing) this led nowhere. Just as poking around about Shiloh seemed futile. There was only one thing that seemed to link these two murders. And I was determined to find it myself.

▽

18

POLSON, MONTANA, IS an odd mix: a reservation town that is also a tourist destination. It can't decide what sort of a place to be. While snuggled onto the southernmost tip of the expansive blue Flathead Lake, replete with boat rentals and marinas and a golf course, it is strangely grim. There is no joy, no liveliness, no fun.

No clumps of pedestrians killing time on the sidewalks, looking in glitzy jewelry stores and junky souvenir shops, like in my hometown. Here the clumps of locals hang out on the sidewalks outside the state liquor store or Social Services or Lake County Chemical Dependency. Reminders of the devastation of the culture of the American Indian, of his hopelessness.

A change from the superficial glitter and plastered westernism of Jackson should have been a relief. But Polson saddened me with its despair hard by its leisure class.

Inside the Lake County Courthouse I waited to see Wade again. This time the room seemed cooler, not like a torture-chamber hot box. I took this as a positive sign. Or maybe they finally turned on the air-conditioning. The pea-green walls still depressed me, looking like mold, reminding prisoners that they were the scum of society.

Wade entered looking surprisingly fit and definitely cleaned up. His hair had been washed and combed into his graying ponytail and his prison scrubs were clean and tucked in. He must have been sleeping better; he looked more rested. He smiled and gave me a quick, surreptitious hug, with a glance at the guard who took up his standard position against the wall by the door.

"Jesus, it's good to see you, Alix." He stopped halfway down into the chair. "Melina didn't come?"

I shook my head. "She couldn't today. She was backed up on her lectures. But I needed to talk to you again."

He settled himself and frowned. "I wish she'd have come." He sat forward, forearms on the table. "Did you find out who killed Shiloh?"

"Not yet," I said. He hadn't heard about Charlotte Vardis so I recounted the story again, just as I had for Paolo this morning. I told him of my connection, my contact with her.

Wade rocked his chair back, a thoughtful look on his face. His beard was as unkempt as ever, and he stroked it as he listened. "So they both were looking for this bluejay pictograph?"

I nodded. "You've got to remember something more, Wade. Anything connected with the bluejay shaman you told me about. Everything was missing from the library. All the old journals."

"Damn students," he muttered. "Too lazy to copy something down so they just swipe it."

"I didn't find anything in your files about it," I prompted him back to the subject.

Wade shifted his eyes to the ceiling corner, twirling his beard through his fingers. "Bluejay pictograph. I've been racking my brain since you asked me before. I just can't remember ever hearing a thing about it. You're sure that's the name?"

"That's what both Charlotte and Shiloh called it. That's all I know." I tapped my fingers on the table nervously. "What about the bluejay shaman? Is there a drawing he might use?"

Wade squinted, then shook his head. "I don't know. There used to be that dance, in the winter, usually January. The shaman would rub himself all over with charcoal and dance for four nights straight, all night. Then he'd bug out and go sit in a tree until the tribe came and rescued him."

He smiled, warming to his favorite subject. "But I don't recall anything about a drawing or painting. A pictograph is usually a painting on a rock slab or a cliff wall."

"Why would these women want it?" I asked.

He shrugged. "Beats me. There's plenty of collectors around though. And lots of illegal collecting from federal lands and reservation land. Down in the southwest mostly."

"Owning such a pictograph wouldn't necessarily be illegal, would it?"

"No. If it's collected on private land or bought from another collector who found it legally."

"Did you know Shiloh had an extensive Indian art collection?"

Surprise flashed across his face, then he nodded slowly. "I do recall seeing her with some dance sticks or war clubs or something once."

I told him about the boxes in her garage that her roommate claimed contained her excess collections.

"That's odd. I wouldn't store my prized collections of Indian artifacts in the garage," he said. "But then Shiloh was strange. She probably got tired of them and wanted to move on."

Neither of us had any answers to that one. The guard behind me bit down hard on a fingernail; the sound of his teeth clicking echoed around the silent room. Wade didn't seem to notice, lost in thought.

"You talked to Tilden about Shiloh?" he asked, breaking our stalemate.

"Yes. But he wasn't much help. All he said was that he assumed she quit the program because you and she had some rift. Some argument."

Wade frowned and let out an astonished chuckle. "Me and her? That's a new one. He probably told the cops that. He's had it in for me since that article." He leaned forward, leering, his eyes wide. "The word around the department was more like *him* and Shiloh."

I blinked. "Are you sure?"

"Hell, no. It was just a rumor. Something for the gossip-mongers. But there's usually a grain of truth to most gossip."

I cocked my head and smiled at him. "Something maybe like Melina and him? A flirtation?"

His eyebrows lowered at the remark but he nodded. "Maybe."

"They were interested in the same area, right? What was it?"

"Religious rites of the Salish," he said.

"And is the bluejay shaman considered a religious person? A holy man?" I asked. Wade nodded. "So where does that leave us?"

"With two or maybe three people who are interested in the bluejay shaman and what is maybe a painting of him."

My turn to nod and stroke my chin. The guard was quiet now behind me, either listening hard or dozing. The room was heating up again with our three warm bodies in its tiny space; beads of sweat wet my upper lip.

Another thought came to mind: "And some antipapists." I had sent him the clippings from the Missoula newspaper about the further vandalism at St. Ignatius Mission with a note about seeing it myself. "That really bothered me at the mission."

Wade scanned my face with his eyes. "Now you know how the Salish feel when somebody cuts limbs off the Medicine Tree or burns down their sweathouses. It's the same thing. The same fucking thing!" He pounded his fist on the table, angry again.

"Do you think it was Tilden? Does he hate Catholics that much?"

"That business with debunking Shining Shirt was a pretty direct hit. That was years ago. But then you say you found the paint can in your car? Maybe that ties in with trying to frame you for this Vardis woman's murder. Like the vandalism was continued to implicate you somehow. To tie you up so you would lose track of whatever it is you're getting close to." Wade raised his burly eyebrows, gripping the table edge with both hands.

A lump of fear settled into my gut. "Would they kill a woman just to implicate me?"

Wade shook his head. "I don't know, Alix. I don't even have an idea of who they are, how would I know what they'd do?"

Driving back I wondered about Mendez—it was two-thirty, and I had missed the lunch date. It was unavoidable; I had no time for chitchat. He didn't need to be seen with me. Bad for his credibility. Besides, he distracted me; I didn't need that. If there was ever a time to concentrate, to cut out extraneous stimuli, to cut to the bone of a matter, this was it.

∇

19

"I CAN'T GET IT." Melina's whisper hissed down the empty hallway. At seven on a Sunday evening between terms, the social sciences building was deserted, its linoleum hallways shining, smooth and silent. A dim malaise filled the unlit hall as we groped in the dark. We had no need to whisper. But the job seemed to demand it.

From my sister I took the pass key to the anthropology offices; Wade had told me where to find it in the mailroom, hidden on top of the cubbyholes. He used it occasionally if he lost or forgot his own office key. It was ironic, his hesitation telling me where the key was hidden. As much as Tilden had tried to undermine him, possibly even let him take the rap for a murder, Wade still had second thoughts about crossing his old mentor.

Melina shivered though the air was stale, unmoving. The air-conditioning had been turned off for the day; the stagnant metallic smell of its residue hung in the air. I moved in front of Tilden's office door, slipped the key into the knob, and jerked on it. The painted metal door moved inward without a sound. We stepped inside and shut the door.

"Nice office," Melina said, still whispering. She was nervous, her hands trembling until she stuck them in the pockets of her shorts. She wore a loose cotton blouse in a thin Indian weave, white and tan. It made her look pale. She had been tugging on her mane again, causing it to stick out. I moved behind Tilden's desk and sat down in his chair, feeling the warmth of its seat. Had he just been here? There was no fresh smell in the air, no aftershave, no cigar or pipe smoke. I looked on the desk for signs of his return: a half-full coffee cup, an open file or book, a burning cigarette. There was none.

"Lock the door again," I whispered. Melina turned obediently and flipped the latch. "You start with the files over there. I'll do the desk."

She nodded, padding over the worn oriental rug to a tall black file cabinet. She kicked off her shoes, opened the bottom drawer, and sat on the floor with the first file. I turned to my own mission, opening the middle drawer of the desk.

The old desk, a lustrous mahogany, was a well-oiled machine, honed by years of loving use. The wood gleamed even in the light from the solitary desk lamp I switched on. The drawers moved smoothly and quietly, a sign of quality construction. I peered at the contents of the pencil drawer: pencils (natch), pens, paper clips, notepads, index cards, cafeteria meal tickets, receipts from restaurants in a little envelope like he was gathering them for his tax return. I glanced in the envelope and set it back down gingerly. Old buttons from presidential campaigns: Reagan '80, Nixon '68, I Like Ike. His heroes? Time to clean out the cobwebs, Mad Dog.

The drawer slid silently in. I opened another, top right, normally a paper supply drawer. Judging from his office, Tilden was a compulsive type, had everything in its place. I smiled, enjoying the guessing game of what each drawer held. Melina shoved a file back into the cabinet and drew out another.

Score one for me. The drawer held typing paper, envelopes, more index cards, manila envelopes, and in the back an index system for the large-format cards he must use in lectures. I pushed the "B" divider forward and pulled out the cards, leaning back to put them in my lap and read one by one.

"Bella Coola," said one. Another Salish tribe, far from

Montana. Basketry; Blackfoot (Siksika) Indians; Boats; Brule Sioux; Burial customs. Nothing on the bluejay shaman. I returned the cards to their place. What else to look under? I pushed to the "S" divider, drawing out the stack of index cards.

SALISH. Its own divider card within the "S." I scanned the headings one by one: Bitterroot Salish or Interior Salish or Flathead. Alliances; Arms; Arts and crafts; Clark, William (and Lewis); Costume; Disease; Dwellings; Enemies; Horse; Hostilities; Hunting; Language; Medicine men.

I stopped and read carefully. Tilden's notes on the "Medicine men" card were brief and choppy; one word used to prod his memory in lecture. One word with no details. "Bluejay shaman," it said. Period. The end. A faded blue fountain-pen scratching, looking many years old. That was all.

I glanced through the rest of the headings. Here was one: "Religion." But again he mentioned only what I already knew: Shining Shirt, Jesuit missionaries, St. Mary's Mission, St. Ignatius, Catholicism. I scanned the remaining "S" cards and replaced them in the index.

"Finding anything?" I asked.

Melina looked up, sighing. "Mostly handouts. Copies of tests."

The drawer below on the right contained files for what I supposed were Tilden's classes for the previous school year. There were six fat files, complete with grade sheets, tests, handouts, and lecture notes. One was a graduate seminar on the Salish and Kootenai. I opened it on the top of the desk and flipped through the notes. Again Tilden used only a memory-jogging key word; the notes were useless.

Melina moved to the middle file drawer, pulling over the chair that I used for my first talk with Tilden. Her glasses slipped down her short nose as her freckled arms rose to grasp another file.

I closed the drawer and turned to the left side. With my hand on the pull the sounds came through the door. Creak,

creak. Melina looked at me, eyes wide. She nodded toward the desk light. I pulled its chain as quietly as possible and held my breath.

Squeak, squeak, the sounds grew louder, closer. Rhythmic. Footsteps. Someone with rubber- or crepe-soled shoes. A bump. The jingle of keys. Melina and I looked at the doorknob, still locked. Who was in the hall? Could it be Tilden?

A door opened down the hall. The shoes creaked a few times, then the door closed. Whoever it was came closer. Pushing or pulling something that rattled as it rolled. The janitor? I looked under the desk for the wastebasket. Where was it?

I motioned to Melina to come over, behind the desk. The wastebasket, a gray metal institutional model with a tan plastic liner, was to the right of the desk. I shoved it around to the front on the carpet. Melina and I crouched down into the kneehole of the desk, cramming ourselves together, holding each other's arms, desperate, cramped, and afraid.

Another door opened, then closed. It was dark under the desk; my bad knee began to ache. Melina's nails dug into my flesh. She dropped her head to her knees. Squeaking outside our door, another bump, keys.

I took a gulp of air, the tension swelling in my chest. The door opened. No footsteps sounded on the rug but the wastebasket scratched away from the desk. A thump as it was emptied; another, close to our heads, as it returned. God, did Mel leave the file drawer open?

I squeezed my eyes together in agony. How had it come to this? It was so damn undignified to be hiding under a desk. We were frozen even as the cleaning person moved away down the hall, the reassuring squishy squeaks of his shoes on the linoleum fading away.

Melina jerked her head up, bumping the desk drawer above. She moaned aloud, then caught herself. We stared at each other, gaping mouths, listening. I counted to one hundred slowly, waiting for a sound from outside the door. At last I let go of my sister's arms.

"Let's go," I croaked. We crawled from the kneehole, stretching our backs and legs, careful not to bump anything. As I turned to sit again at the desk Melina grabbed my shoulders and hugged me, holding me against her chest, my face in her hair. I could feel her shaking still and patted her back. She released me and walked back to her post without looking in my eyes.

Melina had expressed the same hesitations as Wade had about breaking into Tilden's office. At first she had said I should go alone if I must go at all. Then, at dinner, I could see her ruminating, fidgeting with her food, moving it around the plate like hockey pucks.

"Mel," I said. "Come with me. It'll go faster. The faster I'm out of there the less chance of getting caught." She couldn't argue with that. But she had insisted we drive her car and park it far across the campus from the social sciences building. We wore our jogging shorts and shoes as if we were just out for some evening exercise.

The contents of the top left drawer were strictly utilitarian. Markers, chalk, binders, more index cards, pens. I closed it, reaching for the bottom left drawer. Unlike the other drawers, it refused to budge. I pulled hard on the handle. Above the handle was a keyhole, an old brass model with a large opening. The drawer was locked.

My heart began to pound. If only we could open it. Lock-picking was out of my league. Lamely I tried the passkey to the door. No way. I shoved it back in my pocket angrily.

"Mel," I whispered. "Have you seen a big key? Old-fashioned kind?"

She frowned, coming around the desk to see where I was pointing. "I'll look for it. But wouldn't he have it on him? On his key chain?"

"Maybe. But it's possible since it's probably big that he keeps it somewhere here in the room." I shrugged. "Isn't it?"

Melina went back to the cabinet, still frowning. "Sure." She didn't sound convinced. In the next few minutes we ran our hands under every shelf, picked up every stack of magazines, pulled out every book and looked behind it, looked in the bottom and back of every file and desk drawer, and checked underneath the chairs and the rug. And found no key.

We stood in the middle of the small office, looking at the corners of the room. I felt the top of the window frame, the door frame. Nothing. "Go back to the files." Mel went to work on the top drawer as I turned to the bookshelves on the wall near the door.

Books covered the small eight-foot by eight-foot wall completely, top to bottom. There were seven shelves, with books ranging from textbooks and scholarly tomes to paperback popular books. I spotted the trio by Carlos Castenada that I had enjoyed in college myself, and other works on shamanism and spirituality and Indian lore and life. Pulling down a few, one at a time, I checked indexes for Salish and for bluejay shaman, then set them back on the shelf. An old volume in tattered yellow hardcover held stories about the Salish written down in the twenties. In it Lone Pine, Chief of the Salish, is preparing the tribe for two strangers who might be Lewis and Clark. I took it to the desk and read for a few minutes.

All very interesting but signifying nothing. What was in the drawer? I ran my fingers over the brass lock again and shook the drawer handle for good measure before slipping the Salish book back into its place on the shelf.

If I were a key . . . Crossing my arms, I tried to reason it out. Where would I hide? Perhaps Melina was right, he kept it on him. But a big skeleton key like that? It would be awkward. I spun to look behind the desk where a poster of an Indian fancy-dancer was framed and hung on the wall. Next to it hung Tilden's honoraria, his doctorate diploma from Arkansas, another certificate from an anthropological society. Carefully I took them from the wall and examined their backs and edges.

At the desk I opened the drawers once more. The pencil drawer with its ancient history of simpler times: I nudged the buttons and pencils around, trying to make sense of it. The envelope with receipts—that might mean something. I pulled them out, careful to keep their order intact.

The slender stubs of restaurant checks lay in an untidy pile, varying in size from an inch across to four or five inches. Waitresses usually just handed these out and let you fill in whatever you wanted. Handy if you were into defrauding the IRS or your neighborhood bureaucracy. The dates began in January and moved through the months until June. I pulled my notebook from my pocket and scribbled down dates and places on the June ones.

Tilden had said he was in Seattle for a conference at the time of Shiloh's murder. I turned over the receipts until I found the Seattle ones. A professional meeting, he said, so he would be writing them off on his taxes. And there they were, breakfast, lunch, and dinner, from June 19 to June 23. Then there was nothing. The last receipt was for dinner at a bagel house near the University of Washington on the 23rd.

My notebook said he returned two nights after Shiloh's death. I consulted my chronology of dated notes. Shiloh died on Saturday night, the same day her boxes were to be moved into storage. Saturday was the 24th.

Tilden had lied. He left Seattle on the 23rd, in the evening, or early the next morning. But this was only proof he left Seattle, not that he had come back to Missoula. Maybe he had driven straight back to the hills by the Little Bitterroot River and confronted her.

Or perhaps he just quit keeping his receipts? I stifled a moan. This was nothing. I put the receipts back in the envelope and into the drawer, then rifled through the other drawers again. I had to concentrate not to slam the drawers in frustration.

"Anything?" I asked my sister again. Same answer.

Leaning back in the chair I wondered where I hadn't looked for the key. I had felt the bottoms of all the drawers, a likely hiding spot. Time didn't allow me to open every book. Would he tape the key into one? I stood and scanned them again.

Tilden was clever. Which book then? I looked for "Key" in the titles to no avail. Then "Lock." Then "Drawer," then "Bluejay," then "Shaman." There weren't any books until "Shaman," and no keys were hidden in those.

Melina pushed in the top drawer of the file cabinet, wincing as it screeched on its track and thudded shut. She turned to me as I stared at the books, willing them to tell me their secrets.

"No luck with the key?"

I shook my head, disgusted with this whole caper. I knew very little more than when we broke into this office, and nothing that would link Tilden to Shiloh or Charlotte Vardis. Nothing about the bluejay shaman, no stolen library books or monographs or microfiche. Nothing really at all except the fact that he left Seattle on the 23rd of June. Maybe.

Melina seemed calm now, giving me a supportive half-smile, half-frown and squeezing my arm in sympathy at my scowling expression. We were close. I knew it. But no progress was being made here and now.

"Look at this." Mel knelt in front of the bookshelves and touched a row of identical books, all volumes of an old set, *North American Indian,* by Edward S. Curtis. "These are worth a fortune. I didn't know he had a set," she said, glancing up at me with her eyes rounded. "Old photographs from about the turn of the century. These should be in the library." She pulled out a volume and delicately turned the pages to a black-and-white photograph of a medicine man posing on the prairie, fierce and proud. She sat back on her heels as if she intended to stay awhile.

"Mel, let's get out of here," I whispered impatiently. "We're not getting anywhere."

"Just wait. The pictures are incredible. I've never seen them except reproductions in magazines." She looked up again. "Pick one. You might find something interesting."

I sighed and sat down hard on the soft carpet. Glancing down the row of volumes at the flaking pressed-gold lettering on the bindings, I found volume 9, *Salishan Tribes of the Coast*, and slipped it out. It was heavy, like an encyclopedia, though rather thin. On the inside cover was printed "University of Montana Library."

"Look at this." I showed Mel the imprint. She frowned and went back to her book. From the volume I expected little. The Bitterroot Salish were not coastal. I was beginning to think they were rather marginal culturally. But Wade had made his career studying them; so had Tilden.

As I suspected, the volume did not cover the Bitterroot Salish, aka Flathead, only the Chemakum, Quilleute, and Willapa, with some on the Klallam tribes. The photos were impressive, evoking a proud past full of potlatch, slaves, and seafaring canoes: days that were far, far gone. They made me sad to look at them, the Indians in the simple poverty and grandeur of well-made survival and glorious ceremony.

Putting it away, I noticed that volume 10, next to it, was a fat one. It appeared well-fingered; its binding was fraying on the top. The book slipped easily off the shelf despite its heft, and as I cracked it open the binding leather pulled away from the gummed ends of the pages.

Looking down the tunnel the loose binding made, I could see the key taped to the lower end. "Mel," I whispered, as I felt it there, its cold, hard neck under the cellophane. "I found it."

▽

20

As I SAT in the Saab Sister with the flashlight and the copies we had pilfered from Tilden's office, the exhilaration of the escape was still on me. The thrill of discovery, coupled with the frantic tidying up and fleeing the building: It still tingled in my legs well into the night. I tried to calm myself with deep breaths of midnight air, well aware that this little caper, though important, was no more than a minor piece of a larger and more deadly puzzle.

We had found the archival documents, the ones that were missing from the University Library, in the locked desk drawer—microfilm rolled in a small box; monographs from old journals, copied off in duplicate (we had availed ourselves of one of these); and several slim volumes dealing with Salish spirituality, religious rituals, and shamans.

I scanned the books quickly in his office, my head spinning suddenly with our precarious situation now that the goods were in my sweating hands. They mentioned different aspects of the bluejay shaman and his ritual dance. But the copied monograph, a scholarly paper, that I held in my hand in the car told the whole story.

The fact that Tilden had chosen it for duplication seemed important. It had been published in 1932 by a man who taught at the University of Montana, a Seymour S. Smith.

Elaine and Shiloh's cottage, its peach face gleaming in the yellow gold of the full moon ascending in the eastern sky, was dark. The entire street was dark, silent except for the occasional dog bark. The Saab was parked under a huge old elm tree whose leaves were being stripped to their skeleton by some disease or insect, leaving it transparent and ghostlike.

I flipped off the flashlight and slipped it back in my pocket. I'd been reading this monograph since nine; it was now close to one and I had it memorized. Key words popped into my head in the blankness of the view out the windshield down the shadowy street: "quasquay," the shaman, who spent three days of purification in the sweathouse praying to his personal medicine or "sumesh," his guardian animal; no white man's clothes, no shoes, no non-Salish jewelry or adornments were allowed in the medicine lodge, a long hall formed by joining a row of tepees together; and the dance itself, regular hops to music of deer hooves strung onto leather thongs for rattles and a vocal chant. No drums or flutes allowed. The shaman, dressed in breechclout, face blackened with charcoal.

The frenzy of night after night with no sleep, the tribespeople and the quasquays dancing on and on down the rows. Then sickness could be cured. The bad medicine caused by a hostile quasquay could be extricated, for a price. The fee must be good. The shaman could also avenge some wrong done to a tribal member. The payment must make the revenge worthwhile; if the ceremony didn't work, the quasquay might die himself.

I could hear the chanting in my head, rhythmic footfalls of the shaman padding up and down the dirt paths between the seated tribesmen, moccasins hitting the ground. My eyelids felt heavy. O'Brian's voice on the phone came back; yes, he would try to find out the dates of Tilden's travel to and from Seattle. Then Paolo's lilting laugh: Valkyrie the wandering pony had been causing havoc in the Elk Refuge. She would allow no one to catch her and the rangers were furious. I rubbed my eyes, struggling to stay alert.

I turned on the flashlight again and scanned through the copied monograph once more for a mention of a drawing, a carving, a painting, a pictograph. Again, nothing.

I thought of going home. I couldn't have gotten more than a couple of hours sleep last night. My head rested on the back of the seat. Fatigue screamed through my brain, a physical pain, a gunshot of exhaustion. Then a light came on in the upstairs bedroom.

A frisson of excitement left from earlier tingled up my spine. I hunched over the steering wheel as the light went off upstairs, then on downstairs. Finally the outside light came on. I sank down in my seat until I could barely see over the dashboard. Elaine backed her car out of the driveway and drove away.

When she was a block away I started my engine, cursing the choke but getting it going while keeping my eye on Elaine's taillights. I pulled away from the curb with my lights off but turned them on as the Saab joined the traffic lane. Even with the moon the night was too dark under the canopy of elm trees, ghostly thin or not, to drive without lights.

Elaine's vehicle was an ancient Valiant, turquoise, about a 1964 vintage. I made a silent blessing that her car was older than mine; it improved my chances for keeping up. I kept a block back as we turned onto Higgins into the pink mercury lights of downtown. The Valiant stopped at a red light at Main and Higgins. An ornate, buff-colored sandstone bank dominated the intersection with its fancy mosquelike turret.

I stepped on the brake. The light on my block was still green. I glanced in my rearview mirror and to both sides; no one else was around, so I pretended it was red. The day's heat had dissipated from the asphalt of the wide street, leaving serene the refitted head shops and record stores that now served as coffee bars and herb emporiums.

Elaine pulled away at her intersection; now my light shone red. I drummed my fingers on the steering wheel, watching her point south, toward the bridge that spanned the river, toward the Bitterroot Mountains.

When she was two blocks away I ran the light. The street was still deserted; I said another blessing. It occurred to me I was getting downright religious. I smiled to myself and decided it was appropriate on this gig. We were all getting spiritual.

By the time we wound through town, out Stephens Street and down to Brooks, past the new mall and old Fort Missoula, and met up with the Bitterroot River, by the time Lolo Peak gleamed in the moonlight, I was beginning to wish there was more traffic. A car passed us now and then going into town, its headlights a blur. But we cruised along, alone, as fast as our old jalopies would roll, fifty-five miles per hour, solitary on the blacktop, toward the mountains.

Elaine increased her lead. There was no sense in being seen or suspected with the wide open road and a full measure of moonlight to guide me. Flares of red from her brake lights shone bright, then dimmed as she turned right on the Lolo Pass Road, Highway 12. I eased around the corner after her.

The road narrowed. No more shoulders, just a white line. We passed the turnoff to Fort Fizzle on the right. Another unsuccessful army venture. Talk about a premonition of failure.

The road wound through the gradually rising terrain, grassy by the highway but soon becoming tree-covered up the slopes. The gray ribbon was cut extra long here, necessitating many twists and turns. The blue light from the moon gave the landscape an eerie otherworldliness. Lolo Peak was out the left window now, a beacon, an ancient silent grandfather with a toupee of white hair.

I was admiring the mountain's massive beauty when Elaine turned her Valiant onto a dirt road near the crest of the hill. Like a black beetle, it bounced across the plateau of grass and sage, heading toward the forest. I slowed the Saab, watching her car bump and twist over the rutted road, sending up streamers of dust that glowed in the red of her taillights. Almost at the top I slowed more, just crawling along, waiting for her to enter the woods so I could turn off the highway.

The Valiant stopped. It lurched violently, as if it had fallen in a huge pothole, then bounced on its ancient springs, rocking back and forth. Realizing it was stopping, I steered the Saab off the road and cut the lights and engine. With the moon shining in my back window now, I slumped awkwardly, trying to see what Elaine would do next.

The interior dome light of the Valiant turned on for a moment, then went out. Then all the lights went out, and she must have turned off the car. The dome light blinked again as she opened her door and got out. I could see her lean back into the car, then push the door shut. Darkness. Then a tiny spot of light.

Ten minutes passed as I watched her fade into the forest, the beam of the flashlight bobbing dimmer and dimmer across the grass and into the trees. It disappeared and I waited longer, letting her get away. There was no telling whether I would ever find her in the thick forest. But I had come this far; I had no intention of going back empty-handed.

At last the Saab Sister made the turn onto the dirt road at the hill's crest. The headlights were off but at slow speed with moonlight the going was not difficult. The Valiant listed off the primitive road with its nose in a ditch. I circled around it and found a side road that led down the hill into a thicket of bushes.

Bounding back up the hill, I was awake now, adrenaline pumping, scrambling for what was left of my good name. The stars shone dimly, outdone again by the moon. The still, fragrant air reminded me of home: pine needles underfoot, sagebrush releasing its heady perfume as I pushed by it. But how would I find her? I clenched my teeth, running back to her Valiant, ready to track her on my hands and knees if necessary.

With my hand on the car handle, I listened for a sign. An owl hooted, lonely and distant. My chest heaved with the run. Pushing the button on the handle, I was relieved when it opened, swinging out fast with the awkward angle of the car.

The Valiant's interior was spotless, at least in the front

seat. The backseat was apparently where Elaine, a visiting nurse, kept her medical supplies in boxes stacked two feet high. Bandages, bedpans, catheter tubing, all sorted and categorized. The bumpy drive had jostled them some; a few lay on the floor. A box of surgical gloves was spilled.

I slipped behind the wheel, running my hand over the dashboard and under the front seats. Elaine kept her car very clean, like a little old lady who only drove it on Sundays. The glove box opened easily, the door dropping down with a thud. A stack of papers, insurance cards, the warranty booklet, copies of repairs done to the car. And I thought only Porsche owners kept their repair records. I shoved them all back in the glove box.

Did she have a map? Not among the medical supplies. Searching there would take too much time. I sat back with my hands on the steering wheel. Now where would I keep a map—if I didn't take it with me? The seat was bare, the dash was bare, the floor was bare. . . .

As I lowered the driver's-side visor a piece of notebook paper fluttered to my lap. It had been torn in half and folded several times, the folds now flattened by the visor. I smoothed it on my thigh, straining at the penciled scribbles.

The notation read "93 to 12, third dirt road on the right." The map itself was a series of lines that approximated the highways we had traveled: 93 out of Missoula; 12, the Lolo Pass Road; then two stubs of roads and one long road off to the right.

I squinted out the windshield. My reflection hung there, ghostlike. My lucky hat, crushed and familiar, pulled down around my lanky hair. My bangs were getting too long, poking against my eyelashes. I brushed them to one side. Did we turn on the third road? I remembered the turnoff at Fort Fizzle, then this one. Did I miss the second?

The bottom half of the map had been torn away; Elaine must have taken it with her. I sighed. How could I find her in the dark? I folded the paper and returned it to the visor before getting out of the car.

A breeze blew up from the valley, a warm one that reminded me of summer, of heat. The night sky was a velvet screen, close enough to make a person feel insignificant. Was there a reason for living on earth? A despondency clung to me—as heavy as the helplessness of the dead—as I climbed slowly to the crest of the plateau.

If a rattlesnake bit me here tonight, well, that would be it. The thought calmed me: It was out of my control. I felt bolder as I lengthened my stride and reached for my flashlight in my pocket. Some things are just out there, either waiting for you or not. So the events you could control you damn well better jump on. Grab them by the teeth and make them behave. That was how I felt about Tilden and his sleazy tricks. What I wouldn't give to catch him at one tonight.

At the hill's top my rage at Tilden diminished. Fear—for my future, for Melina and Wade's—filled me. Fear, rage—the alternating currents of this night. The other side of the hill dropped off sharply to a flat wetland marsh, then into gentle forest until several miles away the trees stopped in front of a high ridge of rock not unlike Chief Cliff.

The bottom of the valley—the marsh—was shrouded in shadow. It was no bigger than a coulee, formed by the far hill and the one I stood upon. The moon hadn't risen enough to reach its depths. As my eyes adjusted to the darkness I saw the dirt road that came from the highway, winding down the slope toward the marsh. I flipped off my flashlight and crouched behind a sagebrush: Two cars were parked at the bottom of the hill.

▽

21

THE VALLEY WIND blew softly through the grass, kicking up dust and mouse droppings. In the moonlight the little tracks stood out in the sandy dirt behind the bush. A coyote let out a woeful howl in the mountains: The moon hung like a ripe melon in the sky.

I listened, trying to block the sound of the wind in my ears. The air stilled and swirled, a hint of human voice drifting on it. I crawled around the side of the sagebrush, feeling exposed in the lunar glare atop this hill, and peered again into the shadowy valley.

A glint of blue moonlight now caught the corner of a pool of stagnant water near the parked cars. It worked as a mirror, brightening the rest of the scene. The two cars were unfamiliar. I squinted, scanning the forest that began past them, looking for light, for movement, for Elaine.

My legs began to ache as I squatted on my haunches. I put one bare knee, still in shorts from our charade jog across campus, down in the dirt. My hand went down for balance. As it did I caught the movement out of the corner of my eye. The dark and light stripes, long and slender, the S shape.

Rattlesnake! I lost my balance and fell backward on my butt as it slithered out of sight.

I jumped up, hopping three or four paces away across the crest of the hill before remembering I was trying to hide. Bending over, I took a few more steps, caught my breath, and ducked behind a boulder. I closed my eyes, my heart thumping hard in my chest.

The rock was solid, warm, and reassuring. After I was sufficiently calm I peeked over it, down into the valley again. This time a light, a spark of campfire, shone through the trees at the bottom of the tall rock cliff, about a mile away. How had I not seen it before? The angle had improved. The view through the spaces between trees lined up now. Thanks to the rattler. Just like they told us in Lutheran Sunday school about the Garden of Eden. A snake pushing humans into doing something they were not entirely ready for.

I picked my way down the hill, keeping in shadow. Watching each foot placement, pausing to look up and get my bearings, keeping an eye out for snakes and the approach of Elaine, the going was tortuously slow. She must have taken the wrong road in, the second instead of the third. She could be lost. She could be right behind me.

The trees at last: Douglas first, lodgepole pines, a smattering of aspens. I sank against one, feeling its rough, corky bark, releasing a pent-up breath in the cool blackness of the forest floor. The fire I had seen from the hill was little more than a dim glow through the thick growth; had I not known it was there I'd never have noticed it. My hand grazed a damp carpet of moss and paused to sink into its cushioned depth, cradled and safe for an instant. I drew my wet hand across my forehead: The anxiety made me break out in a sweat.

Then a sound. Breaking of twigs downhill. I flattened myself against the tree. Another branch broke, then a whizzing sound followed by a whipping slap: "Ow! Sonofabitch!" It was Elaine, making her way to the campfire and none too pleased about it.

She cried out again. "The hell with it," she muttered and a flashlight beam turned on ten or twelve feet away from me, lighting a small spot on the ground. "That's better."

The density of the underbrush was going to be a problem for me too, even with Elaine's beam to follow. I couldn't turn on my own light. But I would probably alert them with either the sounds of twigs underfoot or my own cursing. I had to smile, thinking of Elaine in her purple sweat suit and little blond curls traipsing angrily through the forest, spewing epithets.

I waited until her footsteps were barely audible, then moved out of the forest again where the moonlight helped light the way. By staying on the edge of the trees, in the shadow of their branches, I could see where I was going yet stay out of sight. It veered me away from the campfire, up the rocky hillside. Soon I reached the bottom of the ridge, a field of granite boulders and pebbles that ran to a small grassy strip, then to the trees.

A chill wind fell from the stone ridge. I hugged my arms against my sides, struggling to get my breathing back to normal. With the wind a sound, faint and momentary, drifted over to me. A pecking sound? Two rocks being hit together? A hard, unnatural sound.

The rocks leading up to the ridge looked ready to roll down on me. They were massive and old. *Intruder*, they whispered. I looked back at the chunks of rock and occasional juniper spread out on the hillside where I'd come. To my right the ridge continued with more rock debris. To my left the wall of rock jutted out and the land below disappeared into the night.

I crept along the granite face of the wall and peered around the abutment. A grassy meadow, nearly flat, sat around the corner, at the bottom of an immense slide of rock. I stepped over a boulder and jumped down into the grass.

Click, clack. There it was. Louder, continuous, rhythmic. No breeze was carrying it here. But I knew the rocks echoed sound perfectly. The direction of this telegraph signal was unclear.

Small outcroppings of rocks, miniature versions of the immense wall around the abutment, rose from the slope. Vegetation grew in clumps and hollows. The meadow where I stood was a handkerchief lawn, apparently a favorite of the high mountain animals, its grasses clipped close to the ground.

The moon had risen over the tops of the trees downhill

from the huge rock face. I stepped across the meadow, into the rocky hillside, listening for the sound. I backtracked into the grass again, covering my uphill ear. Click, clack. It came again. From downhill. I turned. Yes, below.

The forest loomed down the hill, dense and dark, scattered with boulders. Back into it, I listened, then as I tiptoed around a huge rock a light, its source hidden, flickered against the midnight sky.

Edging my way along the backside of the boulder, I moved toward the light. It appeared to be around another rock, but as I got closer I saw there was a cave nestled into the hillside. The light, a campfire—and the noises—came from the cave.

My pulse raced. I moved back toward the high rock face I had come from. Once I lost my balance and caught a yearling tree, bending it nearly to the ground as I fell. I picked myself up and continued until my back flattened against the rock face. I inched along sideways, the sharp crystals of the granite like needles against my fingertips.

The cave faced away from my approach. All I could see was the glow of the fire and a sliver of one side of the entrance. I clung to the rock, cool and gritty. The light became brighter, dancing with an orange glow on the opposite wall of the entrance.

I stopped ten or twelve feet from the entrance. What now, hotshot? Did I stick my head around the corner and yell howdy? The smoke from the fire poured past me. I looked down the hill. This was crazy.

I inched back away from the cave, picking my way in a wide arc to the safety of a lichen-covered boulder across from the cave entrance. The sounds from the cave had changed now to a low chanting. I scrambled up the big rock, finding a place where I could lie on my stomach and see into the cave.

Around the campfire sat three figures. From the distance, some twenty or thirty yards, the campfire light danced on their faces, their features distorted with harsh shadows. I blinked. Why did their faces look so blurry? I squinted. Not blurry. Blackened. Covered with soot.

The figures were all slight, and, I guessed, all women. They wore dark garments, nondescript. I tried to isolate each one, to recognize them. Elaine was easy; her blond curls sparkled in the campfire's yellow light. The smoke from the campfire blew over me. My eyes stung.

The women were chanting, a slow rhythmical chant that seemed to put them half to sleep. Their eyes were closed, hands still on the knees. Then out of the shadows came another figure, a man, dancing wildly, prancing, bringing his knees high. His face was blackened as well, and his chest. He wore only a strip of fabric from his waist, covering the groin. His bare feet shone as he swung them high enough to let the firelight bounce off his pink soles.

As he moved out of the darkness the rest of the cave flickered, brightening. On the rock wall facing the mouth of the cave a painted figure was dimly visible. I couldn't make out the shape of it through the smoke but the color was unmistakable. A bright, jaybird blue.

I sucked in my breath. Would that maniac get out of the way so I could see it better? Could this be the bluejay pictograph? But it was big, three or four feet high. And if painted on a slab of rock, impossible to transport by hand. And hard to hide.

If I couldn't recognize the women, there was no doubt in my mind about the man. Marcus Tilden, the one the students called Mad Dog, pranced around the campfire, doing the Bluejay Dance. It was just like in the monograph. The chanting of the participants kept the dancer moving. The clacking I heard earlier must have been the deer hoof rattles the author had described.

Eventually the bluejay shaman would reach a fever pitch, and the others would suddenly douse the fire. In the darkness he would run into the woods and perch in a tree. The others would persuade him to come down. If they couldn't find him, or persuade him to return, he would lose his mind.

Witnessing it all at last elated me. I couldn't wait to see Tilden flip out and climb a tree. I smiled despite the clammy, cold stone. I watched the hot fire longingly as the women put on more sticks from the pile stacked against the cave wall.

Mad Dog Tilden danced around them, sometimes changing directions or dancing in place. At some invisible signal they picked up the rattles and began the clacking sound, giving their voices a rest.

And so it continued. Not a word was said between Mad Dog and the women. If the boulder had not been so uncomfortable I would have fallen asleep from the rhythmical sounds. I wondered if the women—or Mad Dog—were in some trancelike state. They continued so long, so still, I decided they must be.

I turned my watch to the moonlight. 3:00 A.M. My bones ached on the cold, hard bed of rock. I shivered in my shorts. How long would they keep this up? Tilden must be tiring. I could see his dancing was less inspired, more economical. Then suddenly he tapped one woman on the head and the chanting stopped.

The woman rose. Not Elaine. Another woman. The others hung their heads like they had fallen into a deep sleep. Tilden turned toward the dark recesses of the cave, the woman following. I waited. The women passed over by Mad Dog waited, motionless.

I slipped down from the boulder onto a soft mound of earth. The ceremony (or whatever it was) must be over. I had to get out before Elaine did. Peering around the boulder one last time I saw that the two women remained in the same position, chins on their chests. As I straightened to go, one lifted her face out into the night, toward the moon. My heart leapt; I knew her.

As I methodically retraced my steps to the car I went over and over the night's events. The break-in at the office. The old monographs. The descriptions of the dance and then the real thing.

For a split second I felt a twinge of victory. Yes, he was as whacked out as I had thought. Even more so. Did that mean he had killed two women though? Had they been in this bluejay cult?

Questions, questions. As I reached the Saab one stuck in my mind. Why, on a clear summer night in a cave deep in the Bitterroot Mountains, with blackened face, did Zena Glenn sit chanting?

22

SMITH, ALBERT, SMITH, ZACHARY. Hundreds of Smiths. They were packed in tighter than sardines in the old wooden card catalog drawer. Files of articles, recorded by an overzealous library science major for a thesis project in the fifties: names of all the authors of articles in journals then owned by the University Library.

The research librarian, an officious woman in her sixties with a friendly smile and thick glasses, had shown me the card catalog in a back room. She remembered me and seemed eager to get to the bottom of the mystery of the missing journals and microfilm. I didn't tell her about Tilden's stash. Not yet.

"Graphite," the pencil behind her ear said. I pulled the heavy thin drawer from the cabinet and set it with a thud on a round table. It smelled of dust. The cards stuck together as if the ink hadn't quite dried when our library student had filed them, lo, these many years ago.

Seymour. Smith, Seymour S. I jammed my fingers into the cards. There he was, between Sidney and Russell Smith.

Seymour had sixteen cards, dating from 1923 to 1932. He started out in a local journal about an Indian dig in Minnesota, according to the notes on the card written in a fancy old-fashioned script. Who was this library science major? What a task this person had set up for herself. What an accomplishment. Yet here it languished, unused and forgotten. These were the days of computers and speed-of-light.

Smith's journal articles continued, on topics as narrow as
hunting arrows of the Kootenai and as broad as intertribal
rivalries of the Indians of Montana. He bounced around a
lot those first few years until about 1928 when he wrote his
first article on Salish medicine men. From then on he wrote
about the Salish. Mostly about their spiritual ceremonies.
Sweathouses. Games. The bluejay shaman.

That was the last article, dated May 1932. The one Tilden
had copied off, the one Melina and I had lifted. After that,
Seymour disappeared from the files.

Out in the main library Miss Graphite helped me search
the old *Reader's Guide to Periodical Literature* issues and a
few other such catalogs of journals and magazines. I read
some old monographs about Shining Shirt and his vision for
good measure but learned nothing new. The name Seymour
S. Smith, common but odd enough, never appeared again
after 1932.

What had happened to Seymour? He had been such a
prolific publisher of anthropological articles for ten years.
Then nothing. Had he died? Taken a leave of absence? Gone
insane? He was hot on the trail of the bluejay shaman. Had
one thrown a feather of bad medicine into Seymour? I
wondered if he was like Wade, making friends with the
Indians, joining in their rituals. One of Wade's ancestors in
a way.

Ancestor. I ran down the library steps into the morning
sunshine. The wall of heat greeted me, sucking at my cool
insides as I made my way across campus. I was just getting
used to it when the doors of the administration building
opened and slapped my cheeks with air-conditioned coolness.

"A present for my mother," I explained to the records
supervisor. "It will mean so much to her to have the complete
family history."

The supervisor was an another officious woman, younger
by a hair (dyed no doubt) than the librarian. She was
meticulously attired in a red polka-dot dress with every red
plastic accessory known to woman. Even her red lipstick

matched the crimson of her dress. But her eyes were soft as
she regarded me, weighing my story of the family history of
the descendants of Seymour S. Smith.

"Those old faculty files are boxed in the basement," she
said, scratching her scalp with red-painted nails. "I just
don't have the time to look for it."

"Could I look for Grandfather's file myself? I don't mind.
I really need every scrap of information." I pleaded. I begged.
"You see, he didn't marry Grandmother until after he left
the university. So she never knew much about his career
here." I smiled. "She always told me how proud he was that
he had taught here at the University of Montana." Shame-
less, that's me.

Polka-Dot pursed her lips. She knew I was wheedling. But
her blue eyes squinted and in a moment the keys rattled from
her hand as we descended the dimly lit stairs to the
basement. The long linoleum corridor at the bottom was
quiet, smelling of the battling odors of mildew and Pine Sol.
She unlocked a door to a huge storeroom, rivers of paper in
cardboard boxes and manila envelopes, oceans of messy files,
stacked on rough wood shelves and sleek, chrome wire racks.

I followed the tick of her red heels down the side aisle. We
passed row after row, going back farther and farther. 1957–
1962. 1948–1953. At last we came to the thirties. She
stopped, her bangles clattering against the keys, in front of
a row labeled in faded ink lettering, 1927–1932.

"It should be filed by the last year he was affiliated with
the university." Polka-Dot pursed her lips again. "But you
never know back here." I looked down the row of shelving,
my smile fading.

"Thanks."

"If you want to copy something, you can bring it up to my
office. But I have to charge you ten cents a copy. And you
must put it back in the right place." She turned on her heel,
then glanced back. "You have an hour until my lunch
break."

The row of shelving was forty feet long and stretched to

the ten-foot ceiling. Heavy boxes of files sat covered with black grime. I rubbed the side of one and sneezed. Then I sat down on the floor in front of the very last box on the bottom shelf and said a little prayer for luck.

Forty-five minutes later luck roosted on my shoulder, gazing down on a musty file. I copied down the information in my notebook furiously, then stuffed the file back in the dusty box. Touching Polka-Dot's cool arm upstairs, I thanked her before I flew out the door.

Freddy's Feed and Read sat like a dowdy hen in an old neighborhood storefront three or four blocks from the campus. The exterior was unpretentious, painted brown with a yellow sign lettered with flourishes. As I stepped into the grocery side I caught a glimpse of Freddy heading toward a back room in his signature Hawaiian shirt.

I poured myself some gourmet coffee into a large Earth-friendly paper cup, leaning against a wall by the cash register to sip it and watch for Zena. She worked afternoons, she said. I choked on my coffee when a man with a waist-length neon-green Mohawk haircut turned to show me his surprisingly handsome face.

The lunch crowd thinned. A sprout-and-cream-cheese sandwich called to me from the refrigerator case. I had devoured it with a natural fruit juice that tasted like sweetened sewer water when Zena's black hair flashed by the doorway to the bookstore.

"I don't have time for this." Her words were whispered but hard. I stopped on the last step down to the bookstore as the footsteps of her pursuer approached.

"Please, Zena. I need to talk to—"

Elaine stopped in front of the doorway. Her frightened eyes stared at me, then switched to the direction Zena had gone.

"Hello, Elaine." Bingo: two for one. I stepped down the last stair to the bookstore level. The small room was filled with books, neatly stacked on handcrafted wooden shelves. The summer sun streamed through the huge old plate-glass window, making me squint. "I need to talk, too."

Guiding her by the arm, I pulled Elaine toward the back of the store where Zena had disappeared. She didn't resist. The door at the back revealed a small, dark storeroom with a cement floor, cardboard boxes against one wall, a metal table with two chairs, a sink and toilet. Bent over in front of the sink, washing her face, was Zena.

She rubbed her face with a hand towel nonchalantly, seeing us in the sink's mirror before she turned. I knew before she lowered the towel that her face would be hard. I had underestimated Zena.

"Hello, Alix." Her long black hair was wavy, caught into a band at the nape of her neck. She wore a rumpled cotton skirt that skimmed her ankles and a loose tank top. The towel-rubbing had reddened her cheeks but didn't disguise the dark circles under her eyes. "How's Melina doing? I've meant to stop by again."

"Too busy?"

"Very," she said coolly. "Elaine, can we talk later?" She grabbed her embroidered purse. "I have to go to work. Freddy'll have my neck."

"I'd like to hear what Elaine has to say now," I said. "And you too, Zena."

Zena's eyes narrowed for an instant. "I have to go."

"That's too bad," I said. "I've been hoping to hear all about the bluejay ceremony."

Elaine and Zena exchanged wary looks. Elaine tried to smooth her white slacks but her hand shook so badly she gave up. Zena turned her gaze to me, full of ice.

"The what?"

"Last night," I prompted. "Lolo Pass. Full moon?"

Elaine let a little gasp escape. "You followed us?"

"Quiet," Zena snapped.

"I followed you. I saw your rattles and your charcoaled faces and the bluejay shaman dancing around the campfire. An enlightening evening, I must say."

The two women were silent. Elaine shifted her weight

back and forth. I stepped back and shut the door, leaning against it.

"I don't care what kind of rituals you conduct. I really don't." I wiped the sweat off my upper lip. The storeroom had begun to heat up. "If you need a crazy guru, that's your business." Zena opened her mouth to say something. "Yes, I know it's Tilden. And he is crazy. He may have killed Shiloh, Elaine. Have you thought about that?"

Elaine only stared at me, her eyes widening.

"And someone else is dead too. A woman named Charlotte Vardis. Someone wants the police to think I killed her." I stopped for a moment and sucked in some air, calming myself. "I want to know what Shiloh and Charlotte Vardis had to do with this—cult. Zena?"

She tossed her black bangs off her forehead like a proud horse. "I don't know what you're talking about."

Damn. "Elaine?"

Zena glared at her for an instant, then broke away, walking deliberately to the towel rack and hanging the hand towel precisely on it. Fussing. Leaving Elaine to make her own decisions. Good.

"Shiloh was in the cult, wasn't she?"

Elaine nodded, her hands gripped so tight her knuckles whitened. Her pink sleeveless top began to stain with sweat.

"How long?"

She shrugged. "Couple years, I guess."

"You guess. You haven't been a member that long too?"

She shook her blond curls. "No. No. I went last month for the first time. They needed someone new."

"Who was there?"

Her eyes flashed up at me then surrendered. "Me, Shiloh, Sylvie, Dr. Tilden."

"Not Zena?"

Zena had been fussing with her face in the glow of the low-watt light bulb over the mirror. She turned now and faced me. "This is my first moon cycle."

I checked with Elaine. She nodded. "She took Shiloh's place."

"Whose place did you take?" I asked.

"I don't know," Elaine whispered. "Someone quit over the winter."

"You don't meet over the winter?"

"Only in the summer. May through August on full moons." Her body began to shake. She clenched her teeth as her eyes filled. Her freckled face reddened in anger. "I hate him. I hate him! I won't go back. That's what I wanted to tell you, Zena. I'm not going back tonight."

"Tonight?"

Zena blinked bloodshot eyes. "Four nights in a row."

"All night long!" Elaine shouted, stamping her foot. "I can't do it. I just can't. I have to work. So do you, Zena. He says I have to do it for Shiloh. To give her spirit a peaceful journey. But I—" The tears choked her throat.

My mind raced. "Was there ever a woman named Charlotte Vardis in the group? When you were there?" Elaine shook her head. I looked at Zena. She shrugged. "Have you ever heard of her at all?"

Again they shook their heads. No. No one knew her. No one in the whole damn town. Except me. I took another deep breath. "All right, then. We go tonight."

Elaine gasped and stared at Zena. Nothing seemed to ruffle the cool zinnia, the porcelain flower. Never wilts in the heat, that's the zinnia.

Elaine sputtered: "But we can't take you. He said he would—"

"He would what?"

She shook her head until I was afraid it would come off. We just can't. I'm afraid of him. He might do anything."

"All the more reason to put a stop to it. Zena?"

She blinked slowly, detached from Elaine's emotional outburst. "What?"

"Are you in? Will you back us up tonight?"

"What do you propose to do?" She put her hands on her hips.

"You pump him for information. That's all. Ask him about Charlotte Vardis. You replaced her, Elaine. She must have been a member of the group last year. If we can link the two women to Tilden and to each other then the police can take over. They'll investigate Tilden. As it is there is no proof linking him to either murder."

Zena cocked her head. "Just ask him some questions? All right. For Melina. I have no great ties to the man."

We left Elaine splashing water on her tear-streaked face as Zena and I stepped out into the harsh light of the bookstore. Melina's friend and I only nodded a simple good-bye. We would see each other later. I hoped Zena would show. Elaine I could handle. But Zena's reasons for joining the cult of the hoppin' bluejay shaman remained a mystery to me.

At the door I turned back. Zena stood behind a desk with counters on two sides, serving the bookstore from the center of the room. I stepped back to her as she was putting her purse under the counter.

"I'm curious about something. What is that painting on the wall of the cave? That big one."

She pulled a dustrag out and began to move it over the counter although it was littered with flyers and pamphlets. "That's the bluejay shaman. He's half-bird, half-man."

"Is there a name for that painting? Something Tilden called it?"

Zena thought for a moment. "No, not really. Well, he did refer to it as the new painting." She stopped wiping for a moment and looked me straight in the eye, quite a departure for her. "I got the feeling he dabbed it on there himself," she whispered.

Something about last night's ceremony rattled around in my head as I hit the sidewalk. When Mad Dog tapped a woman on the head and they adjourned to the recesses of the cave, what did they do back there? I should have asked. I would tonight.

The question fermented in my brain. Then another: Where had I parked my car? I stood frowning in front of Freddy's Feed and Read, puzzling about the mundane and the obtuse. Puzzling so hard, in fact, that I didn't see Mendez until he stepped out of the police cruiser.

The sidewalk baked under my running shoes. I could feel the heat rise around me, waves of penetrating vapor, distorting the elm trees across the street and the pots of cascading flowers beside the bookstore's entrance. I wasn't accustomed to this kind of heat, relentless, energy-sapping, day after endless bright day. The temperature turned up a few notches as I stood there waiting for Mendez.

His jaw flexed as he grit his teeth, his face expressionless. They must teach this in the police academy. Show No Emotion 101. But a practiced face-reader like myself could see the tension in his neck, his jaw, his eyes.

"I've got to bring you downtown." Mendez stood squarely before me, eye to eye. His voice was less than official. "I've been looking for you all day."

"What for?"

"Questioning."

He looked away first, shifting his feet and hooking his thumbs on his belt. His tanned arms stuck out unceremoniously below the blue uniform shirt. The .38 sat on one hip, a radio on the other.

"I see." My voice cracked in a way I hated. He looked back into my face, searching for something.

He took my arm like I might make a run for it, opened the cruiser's door, and put me in. At least he didn't handcuff me and push my head down.

The chatter of the dispatcher didn't fascinate me this time. I wondered if I should call Hondo. How deep was this hole someone had dug for me? And was it Tilden? Had he gone to all this trouble?

He knew where my car was the day it disappeared. He

knew because I had just been to see him. He could have
followed me out the building or seen me park from his
window.

What had he said about Shiloh? *I don't think she ever
found what she was looking for.* We had been talking about
finding truth, a spiritual peace, a pathway of knowledge. But
is that what Tilden meant? Maybe he meant she was looking
for the bluejay pictograph. But what exactly was that?

Frustration. I gnashed my teeth as we swung around the
corner and into the police station parking lot. An old gas
station sign on a metal stand read Full Service. Yeah, I
thought, getting out with the aid of Mendez's beefy paw on
my arm, *give me some gas.*

23

THE WELCOMING COOLNESS of the police station made my memory lapse; I forgot my frustrations. My questions without answers. My quandary, imbroglio, pretty kettle of fish. For a moment all I felt was the coolness. The blessed relief. But as the sweat began to dry on my back the reality of the predicament reared its ugly, fiery head.

The interrogation room was one of a million. Cement-block walls. Linoleum floor speckled in gray and slashed with black heel-marks. Institutional gray metal furniture. Crime in Missoula was usually clean. Maybe the occasional revenge slasher. A drug bust, sure. It's a college town. Shoplifting, burglary. All the time. But rarely did a rich out-of-state socialite show up in her Benz with a bullet through her temple.

Knox came in with another man. The second man wore a wrinkled tan suit; he shed the jacket and loosened his tie. His boyish face glistened with oily sweat. I squinted at him from across the table, trying to place him.

The policeman wore the same expression that Mendez had practiced. Knox regarded me for a silent minute, his big face solemn and placid. The eyes that had been so kind yet official at Melina's house now appeared simply official. The air-conditioning had cooled me now and I shivered.

"Miss Thorssen." Knox put his red hands on the back of a chair and leaned forward toward me. His voice boomed around the small room, inappropriately loud. "This is Mr. Albrecht. He's the assistant county attorney up in Lake County."

That was where I'd seen him. Wade's hearing. Lashing

into Wade, making him out as a possible serial killer. I squinted at him. His baby-blue eyes were cold.

"What's he doing here?"

"Observing. Listening," said Knox. I waited. What more did they want from me? My stomach began to tighten into knots.

"Do I need a lawyer?" I tried to match the policeman's voice in decibels, finding the effort gave me strength. "Am I being charged with something?"

Knox shook his big head slowly. There were only a dozen or so hairs left on it, wound around his ears, surrounded by freckles. "We just want to talk."

I nodded and tried to breathe. I wished Mendez had stayed. But I could no longer count on him being on my side. Especially after standing him up for lunch yesterday.

"Tell me about the shirt, Miss Thorssen," he began, leaving the statement hanging as if I had some new information to add to what I had already told them twice.

"What about it?"

Albrecht pulled a chair out, swung it around, and straddled it. How casual. Knox cleared his throat: "Anything you can remember about it. Where and when you saw it last, for example." He sat down in a gunmetal-gray chair and crossed his legs. At least we were on the same visual plane now.

"Well. As near as I can remember I last saw it when I was packing for this trip. But was dark, so I can't be sure it was actually in the trunk. I assume it was." I cleared my own throat, which was suddenly parched.

"It was dark?" Knox said, pulling a pack of cigarettes from his pocket. God, he wasn't going to smoke in this tiny room, was he? "Why was that?"

"Because it was at night." I struggled to keep my voice as even and unemotional as his.

"And when was this?"

"Friday night. A week or so ago."

"The day before your brother-in-law was arrested for murder."

I looked at Albrecht, who returned my gaze. "Right."

"You were hired by the department as a—" He looked at his notes. "A consultant."

"An art appraiser," I corrected. "I own a gallery in Jackson. That load of stuff in the U-Haul trailer?" That stuff I had pushed clean out of my mind. Was that what this was about? My dropping the ball on my job?

The policeman drew a cigarette from the package. "You arrived when?"

"Late Friday night. About two. Early Saturday, I guess."

"And when did you first talk to the deceased? Miss Vardis." It was Albrecht now, wiggling. He couldn't stay out of it.

"On Thursday, I think. My partner called me earlier in the week."

"Mr. Segundo?" Knox referred to his notes.

"My partner." I squirmed. "Check with him. He talked to her in the gallery."

The ring-around-the-collar on Albrecht's white shirt smelled even from this distance. "We have," the attorney said with a triumphant smile. Of course he had.

I glanced at Knox. He hadn't changed positions. The cigarette wrinkled under the rolling of his pudgy fingers. The packet in his other hand looked limp and empty. Maybe he needed matches.

"Your sister corroborates it all too. But she is your sister," the lawyer said.

I glared at him. "What do you mean?"

"Maybe Fraser is taking the fall for her and you're helping concoct the story to keep your sister out of it. Maybe Fraser and Shiloh had a little something going. Maybe—"

Knox sat forward, laying the crumpled pack and the lone cigarette on the metal table. He broke in: "We aren't suggesting anything, Miss Thorssen. We're just trying to get some information about a murder."

I slid a look at Albrecht. What a fishing expedition. His mouth was clamped in a line. Keep it shut, shyster.

The policeman continued. "Tell us about Charlotte Vardis. Everything you know about her."

I sighed. "She stopped into the gallery in Jackson when I was up here," I began, then told them what Paolo had recounted to me, how she had come in wanting a painting researched. Then how Paolo and I had done the calling, and I had returned the call to her at the number Paolo gave me.

"You gave us that number," the cop said.

"Right."

"No such number."

I blinked. "What do you mean?"

"That number has been disconnected for the last six months. It used to belong to a restaurant that went out of business before Christmas."

I shook my head. I remembered dialing, talking to her. The connection had taken a little long, but not so long as to be unusual with long distance.

"You wrote it down when your partner gave it to you?"

"Yes. In my notebook. Do you want to see it?" I reached for my backpack. I pulled out the spiral pad, its yellow cover encrusted with something that had melted. Candy, it looked like. Yech. I fished out a tissue and wiped it. On the fifth page was her name.

"Here. Charlotte Vardis. 307-739-9110." I jabbed a finger on my scribbled writing as I pushed the palm-sized notebook across the table.

Knox touched the notebook with a scarred finger, then pulled glasses from his shirt pocket. He was dressed in polyester western-cut pants and a blue shirt pulled across his broad shoulders. The chrome-framed glasses wobbled on his big nose. He shoved the notebook back.

"Did you know Ms. Vardis was in Missoula?" he asked.

"No."

"She checked into a motel here last Friday. The 23rd."

"She was in Jackson on Monday. Paolo talked to her."

I glanced between the men. So there you have it, gents. She drove to Jackson and back here. Figure it out. Do you want me to draw you a picture? A thought popped front and center. "She was here then. When Shiloh was murdered."

Albrecht jerked his head up. He had been close to dozing in the quiet of the small room. His eyes narrowed. "Do you know of some connection between Shiloh Merkin and Charlotte Vardis?"

I hesitated. Did I? I guessed they were both looking for a mysterious pictograph with a birdman on it. I knew Charlotte was looking for it, a year ago anyway. Moody said Shiloh had asked him about it. Was she looking for it or was she just curious?

"Miss Thorssen?" The attorney had straightened his posture.

"I don't know for certain if there is a connection," I said. "But I can tell you this. When I called the FBI in Chicago, to find out about the Jackson Pollock painting for Charlotte Vardis, I had the agent run her name through their computer." I cleared my throat, visions of water beginning to appear as oases on the tabletop. "He told me she had asked about something called a bluejay pictograph some time last year."

"What is that?" the detective asked.

I shook my head. "I guess it's some kind of Indian rock painting. I really don't know. I haven't been able to find out anything about it, even if it exists at all."

Albrecht stood up. His lip began to curl. "What does that have to do with Shiloh Merkin?"

I took a deep breath. "I don't know."

The ink wouldn't come off my fingertips. I felt dirty, my dignity fouled. Bad enough being grilled by the cops, guilt by association. Then to stand before a counter with a huge hand poking your fingers into an ink pad and onto a card. An official card with all your vital information on it. Like a criminal. And then the ink wouldn't wash off.

"Lava soap," Mendez said. The afternoon was almost expired, exactly the way I felt. At least I had spent a few minutes visiting the drinking fountain on the way out. "I've got some at my place."

I didn't answer. Giving up on my fingertips, I rolled down the window of the cruiser and stuck one arm out. The police said they needed my prints to sort out the ones in Charlotte's car. It made sense. But I still felt dirty. The breeze caught my arm as it hung limply, flapping against the side of the car. I tried to think ahead to tonight, to plan. To forget about the cops and their suspicions. *You'll be staying with your sister awhile. Don't leave town.*

Albrecht must have told them I went to see Wade in Polson. But I was back. Didn't that prove me trustworthy? The warm wind blew my hair off my neck. I ran my fingers through it to get it off my face. Then I got a good whiff of my underarms and dropped my hands to my lap.

Mendez parked in front of his house. The grass grew tall and straight, neat and newly mown. I followed him up the steps and into the house. His bathroom, with old, worn porcelain fixtures, smelled of Comet. God, he was a neatnik.

"There's the Lava." He patted the fat gray bar of soap and shut the door after himself, leaving me alone to scrub on my fingers. I twisted the flaking chrome faucet, letting the cool water splash over my hands. I bent and washed my face and neck, running wet fingers through my hair. The mirror told me I looked like a dishrag.

On this night I needed to be tough, to be strong. I practiced a tough look in the mirror, narrowing my eyes and curling my upper lip. I thought of Mad Dog Tilden. I gnashed my teeth, letting a low growl grow in my throat.

A knock at the door. "You getting it off?"

I froze. Getting it off?

"Is the ink coming off?" he said, louder.

"Oh, yeah." I reached for the forgotten Lava soap. "Little by little."

As I scrubbed the sandpaper soap over my fingertips the mirror told me my face had reddened. I could blush at the drop of a hat. Why had the sexual innuendo of "getting it off" popped into my head?

I scrubbed harder. Ridges began to disappear. All right, face it. Mendez was attractive. He reminded me of all the good things about Paolo: dark, exotic looks, warm, penetrating eyes, strong and muscular. Here I was in his bathroom, his private space. Under other circumstances I probably wouldn't be pushing him away.

I thought about Paolo and his new girlfriend, the rock climber. They seemed so wrong for each other. But it could be just chemical. Sometimes the old beaker just boils over and there's nothing to do but put out the flame.

Paolo had gone on to other flames, namely Ms. Rock Climber. Hell, he had probably put out most of the fires in Jackson. What a jealous thought. I didn't feel that way. Paolo would always be a dear friend, even if I couldn't look at him when he wears those white peasant shirts. May his bunsen burner glow forever bright.

I dried my hands on a spotless blue towel. I couldn't get over how tidy this guy was. My mother would love Mendez. I bet he even does windows.

My hand stopped on the doorknob. What was I thinking? I was running for my damn life here! I needed to be tough, cunning, and smarter than all of them. I needed to be all together in the here and now. I couldn't be thinking about reactions, chemical or otherwise, with an attractive man. I let out another low practice growl as I walked into the hall.

Mendez leaned against the porch railing, smoking a cigarette. I pushed through the screen door, my hands in my pockets.

"Thanks for the soap."

The police cruiser sat by the curb. I had always liked their flashy graphic colors, the bubble tops spilling colors into the night. But now it symbolized the enemy.

"I've got to go."

He took another drag on his cigarette. I only glanced

at him, then looked away, concentrating on my growling attitude.

"Where to?"

"Back to my car. Over by the bookstore."

"Then where?"

I bit down harder on my molars. "Back to my sister's." I flashed my eyes at him to show my anger.

He slid down the railing toward me. I stiffened. "You didn't show up at lunch. I had to eat with a couple of suits. Kept talking about some Japanese movie they saw—a samurai thing."

"I like samurai things—ah, movies," I said.

He looked in my face. I looked away. "I wanted to tell you something I heard about Vardis." My ears perked up. "Yeah, I thought you'd be interested," he smiled. "She was involved in some kind of art deal that went sour down in Oklahoma. We got a sketchy report about it from the cops down there. No charges were filed against her but the auction house made a complaint."

"What happened?"

"Seems she was hot on something they were auctioning. One of those big, fancy auctions with a catalog and all. I think they said it was an antique rug. Navajo. She got obsessed with it. Came by every day to study it, touch it. The dealer had to warn her to restrain herself a few times because she was going to wear the thing out fingering it."

Mendez took another drag on his cigarette, blowing out the smoke as he continued. "So finally the auction starts. She bids on the rug. But somebody else wants it too. The bidding goes up and up. At the end, she gets it. She's delirious. But she doesn't have the cash. She went too high. So she had to give up the rug to the other bidder."

I waved away a haze of smoke with my hand. "How did she take it?"

"Not well. The auction was over and the bidders were doing their paperwork, picking up their items. They give her

the bad news, she goes nuts. Has to be driven home by the
security guards."

My nose started to sting from the cigarette smoke. So—so
she was nuts? She was rich but not rich enough? She liked
Indian artifacts? Maybe. But what else? I had the feeling
there was more to it that was beneath the surface.

"So why didn't you show for lunch?" Mendez asked,
breaking into my thoughts.

"I was busy."

He let out a laugh. "I bet. Doing what?"

I stared at him. Didn't he get it? This wasn't some social
trip, a girl's vacation. What was he laughing about? "What
difference does it make? I didn't show up because I didn't
want to show up. All right?" I stamped down the steps. "I've
got more important things on my mind than having lunch
with a cop who will probably bring along his handcuffs for
dessert!" I turned on the sidewalk. "Now, do I get a ride back
to my car or do I have to walk in this god-awful heat?"

Mendez tossed his cigarette into the bushes and stood up.
I didn't look at him as I marched to the cruiser but I knew
his jaw would be tense again, his eyes hard. Good, I thought.
That'll make it easier. I reached the car before he did.

Even the dispatcher on the radio was silent.

$\triangledown$

24

THE NIGHT WAS clear again. The moon rose late, after midnight, just past full. A goose egg swathed in a misty nest of angel-hair clouds over the Clark Fork River as it came down the divide east of Missoula.

The eerie light streamed in the side window, then the back, as I drove Elaine's ancient Valiant south along the Bitterroot River, then west into the mountains. Zena drove her own car, with Elaine along. It was the one thing she insisted on, that she drive Elaine up and that I follow in Elaine's car. She wouldn't listen to reason. I had more questions for Elaine. She needed to be drilled for the questioning, to be pumped up.

Now that was impossible. I had done some drilling at Elaine's before we left. But the silence of my own thoughts and the divergence from my plan made my guts wrench. Zena had her own ideas. She would ask him whatever I wanted for Melina's sake but she seemed detached from the whole caper. Unreliable, was what I was thinking.

As we turned off the highway on the third dirt road, making our descent into the narrow canyon with the marshy bottom, I resigned myself. If we found out nothing tonight I would try another tack tomorrow. There was no turning back now. I could do nothing but rely on the two women. The thought made my stomach flip.

At the floor of the canyon frogs were singing. Scents of pine, sagebrush, and fish settled in the cool bottom. I slipped on the hunting jacket that had been my father's, pulling it tight. *No game birds tonight, Rollie. No runty quail. Big game tonight. Big game.*

Zena flipped on a flashlight. Elaine began to protest. "But he said no lights."

I remembered Elaine had turned on a light in frustration last night. Now she tried to get her comrade to stick to Tilden's crazy rules. Zena turned toward the dense woods and started walking. Elaine looked at me, her eyes wide with fright, and hurried off. I had no choice but to follow.

The moonlight disappeared as we entered the trees. The beam of the flashlight bounced ahead of me. If anything it made things worse, drawing my eyes to the light and away from my feet, making the shadows around me blacker. I stumbled on roots. Branches scratched my face, bumped my hat off my head, slapped my legs.

No time to worry. No time to plan. Put the right foot down on solid ground. Bring the left foot over that rock. Don't step on the rotten log. Look up, a tree dead ahead.

The route Zena plotted for us was direct. At least more direct than my circuitous one the night before. This time I was just a shadow of the other women. I struggled to keep close to Elaine's back as the trees began to thin and we came into the open.

I had been following so close that my nose came within an inch of Elaine's blond curls when she stopped beside a boulder. I remembered this boulder-and-tree field as just below the cave. Over Elaine's head the moon shone on the high rock cliff.

Zena clicked off her flashlight and handed it to me. I slipped it into my pocket. Here the moonlight was bright, turning the rocks into strange bluish forms that seemed capable of springing to life. One to my right took on the form of a huge slab of blue Jello.

"I'll split from you here," I whispered. "There's a boulder over there I'll climb up on. I can see the cave from there."

Zena and Elaine nodded, their faces solemn and tight. I touched Zena's arm as she began to move away.

"You know what to do, right? Bring up Shiloh first," I said. "Then, Elaine, try to find out whose place you took last year. I'm sure it was Vardis. If that doesn't work, bring up the murder. You read about it in the paper. Mention Charlotte Vardis's name. See how he reacts. Ask him if he knew her."

Elaine nodded. I looked Zena hard in the eye. "This is important. For Melina."

Her face was illuminated by the moon, with purple shadows under her eyes and nose. She looked away at the moon, blinked, then turned to go. Elaine followed her around the rock and its neighboring trees, up the hill to the cave.

When I found the boulder that had cradled me last night I leaned against it for a moment. The surface was cool and rough, with lichens that looked green and gray in the moonlight. Tiny crystals sparkled in the gray granite. The rock felt like the Lava soap that had decimated my fingertips.

My breathing slowed from the hike. At last I pulled myself up on the rock. We had timed our arrival for an hour earlier than the others; my watch said one-fifteen. We were late but still they wouldn't arrive for forty-five minutes. I settled in, pulling the jacket tighter. I found a pile of needles that had blown into a shallow of the rock and sat on them.

In the cave I could see Elaine and Zena changing into the sacklike costumes and putting the black paint on their faces. Their voices sometimes floated down, too low to hear the words. In fifteen minutes they were finished and sat down on the floor of the cave to wait for the others.

At one-forty-five a distant rumble startled me. I wasn't sure what it was. Their cars maybe? An earthquake? Then it came again, stronger and closer. I peered through the treetops toward the ridge. A black cloud the size of a blimp, tinged with moonlight but dense and forbidding, moved quickly toward us.

I swore. A thunderstorm was not in the plan. Would they go on with their ceremony? The cave would stay dry, I supposed, and cozy with the fire. I, on the other hand, would be a drowned rat in no time.

Before I had time to think of preparations for rain I heard footsteps in the forest below. Two figures moved quietly, only a twig breaking or a pebble rolling away to announce their arrival. My viewing rock was forty feet or so north of their path; they passed me without a glance.

When they reached the cave Elaine and Zena had built the fire, its first flames licking the wood. Tilden and his wife's faces were already blackened. They slipped off coats and stood in their ceremonial outfits: hers a sacklike dress, his the skimpy breechclout.

Sylvie began applying black makeup to her husband's arms and legs. He stood like a statue, arms extended, while she painstakingly rubbed the black over him. She moved expertly across his arms, then his back, and down his legs. She stooped to do his ankles and feet before putting the black away.

The thunder rumbled above the cliff again. The clouds had moved quickly, now covering almost half the sky in a gray blanket. The moon shone from the east under them, like the proverbial silver lining.

They were ready to begin. The women sat cross-legged around the fire now. Tilden had his back to them, facing the rock painting of the bluejay shaman on the back wall of the cave. I wanted a better view. Neither the moonlight nor the firelight penetrated far enough to get a good look at it. For now the dim outline of the stick figure would have to do.

The stiff wind that swept down over the ridge, smelling of rain, took me by surprise. I was crouched behind part of the boulder that rose gently into a prow like a ship's. Then suddenly the sky burst with light. The scene went from thick black to strobe-light blue, turning the hillside into a stark postcard moonscape.

I hunched down reflexively. The lightning felt like a spotlight. One, two, three: I counted the seconds until the crack of thunder hit. Four, five. The deafening clap echoed off the granite ridge, doubling its power. I held my ears, the deep-bellied roar bombarding me. It rattled around inside my head for long seconds.

When it finished and the woods grew silent, the wind again brought the promise of rain. I huddled on my rock, wondering what to do next. Could Elaine and Zena carry on if I went back to the car? Would they even know if I did?

I swore under my breath. Nothing was going as planned. A drop of rain hit the boulder beside me. A tree would do for shelter. Maybe I could still see the cave, send the women telepathic messages to keep them on course. Right.

Another raindrop. Gotta find a tree. I crab-walked over the top of the boulder and readied to slide down the side of it to the ground.

Without warning the clouds crashed together and performed their light show. Blue, blinding flash—light everywhere. I should have been ready. Instead the suddenness of it made me hurl myself off the boulder in a giant leap instead of the dainty seat-of-the-pants slide I had planned. I landed in a crouch position in the moist dirt.

The thunder hit, a rumbling, earsplitting din, echoing off hard rock, absorbed by the pine trees. My hands clapped over my ears, I waited until all the vibrations shivered away. The moss where I had landed felt soft and damp.

"What do we have here?" The voice came from behind me. I toppled over from my crouch, feeling the wet ground soak through my jeans.

"Get up."

I obeyed, getting a look at Sylvie Kali, in black face and burlap sack dress, standing like a sentinel before me, hands on hips.

"Hello, Sylvie," I said, trying to keep things light.

She said nothing, grabbed my arm and pulled me up the hill toward the cave. We stumbled around stumps and downed trees, rocks and rabbit burrows as she pulled my jacket off my shoulders.

The campfire grew brighter. At the mouth of the cave we stopped. I gasped for breath. Sylvie appeared to be in better shape; she was surprisingly strong. I got my first good look at her. She had dyed her gray hair black and braided it. Strips of leather held the ends. Her eyes shone from the blackened face, white and glistening in the firelight.

"Look what I found hiding in the bushes," she said to the group. "Melina's sister."

Elaine and Zena gave me wary looks. Mad Dog Tilden stared at me blankly, then turned his gaze to his wife. "The ceremony must continue. You have broken the circle."

Sylvie's jaw went slack. "But she was out there spying. She could hurt you, Marcus."

Tilden didn't seem to hear his wife. "Get her dressed."

"Wait a minute, I didn't come to dress up in a sack. I'll just go now and let you do your thing in peace. I'll—" I began to edge away toward the mouth of the cave. Sylvie put her hand on my sleeve and held tight.

"I think we should tie her, Marcus."

Tilden had dropped his head to his chest as if praying or meditating or something, and said nothing. Sylvie took that as a yes.

In a moment I was down to my underpants and bra, my wrists and ankles strapped with twine, and a burlap bag with slits over my head. Sylvie threw my clothes into a corner with the others' and pulled out the black makeup. I let her slap it on my face. I didn't fight. I wasn't really afraid. This was such a great opportunity to see this craziness close up. Now I didn't have to rely on Zena and Elaine, the unreliables. I could question Tilden myself.

As Sylvie shoved me over to the campfire next to Elaine I got a look at the rock painting. Zena was right; it looked new. The bright blue paint looked fresh. Drips from the careless job still clung to the rock. It was big, four or five feet tall and three feet across. And it was crude.

No one could steal that, nor would they want to. I squirmed to get comfortable, loosening the twine on my ankles, so I could sit cross-legged like the rest of them. My hands were inside the sack, tied together in the front. I felt a breeze between my thighs, barely covered by burlap. The fire burned low now.

Tilden stamped in the dirt behind me.

"Very good." His voice was shallow and flat. "Four spirits. The four directions. The circle is complete. Tonight is the night of all nights." As he began to move around us, Sylvie picked up the deer hoof rattles and found a beat. Elaine and Zena followed suit.

The mad professor was a sight. His hair was smeared with black makeup and stood at odd angles on his head. The black on his face made his unpainted eyelids stand out like an owl. The breechclout hung on his bony hips, flapping indecently.

"We begin again. No more interruptions," he said. He lifted his knee then and began to prance to the beat. I watched him go around a few times until the novelty wore off.

Elaine stared at the fire, her deer hooves in one hand, tapping against the other palm. The flickers of the fire lit up her smeared face, especially around her nostrils where she hadn't applied any black. She seemed to be in a trance, her shoulders slumped forward, eyes wide.

Zena, on the other hand, seemed very much awake. Her eyes flicked from place to place as she kept her head completely still. Her black hair was braided now by each ear. She told me she had taken a nap earlier in the evening; she did look rested. Her rattle tapped against her palm.

Sylvie sat opposite me, in the position closest to the cave opening. She stared over the tops of the flames at the bluejay painting on the rock wall. Her face was a fortress. Without warning she put down the rattle and began to chant. I had heard it before, in Tilden's sweathouse.

Zena and Elaine took the cue, setting down their rattles. They joined in the low, three-note chant, rhythmic and soft. It reminded me of rocking a baby to sleep with nonsense syllables. Sort of a "oi-ya-ya." The lull of the words without meaning, droning on and on.

I wanted to ask him about Shiloh and Charlotte, but when? Had Elaine and Zena already done it?

Tilden pranced around the circle. He paused behind Sylvie and looked at me with his owl eyes. "You will chant. You will all chant."

He continued his dance. I sat taller. "I don't want to chant." Maybe I could get him talking.

Tilden was behind me. He came high-stepping around again and repeated himself: "You will all chant."

"No, I will not."

Even Elaine flashed me a look from the corner of her eye. Tilden continued dancing as if I had said nothing. I tensed, waiting for his reply.

It came unexpectedly, a sharp kneecap down on my back, raking my rib cage. I moaned and leaned forward from the blow. Quickly, though, I gasped for breath; it was an angry one. "Hey!" I said. "Cut it out."

The chant had almost died out. Sylvie was the only one left, a whisper. Mad Dog rounded the circle again. His makeup was smeared on one knee.

"You will all chant," he boomed. Zena and Elaine picked up the chant, eyeing me.

I said nothing. Mad Dog padded in the sand floor, a small scuffing sound. He twirled once, a flourish, then continued. I tensed as he was behind me but he kept going around.

His face was set in a stoic pose. Some divine grace. His night of all nights? What a case. And how did he get these women to do his bidding? Were they as frightened as I knew Elaine to be? Tilden moved around again, the chanting soft, the beat even. I gritted my teeth, moving my back to feel the pain in my ribs. I kept my eyes on him as he pranced to the rhythm around again toward me.

This time I was ready for him. A glimpse, a minute one, just before he rounded behind me, told me to beware. I leaned to one side just as his knees came down. One knee caught my shoulder, the other missed. Mad Dog reeled into the sand, catching himself on his hands and knees, leaning against Elaine. She let a small scream escape and pushed him off her.

Thunder crashed outside the cave. The walls of rock cushioned the sound, a freight-train rumble passing deep below us in the mountainside. The rain began falling, heavy wet drops bouncing off the earth.

Tilden picked himself up. Sylvie began to chant loudly. Zena and Elaine chimed in. Mad Dog took up the dance again as if nothing had happened.

Something snapped in me. This whole scene revolted me. Why were these women doing this stupid ceremony for this deranged man? What hold did he have over them? Even Elaine's explanation was weak. But she was weak, and afraid. Were they all afraid of him? Was it because they knew he killed two women and were afraid he would kill them?

Whatever their reasons, I hated this submissive crap. No man ties me up and makes me sit in a cave all night. I began to wiggle in my twine while looking out for the kneecapper. The rope cut into my skin. My blood began to boil. I could keep my mouth shut no longer.

"This is no bluejay dance," I declared, my voice loud over the chanting.

Tilden was opposite me. He gave me a bored look.

"Quiet," Sylvie said.

I let Tilden dance around behind me. "Where is the bluejay pictograph, Dr. Tilden? Did Shiloh steal it?"

Elaine stopped chanting and looked at me, her mouth agape. No, she hadn't brought up Shiloh before I arrived. Zena pretended I hadn't said a thing. The reaction for Sylvie and Tilden was just what I had hoped.

Both stopped what they were doing. They froze in place. Took them by surprise, I did. I smiled.

Then Sylvie began to chant again. She gave Tilden a look I couldn't comprehend from my angle, a look that started him dancing. I guessed they weren't going to dignify my question with a response. That was all right. I had my answer.

Tilden pranced around again. "Or was it Charlotte who took off with it?"

The reaction this time was muted. Surprise only works once. Sylvie closed her eyes and chanted louder. Zena and Elaine chimed in. Tilden bent over, dancing furiously.

I worked on my wrists. They felt raw but the twine was loosening. My eyes followed Mad Dog, the high-stepping, jiving, jamming bluejay shaman. He seemed to hunker down now, serious at last without my impertinent questions. He made no attempts to kneecap me again but I kept a wary eye on him.

The twine broke with a snap. I glanced at Sylvie but her eyes were closed. She hadn't seen the twitch of my sack dress as my wrists popped free; my arms were free, my legs weren't. Not much chance of making a run for it. The short sack dress didn't provide any cover to work on the ankle twine. And my arms were still inside the burlap sack, with little chance to make a quick getaway out the armholes.

I racked my brain for a plan, trying to think of a way to communicate with Elaine or Zena without rousing suspicion. I rubbed my sore wrists. I stole glances at my two compadres. They appeared asleep except for their moving lips.

And all along the three-note chant, *oi-ya-ya, oi-ya-ya,* the padding of bare feet on the sand floor, the smell of the rain pummeling the hillside and the rocks, the flash of lightning and its mate, the rolling thunder. The fire popped and flickered. It should have warned me. But it didn't.

Tilden stopped behind me and let out an incomprehensible sound. A foreign word. And tapped me hard on the top of my head.

"Untie her feet."

Tilden stood behind me, his knees pressing against my back. I leaned forward but he pushed harder. I sat up straight, pushing his goddamned bony kneecaps back. In the lull that came when the chanting stopped, we played seesaw. With each push I lost more playfulness.

The three women looked at us from their grotesque blackened faces. To me they looked pitiful; it made me wonder how I looked. I threw my hair back off my face. Sylvie stared at her husband.

"That's not a good idea, Marcus," she said, low but firm.

"I am the bluejay shaman!" His deep voice bounced off the rock walls of the cave, gaining with each echo.

Sylvie stood up and came toward us. "She will ruin everything," she whispered.

"I am the bluejay shaman!" His voice was louder, and off-key.

Sylvie's hand shook as she brought a Swiss army knife from the pile of clothing and opened a blade. I held my breath as she brought the blade near my white ankles. She slipped the blade under the twine and snapped it.

As she stood Sylvie grabbed my arm through the rough burlap and pulled me up with her. My legs ached from sitting on the cold dirt floor; red lines ringed my ankles where the twine had cut into the skin. Sylvie turned me toward Tilden by the shoulders.

He stood facing the rock painting again, his head bowed in reverence. Beyond him, around a bend in the cave, I could see a dark recess that appeared to have a pile of straw on the floor. A small, fat candle burned in a metal can, flickering on the cave walls.

Sylvie gave me a push from behind toward the recess. I stumbled, brushing into Tilden. The flap of his breechclout brushed aside, baring a white cheek. A half-moon, sickeningly bright with scraggly black hairs curling on it. Was it the sight of that one white cheek that made it all come clear? Or the private, romantic glow of candlelight in his little love nest?

Whatever it was, it came clear: Tilden got these women to do his bidding in more ways than one. And the big one occurred back here. The whole enchilada, the nine yards. Spread it, baby, let the bluejay come to roost.

The revelation hit me square in the gut, followed by blinding rage. I thrust back my elbow into Sylvie's stomach as hard as I could, sending her backward, bent over, gasping for air. Tilden spun around and came toward me. I struggled my arms out of the slits in the sack dress but he was on me before I finished. My knee connected with his breezy little breechclout, but he turned, protecting his groin with his leg.

"Sit down!" he commanded as he took my shoulders and tried to push me to the floor. My arms finally free, I batted at his while kicking his shins with bare feet. My toes felt like mincemeat before I gave up. I tried to twist away but his hands tightened like iron on my shoulders. I gasped in frustration.

"Let me go!"

Sylvie came back to life then and tackled me from the side, her arms tight around my knees, sending me sailing back against the straw. I landed hard on my butt. The blow shivered up my spine and rattled my skull. Tilden followed her, trying to get hold of my arms. I doubled my fist and tried to punch him but I must say I never learned to fistfight. I was flailing, grunting, using my elbows, my fingernails, pulling hair, anything.

"Elaine! Zena! Help me!" I yelled between pulling Sylvie's braids and trying to get hold of Tilden's ears. I connected on his face with a long scratch down his left temple that didn't slow him.

"Bring the twine. Elaine!" Sylvie said. I looked toward the campfire, half-hidden by the bend in the rock wall. As I did Tilden grabbed my wrists. I groaned, trying to pull them away.

"Elaine! What are you doing?" She appeared with the rope. "Help me!" Tilden shoved me back on the straw. "Help me!" Tilden shoved me back on the straw. I was now flat on my back with Sylvie on my legs and Tilden holding my arms down at my sides. He bent over me, his face reddening under the makeup, his breathing heavy.

"You'll never teach again." The anger swelled in me, trying to escape. The twine circled my ankles, tight and cutting.

Lightning flashed, sending an electric charge through the cave. The thunder came quick on its heels, cracking open the sky right outside. It sounded like a tree had been hit.

Then the rain came down in torrential sheets, pounding everything in its path. The wind blew in the cave over the campfire, sending sparks flying.

"Zena, tie her wrists. Elaine, you hold them," Sylvie said. With my ankles bound, she stood up. Her face was in shadow from my vantage point but it probably would have shown nothing but the fury I had produced by disrupting the professor's cozy cult.

The two other women came toward me. "Elaine. Zena. You can't be serious. Don't do this. Don't let him do this to me." I searched their faces, trying to plead with them without letting Tilden know we had prearranged this meeting. I didn't know what danger they might be in if he knew.

Tilden held my shoulders down as Elaine took my wrists. "Elaine," I whispered. "Please." I began to panic. I could feel it growing within me as if the thunder had entered my body and was fighting its way out. A roar rose in my ears. A scream collected in my throat. This couldn't be happening to me. It couldn't.

Then the voice: "All right, everybody. The party's over."

25

MENDEZ STOOD IN the cave, both hands on his gun leveled at us. The gun was the first thing I saw, glistening in the dim light, hard, metallic, and cold. Mendez stood astride, feet firmly planted in the dirt next to the campfire.

His face held no emotion. It was as cold and hard as his Police Special. My first instinct was that he had come to kill us all. *He is the killer.* The panic that had been rising in me began to flood my eyes, my nose, my ears. This is it. This is it.

The people around me had frozen in place. Then suddenly Sylvie turned to her husband, a look of unmistakable terror in her eyes. She knows Mendez is the killer, I thought. She knows he will shoot us all.

Tilden rose slowly, gathering himself to a dignified stance. As dignified as possible with black smeared all over your skin and your privates flapping in the breeze. "What do you want?" His voice was condescending. He *was* the bluejay shaman, after all.

"I want you to move away from her. Slowly." Mendez twitched the gun to his right, toward the rock painting. "Over there. All of you."

As if in a state of suspended animation Sylvie, Tilden, Elaine, and Zena stepped away. Sylvie came behind my head, stepping up beside her husband, her hand on his arm. I lifted myself up on my elbows, then sat up.

"Are you all right, Alix?" Mendez asked, glancing away from the others for an instant. I tried to clear my head. Why

is he concerned about my safety if he has come to kill us all?
I shook my head to clear it.

"Alix? Are you hurt?"

"Umm," I stammered. "No. I'm all right." He had come
here to rescue me—not to kill us all. I tried to sink into the
dark recesses of the cave to hide. But as I put my hand back
on the straw I felt the heat.

Gasping, I pulled my hand back. A pile of straw sat on the
candle. As I looked back it flashed up, a golden rocket of flame.

"Fire! Fire!" Someone yelled.

Confusion followed, running, shouting, stamping,
screaming. Mendez kicked away the straw and stamped it
out with his shoes. Elaine took up a wail, sinking against
the side wall of the cave with her hands over her ears. Sylvie
pulled Tilden past the campfire into the night. For an instant
I saw Zena hesitate. Her eyes were wide with fright. Then
she bolted out of the cave.

When the fire was out I realized I had sat immobile
through the melee, doing nothing. I was scared shitless,
frozen to the spot. Totally useless. I pulled my knees up to
my chest and hugged them. My forehead dropped against
them. I swayed to the sound of Elaine's screaming. My mind
was a void. A great black void.

Mendez was shaking me. "Alix. Alix!"

I lifted my head. Everything was blurry.

"Alix, it's over."

He whispered my name. It sounded like Rollie's voice, my
father's voice. My cheek was on his shoulder now, his hands
on my neck. Tears streamed down my face. I swallowed hard
and pulled myself away, wiping my face.

"Can't you get her to stop?" I got my first good look at
Mendez. He had been drenched by the thunderstorm.
Everything he wore—a dark windbreaker, jeans, chamois
shirt, boots—everything was soaking wet. His black hair fell
over his forehead in wet ringlets. His hands were damp as
he wiped my face with a handkerchief.

He glanced at Elaine. She sat slumped in a heap, wailing

her lungs out. It echoed around the cave, bouncing off the craggy angles. A smile crept onto Mendez's lips, a slightly mocking smile, as he got up and walked to her.

"Miss?" He shook her shoulders very lightly.

"Her name's Elaine," I shouted over the wail.

"Elaine!"

Elaine paused. She opened her eyes for a minute, saw Mendez, and opened her mouth to scream again.

"Wait, Elaine. It's over now. They're gone." His voice was gentle and soothing.

She closed her mouth. "Gone?" Her eyes darted around the cave. "Did you shoot them?"

Mendez shook his head. "They ran out."

Elaine took another look, then heaved a sigh of relief. "Thank God." She stood up and walked to the corner where the clothes had been heaped. The Tildens and Zena had grabbed things on their escape. "Oh, no. I hope all my stuff's still here." Without a thought to Mendez's presence she hiked the burlap sack dress over her head and began to dress in her civilian clothes.

Mendez stooped down to untie the twine from my ankles. The knots were still loose. In a moment I was free, standing in the pile of straw that I had dreaded so. I kicked it off my bare feet and looked away from Mendez to Elaine.

"I have to get dressed," I said.

Does humiliation flow from humility? I never considered them the same thing. To have humility means you don't take yourself too seriously. To be humiliated is something else entirely. It is demeaning, degrading. You are crushed, flattened.

That was the way I felt on the drive back to Missoula. I drove Elaine's Valiant again, since she was shaking all over, wet and hysterical after the walk back to the cars. Besides, I couldn't ride with Mendez. He had come to rescue me and I thought he meant to kill us! The thought was base and humiliating in itself. Even if he wasn't the gloating,

I-told-you-so type (and I didn't know that for a fact), I could feel the message in the air around him.

Oh, I was grateful he had come to the cave. A rescue by anyone was preferable to being raped by a maniac. But it humiliated me. Just being in the entire situation, tied up, helpless, was almost unthinkable. I considered myself a resourceful, independent woman. I could get along. I had been getting along. It wasn't that I didn't like men, I did. I liked them a lot. But I didn't need them for my work. That I could do quite well on my own, thank you very much.

That's what I thought. But I had gotten myself in too deep. I could have been hurt or killed. Just like Melina had told me at supper. We had argued about going up to the cave with Elaine and Zena. I won the argument but she made me tell her all the details, where I was going, when I would be back, everything. So she could tell the police where to look for me when I didn't come back.

The police. She had told Mendez. Of course. But how, when? I slowed to a stop before entering the main highway. The El Dorado shone its headlights through my back window. I squinted into the rearview mirror and made the turn.

Elaine shivered against the door. We had all gotten soaked in a last downpour of the thunderstorm before it moved off onto the plains. The hike back was helped by Zena's flashlight until it burned out in the middle of the forest. Wet branches slapped us, scolding us for our defective judgment.

Exactly what Melina would say. Could get you killed. *I couldn't live with it if something happened to you because of me, Alix! I talked to Wade about it this morning when I visited him. Don't take any chances because of him. Don't take any chances.*

She had been upset by the visit to Wade. Hondo had told them the trial may get delayed by the investigation into Charlotte Vardis's death. The police thought they were linked. I knew that. I also knew they didn't know how they were linked.

I looked at my watch. It was just after four. As we entered

the outskirts of Missoula Elaine sat up. The heater in the old Valiant had warmed her up.

"I'm never going back. Never," she muttered.

I glanced at her. The black on her face gave her an ashen, muddy look. She was a mess. "I don't think you'll ever have to go back."

She wasn't listening. "I hate him. I hate him!" Her hands gestured wildly in circles. "That man and his poetry! He's crazy!"

I glanced at her. "Poetry?"

Her wet curls sprayed droplets onto the car seat. "In that cubbyhole back there. Where he tried to get you to sit? That straw pile."

"But what about poetry?"

"He makes you listen to poetry. Salish poetry."

I gripped the wheel tighter. "On the straw?"

She nodded. "For hours. You have to sit there while he recites Salish poetry or something. Stories. It goes on for hours and hours. He makes you sit there staring at him, like you could even understand one word!"

The pit in my stomach hardened. "That's all that goes on back there? On the straw?"

"That's all?! Isn't that enough? He picked me last month and I thought I was going to die before he finished. It was agony. Pure agony. Torture! I'll never go back. Never."

The lights of Missoula grew brighter. We passed the mall, pink mercury lights blazing in the barren parking lot. The streets were empty. The sane people were all in bed.

Melina had waited up for me. The house was ablaze with light on the dark-windowed block, streaming white onto the burnt lawn. As we reached the house the sky began to lighten in the east. The moon set in the west.

The Valiant chugged to a stop by the curb. I put it into park and left the engine running. Heat blasted from the vents; I turned down the fan and faced Elaine.

"You can get home all right?"

She dabbed her dirty face with her sleeve. Black stuck to the fabric but her face did not improve. "Sure." Her voice was barely a whisper but I was too beat to argue with her.

"I'll call you later." I stepped out into the street, the cool freshness of the air surprising me. The sidewalks had been washed by the rain. Leaves and broken branches lay in scattered heaps as testament to the wind's fury. I rounded the car and gave her a wave in the headlight's glare.

Mendez's El Dorado pulled up, mud sprayed up its sides from the slippery drive out on the dirt road. Beads of water clung to the hood's waxed surface. I stood staring at it for a moment, my head clogged with fatigue.

He got out of the car as the Valiant pulled away. In the light from the porch and windows he looked pale, his lips purple. I squinted at him, then saw the shudder convulse through his body.

"You're freezing," I said. "You're getting hypothermic. I've seen skiers. Didn't you have your heater on?"

Mendez looked vaguely toward his car. "It, ah, it doesn't work." He stuck his hands in wet pockets, then brought them out again.

The air blew down the street, not quite a wind, but with a chill on it. I frowned. I hadn't planned on asking him in. Just looking at him reminded me of the stupid mess I had made of tonight. And then what Elaine had told me? I didn't want to think about it.

"You better go home and change into something dry," I said. Melina's face came to the window. "My sister's been waiting up. I'll have to explain it all to her. It'll be boring."

He looked up at the house, saying nothing. I knew you could get a little weird with hypothermia, like you couldn't decide what to do next. His jaw began to shake, chattering.

"You can get yourself home, right?"

He frowned at the street behind me. A policeman ought to know every inch of this town. But his eyes seemed clouded. His teeth clacked together convulsively.

"Oh, shit, come on." I grabbed his arm and led him up to

the house. He was strong. His feet didn't seem to work too well so it was almost like dragging him. Once we got to the steps he seemed to liven up, grabbing the railing and hoisting himself up. Melina met us at the door.

"What happened? Are you all right?" Melina fretted as we stepped in. "Jesus, I've been out of my mind!"

"You're not the only one," I said, depositing the shivering Mendez on a small throw rug. "I'll tell you about it. First we've got a case of hypothermia to take care of."

Melina stared at me, then at Mendez. "Hypothermia?" She stepped up to him and began to feel his windbreaker and tousle his hair like a mother would a child. "God, you're blue." She took his shoulders and led him to the stairs. "We'll get you in a hot shower. Alix, put on some coffee."

Twenty minutes later Carl emerged in an old pair of Wade's flannel pajamas and robe. They hung on him like he had shrunk in the wash. Melina and I sat at the kitchen table drinking coffee. I had washed my face and changed into a pair of sweat pants and a turtleneck and wool sweater borrowed from Mel. I took one look and burst out laughing.

He stood in the doorway, his hands vanishing up the voluminous plaid sleeves, his bare toes poking out of the pant legs. His face had a wounded look on it as I guffawed, covering my mouth. Melina shot me a look, then set Mendez down in her chair. She poured him a cup of coffee as I tried to control myself.

"Now drink this, Carl," she said, setting a steaming cup in front of him. I thought she was going to put the cup to his lips herself, she was being so damned maternal. But he smiled up at her and did it himself.

"Tell me all the details tomorrow, Alix." Melina stood in the kitchen door. I started to protest her leaving but she turned to go. "Good-night."

My laughter was gone now. The tension, humiliation: I felt sick suddenly. I stared out the window at the dawn creeping into the big elm tree in the backyard.

Mendez just sat sipping his coffee, his hands around the hot mug for dear life. He hadn't said a word since he'd been in the house. He didn't have to. I knew what he would say. The sentences would all have "should have" or "could have" in them.

I shoved my chair roughly across the floor behind me. My feet wouldn't stay still. The silence was killing me.

"Listen, just don't give me any lectures, okay? I know I screwed up. So just don't tell me all the things I should have done. Okay?"

His face was getting pink again. He turned to me from the steam of his cup and spoke at last. "Are you all right?"

My jaw dropped. "Am I all right? Yes. You asked me before. There are other things, bigger issues, things I haven't told you, things I have almost figured out." I paced back and forth on the small linoleum floor. "I don't know why . . . Is that all you can say, 'are you all right'?"

Mendez sat back in the chair and began rolling up the pajama sleeves. Melina had put his clothes in the dryer on the back porch; I could hear them going round and round. His gaze when he turned to me was free of hypothermic clouds. "It seemed like the safe thing to say. Besides, I meant it. I was worried about you."

I folded my arms. "Well, don't be." He looked at me with those dark eyes. "All right." I took a deep breath. "I'm grateful. Okay? Okay, thank you." There. You said it, now shut up already.

I turned and put my hands on the edge of the sink. What a coward I was. Turn around and look him in the eye and say it. But I couldn't.

The coffeepot was almost empty. I poured the dregs of it into my cup, more glad to have something to do than to drink it. But I did, sip by sip, staring out the window over the counter at the house next door as its summer colors came to life in the morning light.

"I'm glad you're not hurt," Mendez whispered behind me. I hadn't heard him pad up; I jerked my head at the sound of his voice by my shoulder. I was still jumpy.

"Hurt?" I put down my cup. A laugh that was more like a snarl erupted from me as I turned, took three paces away from him, and leaned against my chair. "That was hardly likely. You know what Mad Dog Tilden does to his victims back there on the straw? What evil torture he has devised? What perverted act he makes them do?"

Mendez turned to face me.

"I bet you can guess though, can't you?" I waved my arms around like a TV preacher. "You see it all in police work. Molestation, sodomy, rape, mutilation, murder. The mind boggles with possibilities. I know mine did!" I couldn't stop. The knife, my tongue, just kept plunging into me, again and again. "I didn't try to guess too far. I figured a simple S&M bondage thing, maybe more S than M, but rape for sure. I had it all figured out, like I've got everything in this whole mess so figured out! So I fought, I kicked, I pulled hair, I scratched. He wasn't doing that to me! Not to me!"

I pounded my chest with my fist, my voice having lost all control. Mendez looked up from his cup. I couldn't stop.

"They tied my feet. The women who are supposed to be helping me get information are helping tie me up! I've been betrayed! I start to panic. The twine is cutting into my ankles! But then, *viola!* My knight in shining armor shows up to save the damsel in distress."

I walked to the window, then turned to finish. "But what do I find out on the way home? There is no S&M. There is no rape. That's all a figment of my imagination. What there is, is a madman." My voice dropped to a whisper and I seemed breathless suddenly, sapped. "A madman who tortures his victims with poetry."

Mendez stepped closer. "Poetry?"

"Salish poetry. Endless, incomprehensible Indian poetry. He makes them sit . . . and . . ." My breath came in gulps, convulsive gasps. "And listen to . . ." I doubled over then, holding my stomach, moaning, afraid I would be sick.

"Sit down," Mendez said, pushing my chair under me and

guiding me down. I kept my head over my knees, gasping for air. After a moment the spell subsided.

"So you see there was no reason for you to come after me. No reason at all." I was looking at the ceiling when it went blurry. Tears began to stream down my face. To spite me, I thought, since tears were weakness, inner pain that should be kept inside. But they wouldn't stop.

Then Carl was holding me, just holding me against Wade's ratty old robe with the coffee stains and the dandruff. Holding me against his warm chest, muffling my cries. Even as I cried I scorned myself. I tried to tell myself I was crying for Wade, for Melina, for their marriage held in fragile balance, for Rollie long since gone, for the spirits of Shiloh and Charlotte floating unexplained somewhere around us, waiting for retribution. But it wasn't true.

We held each other for the rest of the night on the couch. Arms wrapped around each other, the thin purple Indian blanket over us, belly to belly on the Danish modern sofa, Carl and I slept. I smelled the campfire in my hair and soap on his neck. His breath warmed my ear, tickling it. He massaged my neck until I relaxed, feeling the *oi-ya-ya* in my brain as sleep swam over me.

The birds chirped morning songs. There were lips on my neck. I opened my eyes and felt a ton of bricks on my forehead. Like a hangover. But I hadn't been drinking so this must be what a fuck-up hangover feels like. Before I could concentrate on it distractions came. The lips searched further, moist and curious. Then cool hands on my ribs. Then breasts, hips, shoulders, thighs, every part of me. I was awake.

Carlos, I whispered in his ear. He had the softest eyelids in the world. When we were together, one being, the walls inside me fell down. I was no longer a cunning businesswoman with a wicked eye for color and a vengeance for justice. No longer a strong sister who made it without daddy's love. No longer the daughter who propped her mother's head with a tiny hand as she cried lonely tears. No longer any of them.

The love we made was like in a dream, slow and sure and gentle. Savoring, unhurried, natural. And incredible, did I mention that? Yes, incredible. *Oi-ya-ya.*

$\triangledown$

26

CONCENTRATION WAS OUT. The spread on the top of Wade's huge desk had been straightened, restraightened, copied, reorganized, and filed. But still the answer eluded me. The fuck-up hangover returned in spades, only now it seemed a prediction of the future as much as a reflection of last night.

Mendez—Carlos—was the reason, of course. Now I cursed him under my breath, even though I had said quite opposite things in his ear. I didn't need distractions. I couldn't work that way. One-track mind, and all that. I had to be obsessed.

I stared at the piles of papers, willing them to speak, to crack open, spill their secrets, their guts. Picking up Charlotte's stack, I read through it again. There was so little on her. I wondered if the cops had found out anything more. How had she arranged that phone call I made to her when I thought she was in Jackson? The phone company could have forwarded it. But wouldn't the cops have those records? And why? That's the real key. Why had she called me? Was it an alibi for Shiloh's murder? Why would she kill Shiloh? For the bluejay pictograph?

I picked up Shiloh's stack. Clipped to the back was the journal that Tilden had given me about Manitou Matrix and its leader Orianna Gold Flicker. I unclipped it and read it again.

* * *

Search for Inner Beauty and Wisdom Drawn
from Native Religions
When Orianna Gold Flicker was a child she spent
hours each day in a tête-à-tête with Mother Nature in
the woods behind her parents' house in upstate New
York. She found strength in the order she found there,
in the plants' intricate structure and the insects' life
cycle. In the balance of day and night, winter and summer. When she grew up she dreamed of being a biolo-
gist or a naturalist, or perhaps working in a zoo with
animals.

But after a chance meeting with a psychic when she
was a teenager Orianna's life was changed. A fork in
the road, she says. A new path chosen. A path toward
transcendental perception drawn from the earth and
from the native religions that celebrated the seasons,
the earth, moon, and sun.

My eyes scanned down the close type. I frowned. Dreck,
tiresome dreck. But maybe later on, something buried deep
in the article.

"We are fiercely protective of our friends in the movement," Orianna says, caressing her hand-carved wooden
flute. "And we are sensitive to their need for privacy. We
are not out to exploit our brothers and sisters on reser-
vations or wherever they may live. We have a common
bond. My Indian blood runs hot in my veins. . . ."

I slammed the journal closed. I should have talked
privately with Orianna. She might have let something slip,
something about Shiloh. Maybe a rivalry between them.

But the big woman wouldn't let me close. I realized that
early on. Aligning myself with Tin-Tin and Moody had
barred me from being her friend. Her secrets were carefully
guarded, her persona carefully manicured. If she hated

Shiloh she would have one of her henchwomen do her in. She wouldn't sully her spiritual hands with someone's blood. She had too much to lose.

The iced tea on the corner of the desk was beaded up, sweating in the office. Outside the day was cool, refreshing after the terrible heat. Low clouds came and went like the clouds before my eyes. I struggled to see the whole picture. The last pieces would surely make it all come clear.

I had showered the smell of Mendez off my skin but I couldn't get it out of my nostrils. I drank iced tea, trying to ignore it, to keep my mind on the problem. Wade's problem. My problem. Shiloh's problem. Charlotte's problem. They wouldn't rest until their murderer came to justice. I felt it. I knew it. I wouldn't rest either.

I picked up Seymour Smith's file and stood up, pacing the room, talking aloud to help me concentrate. "Seymour S. Smith, born 1885, died who knows when. Joined faculty of department of anthropology at University of Montana 1922, taught there until 1933. Previously taught at University of Wisconsin where he received his doctorate in 1919."

Flipping the page of my notes, I read the part about his articles. "Published in various anthropological journals, starting in obscure ones and moving up to his final article published in *Annals of American Anthropology* in 1932. After that Seymour began to be sucked down into the quagmire of his fabricated life." I swept the sweat off my lip and longed to be outside in the cool air. Kicking the rattletrap fan, I kept pacing.

The student newspaper began researching Professor Smith's background based on a tip from another instructor recently moved from Wisconsin. As school began in the fall of 1932 he taught his usual courses: Intro to Anthropology, Statistics and Research, a graduate seminar on Montana Indians. Then the newspaper published its exposé: Seymour had never gotten a doctorate from Wisconsin. In fact he had no doctorate at all, merely a master's in education from a small college in Mississippi. An investigation erupted. By winter term he was suspended from teaching. He hung on through appeals until summer, when his position was eliminated during "budget cutbacks."

I gulped down iced tea and turned a page in the file again. This was the best part.

Hearings into Smith's competency were heated and emotional. Every faculty member in his department testified in his favor. Students cried and pleaded to let him stay. He was well-regarded in the anthropology community nationally for his publications and research. Everybody loved him. But he was a fraud.

The icing on the cake at the hearings came when the dean of the college—a close friend of Smith's—reluctantly called in the editor of a prominent academic journal to testify. Smith had submitted a manuscript for publication that had been heavily scrutinized by the editors. Smith claimed that he had found a certain native painting that illustrated the Salish Indians' bluejay shaman. He described it copiously in the article, the editor said, including where it was located in the Bitterroot Mountains.

Something in the article rang false to the editors. They decided to dispatch an independent researcher to hike to the spot described in the article. Not only did the researcher not find the painting but the terrain where Smith said the painting existed was flat and green with meadows and a small creek, hardly territory for a large rock painting on the side of a cliff wall.

I sank back into Wade's old desk chair, running my fingernail down a gash in the wooden arm. What did it mean? This mention of the bluejay pictograph was the first anywhere I had found. The controversy surrounding it even sixty years ago was exciting. But was there a real pictograph? If so, what happened to it? It sure wasn't the new one in Tilden's cave. How was Tilden related to Smith? Were they both frauds? Did they both want to be someone else so badly they made up new lives for themselves?

Back to the piles. I reread each one, making myself go slowly through each line, letting it sink into my head. Shiloh, Charlotte, Elaine, Zena, Sylvie, Tilden—where were they?— Orianna, Moody, Tin-Tin, Smith. Who else? Melina, Wade, Mendez, me. Again and again, I read them.

The phone rang while I made myself a tuna sandwich. My hand hesitated over the receiver. If it was Mendez I would have to make an excuse and I didn't really want to. Just the phone ringing sent a little ache through me. I pushed it down, steeled myself, and answered the phone gruffly. "Yes?"

"Yes, yourself." It was Melina. I relaxed at the sound of the lilt in her voice. "I guess the night didn't turn out so bad after all."

I took a bite of sandwich and said, "Mmmm."

A frustrated pause. "So? Are you going to tell me about it?"

I swallowed. "What's to tell?"

"Alix."

I laughed. My sister loved to listen to my sexual adventures, since she'd been married forever. "Well, first he nibbled my ear, then my neck, then my—"

"Wait, wait. I guess I don't need the details," she laughed. "You two looked so cozy all curled up together when I left for work. Did he have to leave?"

"Yeah. He had some extra shift today."

"If he feels as bad as I do I hope it's a light crime day," Melina said. "I've got a splitting headache."

"Me too. Take two aspirin and call me after my nap."

Melina moaned. "Oh, that sounds so good. I wish I could

curl up right now. I'll be home early, about four. Then tell me everything."

"Yes, boss." I hung up the phone and finished my sandwich, wandering out into the backyard where the dappled shade of the elm invited me to linger. Next to it an ancient mountain ash fluttered its leaves as if batting eyelashes. I dragged over an old webbed chaise that looked like Wade had sat on it once too often. The little round leaves of the ash lined up in exquisite order on each spray, then shivered in the breeze. The thunderstorms had drenched everything, charging it all with renewed strength. Even the dead lawn showed signs of life.

I stared at the sky in the spaces between the leaves. Spaces between facts. Answers, blanks. My fingers laced over my belly. A feather-gray cloud drifted in, obscuring the blue. Then another, and another.

Melina shook me, her hand hot on my arm. "Alix, wake up. The phone's for you."

I jerked up as if I'd never been asleep. "Phone?"

"A woman. Sounds upset."

I followed my sister up the swaybacked wooden back steps, looking at the overcast sky and getting my bearings. My head felt surprisingly clear yet I knew I had been dreaming about bluejays and charcoal faces and rain and rocks and—and—and what? Whatever else it was lay just outside my consciousness, like a cloud I was trying to grasp.

"What time is it?" I asked.

"Five." Melina opened the refrigerator. The glow from the old fridge's bulb lit the kitchen. A rumble in the heavens promised another rainstorm. "God, I should throw some of this stuff out. Without Wade to eat up the leftovers they're starting to collect."

I touched my forehead on the way to the phone. Wade, poor Wade. Already it seemed like he'd been gone forever. I put the receiver to my ear.

"Hello?"

"Oh, Alix. I'm so glad you're there," the woman said.
"Elaine?"

"I had to call. I hope you don't mind."

"Of course not," I said. "I meant to call you today." Melina
took something out of the refrigerator that looked like an
embalmed rodent under plastic wrap.

"It's Zena," Elaine was saying. "I just don't know if I can
trust her."

"Trust her?"

"She called this afternoon. She wanted to come over and
look through Shiloh's artifacts. Her Indian artifacts. She
says she's writing a book about Shiloh."

"Oh, really."

Elaine clucked her tongue. "That's what I thought. Sure,
a book."

"What did you tell her?"

"I told her the things were all in storage. And her stuff all
has to go through probate and all that. She didn't leave a
will, you know."

"No, I didn't."

Melina had emptied four Tupperware containers and held
out a fifth over the garbage can. She opened it and made a
face.

"Well, she didn't," Elaine said. "I don't know if I can even
touch her stuff. Maybe I should be boxing it all up. I don't
know."

"I think you did the right thing about Zena." It sounded
like Elaine was sipping a glass of her jug wine. "How are you
feeling after last night?"

"Oh, pretty good. I took a long nap." She giggled nervously.
"Actually I called in sick and slept all day. Isn't that sinful?"

"I think I'd do the same thing after—what?—three nights
in a row in that cave?"

"Tonight would have been the fourth."

"Listen, Elaine. Remember when I asked you about a
bluejay pictograph and you said you didn't know about one?
Could there possibly be something like that, maybe not a

bluejay but some other rock painting or rock carving in Shiloh's collection of artifacts? The ones in the garage?"

"Well, I suppose. Maybe."

"What if you and me were to take a look? It wouldn't be like Zena. Just you and me out there poking around in the garage. We wouldn't take anything, I promise. Just look in those boxes."

"I don't know, Alix. I just told Zena she couldn't."

"This bluejay pictograph might really exist. Something like the one Tilden has in the cave but smaller maybe. A professor back in the early thirties might have found it and hidden it somewhere. Shiloh could have found it. That may be why she was murdered."

"For a rock painting? Murdered for a chunk of rock?"

"I know how it sounds. But I really think it could be there in those boxes."

I left Melina on her knees, worshiping the god of Freon. Half an hour later Elaine and I pulled open the warped wooden doors to the old garage. More convincing of Elaine was in order when I arrived; then I had to wait for her to finish washing her dishes. I dried. She put away. Eventually we got to work.

"Is there a light in here?" I whispered, staring at the huge lump of boxes covered with the tarp. There was nothing else in the old building, no rusty shovels, no ancient bicycles, no mousetraps rotting in corners. The floor was clean around the perimeter of the pile. Very clean.

A fuzzy light came from the window by the lilac hedge. The one I had peered into a few days—a lifetime—ago.

Elaine moved around the stack of boxes to the right, batting at cobwebs. "I think there's a string." She squinted into the ceiling, found the string, and pulled it. A twenty-five-watt bulb flicked on, shedding a weak golden glow on the olive tarp.

We pulled the tarp outside. The sky darkened more, threatening rain. Inside the garage the tape holding the box

flaps down yielded to our fingers as we began exploring
Shiloh's stash. Elaine started on the right, I on the left,
pulling out packing paper, unwrapping dance sticks, kachina
dolls, delicate painted pots, beaded bracelets, every conceiv-
able artifact of American Indian culture. From the utilitarian
to the exotic, from feathers and fur to elk teeth and turkey
bustles, Shiloh had it all.

"Oh, my God," Elaine gasped, digging into a box.

"Did you find it?"

"Depends on your idea of 'it,' " she said, drawing something from a cardboard box. "Look at this." Carefully she let
a buckskin dress fall from her fingertips. It was a full-beaded
Sioux dress, resplendent with blue and silver beads against
the soft white buckskin.

"It's beautiful. Haven't you seen it before?"

"No. I've only seen a few of these things. Shiloh was very
guarded about her collection. I always suspected she had
some treasures though." Elaine lowered the dress back in
the box, pulling the packing material back around it.

"Too bad she didn't will it to you. That must be worth a
small fortune. I wonder where she got it."

"She had lots of friends among the Indians. But I don't
care how much it's worth. It's so incredibly beautiful. I'd
almost be afraid to own it."

"Maybe that's why she didn't display her things." I set
aside the box I'd been working on, one containing rather
plain beaded belt buckles of recent vintage and a couple of
watercolors that didn't seem important. "Find anything at
all on rock? Carving or painting either?"

"Nothing." Elaine opened another box, using her fingernails.

Rain began to fall outside, lightly at first then pounding
the roof in earnest. A drip developed, wetting the old wooden
roof boards. I shoved a box aside to get it out of the trajectory
of the falling water. Elaine began to slow down, pushing her
blond curls off her forehead, making little sighing noises. I
kept ripping open box after box, hopes rising with each new

one only to be dashed as I set it aside for another.

"What good is it going to do if we do find this bluejay thing?" Elaine sighed, dropping her hands to her sides in disgust. "What good, can you tell me?"

I looked at her. It was a good question, one I had been both struggling with and trying to ignore. I told her all I had figured out. "It will give us a motive for her murder. From motive we find the murderer. We also know Charlotte was looking for it. Then Charlotte may have killed Shiloh." Elaine looked at me, incredulous. "Maybe."

"Maybe, maybe! The only thing I'm sure of is that Shiloh is gone. Dead. I don't know about anything else anymore." Her voice rose like she might be getting ready for a good cry. I tried to think of some comforting words but again they eluded me. "And to think that a wonderful person like Shiloh would die for a stupid slab of stone?! That is the most ridiculous thing I ever heard! Why would anyone even want this bluejay pictograph? And kill someone for it? Two people even? I just don't understand—I just don't!"

With that she sat down on the nearest box and buried her face in her hands, not quite sobbing but close to it.

I stared at her, feeling inadequate. My heart was worn out with death and all the minor tragedies in its wake. But what had she said? Her words pounded in my head. *Why would anyone want the bluejay pictograph? Why would they kill someone for it? Why??* Before I knew it I had her hands in mine. "Come on, Elaine." I pulled her to her feet as she questioned me with her eyes. "We have some phone calls to make."

$\triangledown$

27

THE GARAGE SMELLED of wet wood and cockroaches in the aftermath of the storm. I wiped the sweat off my face with my shirttail as the tarp floated down over the boxes as it had before. Surveying it, kicking a box or two under the tarp, I sighed and looked at my watch. 8:45. I pulled the string, plunging the garage into darkness.

The two-days-past-full moon didn't stream its welcome light through the dirty panes of glass. Tonight would be starless, moonless, a sky sheathed in gray. The rain had stopped but the humidity rose from the pavement outside as if from a steam iron.

Stumbling around the Volkswagen-sized stack of moving boxes, I found my spot in the back. I had restacked the boxes to give me a sheltered hiding spot here. Crouching, immediately damp and uncomfortable, I waited, listening to the night.

Our visitor was thankfully prompt. I heard them talking as they came out the back door of the house. Their voices were too low to catch the words.

The wood doors scraped across the weedy dirt as they pulled them open one at a time. I felt the scrape in my guts, tightening. My breath came shallow and quick. Elaine whispered something and the tarp moved by my head, slinking away toward them as they pulled a corner. In another minute I would be exposed. My flashlight felt cool in my hand. I extracted it from my pocket, got my feet under me and stood up.

Click. The beam froze all movement except its own, wagging from side to side, searching until it homed in on the face. Before it settled I growled my line: "Find what you're looking for?"

The flashlight stopped on the face. The round face with the blue eyes and blond curls framing it like a cherub. Elaine. Elaine? She was supposed to— "What the hell, Elaine?" I hissed.

Her wide eyes blinked furiously, shining with fear, then flicked to her left. From the shadows behind her came another figure, slender but steady with a strong step.

"What the hell indeed." The voice from behind Elaine purred in the darkness. I kicked the box in front of me involuntarily, stumbled, disoriented in the dark, then moved the beam toward the voice, the corner. Cool blue eyes and tinted black hair shone in the light. It was Sylvie. In her hand she held a small gray handgun with the barrel pointed at me.

For what seemed like several minutes we stood pointing our respective weapons at each other. It was ludicrous. My silver chrome flashlight, no bigger than a banana and about as lethal, with post-modern ribbing and a tiny black button. Against her hard, cold steel with imminent projectiles. Ready to fly at me, through me, at any moment depending on the caprices of a slim white finger poised on the trigger. I tried to wrench my eyes away from her finger, to think, to say something, to act.

My hand began to shake. I caught the flashlight with the other hand and found Elaine in the darkness.

"What happened?" I whispered stupidly, as if Sylvie were not there. Elaine's eyes shone in the dark as she looked at the gun.

"I'll tell you what happened," Sylvie said smoothly. I spun the beam to her face. She squinted but her smile was pitiless. "Elaine called me back. She warned me about you. We're old friends, Elaine and I. We go way back, don't we, Elaine?" She glanced toward her in the gloom. "Don't we?"

Elaine scuffed her feet, looking down. "I've been going to Kali for about seven years."

I stared at her. "She's your *therapist*?"

"Seven years."

The scene before my eyes went hazy for a second. I felt the blood rise to my forehead, throbbing. Why hadn't she said so? "Thanks, Elaine," I spat. "A heap."

"She said no one would get hurt," Elaine squeaked. She glanced at Sylvie. "You said so."

The older woman bared her teeth savagely. "I did, didn't I?" A cold chuckle. "You shouldn't be so trusting, Elaine. We've talked about that many times, haven't we?" The mocking counselor tone was unbearable. The whites of Elaine's eyes flashed toward the light, then at Sylvie, then everywhere. I flicked off the flashlight.

A scuffle in the sudden darkness. I had the advantage since my pupils weren't quite so constricted as theirs. But the boxes made a huge obstacle course, tripping me, sending me at odd angles, awkward. When I struggled upright Sylvie stood beside me, the gun to my ribs.

"What do you want?" I snarled, my fear giving way to anger, betrayal, indignation. How dare she poke a gun barrel into my side? How dare Elaine double-cross me when I was just trying to find her lover/friend's killer? How dare they blame Wade for her madness?

"Are you going to get rid of me like you did Shiloh? Or perhaps a little cleaner, like Charlotte?" My eyes adjusted to the dimness. I surveyed the garage as Sylvie breathed hard by my shoulder. She was no longer so cool and calm.

"I want the pictograph," Sylvie said, her voice low, clipped. "You will find it now."

She shoved me into the nearest stack of boxes, keeping the gun leveled at my chest. I had to know about Shiloh.

"Wouldn't Shiloh tell you where it was?" I said. "Is that why you killed her?"

Another twisted chuckle. "Open the box. Find the pictograph for me!" She waved the gun to get me to turn and get to unpacking boxes. It worked. I moved as slowly as humanly possible. Elaine stood paralyzed by the door. I wondered how long it would be until she bolted through it.

"Shiloh stole it, didn't she?" I said, trying to get her to talk.

"Shiloh Merkin was a fool. A self-important fool!" Sylvie said behind me. "She wanted to donate the pictograph to the university. Make a great name for herself along the way. When Marcus found it himself. It belongs to Marcus!" The pitch of her voice rose with each exclamation. "Now find it!"

I opened a box, pulling the tape back slowly and carefully, dropping it at Sylvie's feet. Then I pulled out a wad of old newspaper. "I can't see a thing. It could be in here and I'd never know."

Sylvie considered, then barked, "Elaine, turn on the light."

I picked up the thread of conversation, slim as it was. "But the man who found the bluejay pictograph took it illegally. Tilden has no right to it."

"He has every right to it!" she cried. "No one knew it existed for sixty years. Shiloh was the one with no right to it."

I laid another wad of newspaper aside. "So you killed her?"

Silence. Then Elaine piped up: "Did you, Kali?"

"Find it. Now!" She poked the gun in my ribs from behind. I lurched forward against the box. I wanted to tell her I didn't think it was here. To say I knew nothing. But looking bought me time to think. To figure out a way to get her to talk.

I moved the box aside and leaned down to undo the tape on the one underneath. The barrel on my ribs followed me, sure and steady.

"Donating the pictograph would have exposed the cult, wouldn't it? Tilden must have been frantic about that."

Sylvie said nothing, digging the gun into my ribs harder.

"His reputation as a scholar would have been tarnished by her revelations. Dresses up in leather and smears black all over himself. Hops around a campfire under a full moon. Coerces women to join the cult."

"There was no coercion!" Sylvie hissed. "We had to turn women away. Women whom we couldn't trust. When we began there was a waiting list of twenty women who wanted to join."

"When you began," I said. "But now?"

"Now it is the same," she said quickly.

"Is it? Then why did you have to approach Elaine to replace Charlotte Vardis? She didn't even want to go."

The answer was another dig with the gun barrel.

"Charlotte wanted the pictograph too, didn't she? She wanted it bad. She would have done almost anything to get it. But you thought she had given up, didn't you, Sylvie? She went home to Oklahoma for the winter. But then she showed up again. What did she offer in exchange, Sylvie? To keep her mouth shut about the cult?"

"You keep your mouth shut. Find the pictograph. No more talking."

"And if I refuse? You'll deal with me like you did Shiloh and Charlotte?"

"If I have to."

Elaine gasped. I looked at her across the stack. "In front of Elaine. She'll be a witness. Or will you kill her too?"

"Elaine won't say anything, will you?" Elaine shook her head. "Then get out of here! Now!" Elaine put out her hand toward the door handle. "And don't say anything to anyone or I'll come after you next."

The door scraped open. Elaine slipped through and shut it behind her. We could hear her feet pounding toward the house, and her sobs as well. With a deep breath, calm on the surface at least, I turned and faced Sylvie.

"You don't mean to kill me or you wouldn't have let her go. She's probably in there calling the police right now."

A flicker crossed Sylvie's face. "So open the box with the pictograph. Now."

I shook my head. "It's not here. Elaine and I went through all the boxes. Shiloh must have hidden it somewhere else." I smiled at her and the gun she held loosely in her hand. Her wrist was bent, pointing the gun toward the boxes. I thought of running but she tightened her grasp on it then, pointing it toward me again.

"I don't believe you."

"Look for yourself. Here," I said offering her my flashlight. "Use mine."

Sylvie stepped forward and grabbed my outstretched arm at the wrist, twisting it fiercely. She poked the gun into my stomach. I gasped, feeling the barrel against my diaphragm, the cold reality of it. Then the hot breath of Sylvie, expelled through her clenched teeth, made me blink, fear rippling through me.

"You will find it right now or have a hole in you big enough to walk through." She was so close I felt her saliva on my chin as she spat out the words. She loosened her grip enough to spin me around toward the boxes. Her gun took up a position over my kidneys.

The loud scrape of the door opening sounded like the gun going off. I flinched, waiting for the searing pain of the bullet. Only after blinking did I realize that the garage door had been opened. A man stood silhouetted in the streetlight at the end of the driveway.

"What are you doing, Sylvie?"

Marcus Tilden stared at us, his bulging black eyes uncomprehending. His deep voice seemed out of place.

"M-Marcus. Get out of here." Sylvie tightened her grip on me, digging the gun barrel in.

"What have you got there?" Tilden took a step forward. "Is that a gun?"

"Get out of here, Marcus," she repeated. "I'm looking for the pictograph. If you leave I will find it for you. For us."

He took another step forward. "Elaine says you killed Shiloh. Did you, Sylvie?"

"Please, Marcus. Leave," she pleaded.

"Why, Sylvie? Why did you kill Shiloh? She was like a daughter to me." His voice broke and I saw the tears well in his eyes.

"More than a daughter, I'd say." Sylvie's voice was back to its original venom level; she ground the gun into my rib cage. "I knew about you and her. You didn't think I knew, but I did. You just couldn't leave them alone."

"You're tired, Sylvie. We haven't had much sleep. Give me the gun."

I felt her arm shaking. "You screwed them all, didn't you, Marcus? You don't even have the decency to deny it! When we began the bluejay dance I thought I could help you, bring you back to me, be a part of your life. But you just kept screwing them, didn't you?"

"Sylvie, please. Give me the gun," Tilden said smoothly.

"Give him the gun!" I pleaded in a whisper.

"Give, give! I give you everything, Marcus. Everything!" Her voice began to break. "And what do you do to repay me? Fuck everything with two legs. Even that bitch Shiloh. She was going to ruin you, Marcus. She would have told everyone you stole the pictograph."

"No, she wouldn't. Shiloh cared for me." Tilden's voice sounded strange suddenly.

Sylvie shoved me against the boxes. I felt the corner of one in my gut, expelling my air. The hand I had in front of me kept me from tumbling headfirst onto the cement.

"SHE cared for you?! HER?" Sylvie backed away from Tilden, waving the gun wildly. He dodged its trajectory but kept his advance. "Stay away from me, Marcus! You don't care about me."

"I do care about you, Sylvie. Put down the gun."

"You don't care." Her hard face began to dissolve in misery. "I did so much for you. I killed her for you, don't you see?" She was crying now, tears streaming down her cheeks. She held the gun with both hands. "For you, Marcus. So we could go on together. Just you and me, Marcus."

"We can still go on if you put down the gun," he said with no emotion.

"No, no, we can't now, Marcus," she cried, still backing slowly away. I turned, sinking lower against the boxes. "It's too late. You never cared enough. And now it's too late."

In a swift movement she turned the gun around and put it in her mouth. Time stopped for a second. I will never forget the blueness of her eyes, the whiteness of her skin in the eerie light of the dank garage. The artificial blue-black glints of her hair in the outrageous braids. Outside the city lights reflected off the low clouds, giving everything a close, claustrophobic intensity.

There was no time for Tilden to grab her, to stop her from pulling the trigger. He yelled "NO!" but she was right. It was too late. She was gone.

Gasping, deep, pained, and rhythmic. In the dark I couldn't be sure if it was me or someone else. Sirens pierced the night. Feet pounded on the cement, then a cry took up its place in the unholy scheme of the night.

My eyes were shut. I sat trembling on the floor, my back to a box, my hands over my face. I didn't want to see. I never wanted to see again. But when Mendez came, rubbed my arms to bring me back to life, pulled me up onto his chest and held me there, when the sounds began to crowd out the silence and chaos, confusion, shouts, cries, voices everywhere filling the old garage, my eyes opened. I saw her. I could not help myself.

At the police station I tried to keep my eyes open all the time. That way the visions of gray steel tables and chairs, flat white walls, and policemen smoking cigarettes and taking notes blotted out the memory. Even a blink was enough to open the window to the memory that clung behind my eyeballs like an old piece of gum that you never can get off your shoe. Scrape all you want but it'll still be there. Use some fancy cleaner and the stain remains. Only time, and a lot of walking, can erase it.

Melina came, sitting with me as I told the story again to a different set of cops. They asked me questions. I told them everything I knew, babbling on like they were interested in my father's old Impala that sailed into Flathead Lake or my hunches that caused the eventual arrest of the Andy Warhol forgers back in '87. They nodded and brought me back to the subject. I could see them, hear them doing it, yet I talked on.

Melina called Hondo, who sat close to me, pressing my knee whenever he wanted to interrupt. He did that a lot; it took most of the night. At three they all left the room except Melina and me. She sat with her head propped against the wall, eyes closed. I wanted to tell her how I hadn't wanted Sylvie to die, how I didn't know that would happen. But I remembered she had heard me tell the police the same thing.

Mendez stuck his head in the room. I smiled at him. My eyes were getting harder and harder to keep open. He slipped in, his brown eyes weary. His uniform had lost its creases long ago. I touched a button on his shirt pocket.

He glanced at Melina and whispered, "I think we're done for tonight. Elaine told them everything that happened." He shook his head. "She's pretty hysterical." He rubbed my leg tenderly. "How are you doing?"

"Okay," I whispered even though on the inside a horrible battle raged, a battle that would continue at least through the night. A maelstrom of guilt and justice, of victory and agonizing defeat, of relief and searing pain. He looked into my eyes. I wondered if he could see it raging.

"You sure?" he asked. I nodded, looking away. I didn't need any soul-searching eye contact tonight. He rubbed my neck the way he had the other night. I closed my eyes at how good it felt but opened them quickly again as the memory of Sylvie came flooding back.

I took his hand, pulling him around in front of my chair. He sat down next to me. His fingers were so soft. "What will happen to Tilden?"

He shrugged. "They're questioning him about the other two deaths. But he probably wasn't involved. Except that he was boffing them, of course." He pushed my bangs back off my forehead. "I'd say his career at the university is over." Detective Knox came into the room then and cleared his throat. Mendez dropped my hand and stood up.

"You're free to go, Miss Thorssen," Knox said. "We know how to reach you." He turned and left the room.

Mendez took my hand again and drew me up. "I'll take you home."

"What about Melina?"

She opened her eyes. "I can get myself home. I'll see you there, Alix." She gave me a small kiss on the cheek and shuffled out.

We took the El Dorado. His shift, even the extra one, had been over hours ago. I was thinking again about the call I'd made to him before everything happened. It was an afterthought, and even then I hadn't gotten him directly. Had to leave a message with the dispatcher. If only I'd tried a little harder, maybe Sylvie would still be alive.

Could I have saved Sylvie from herself? From the demons that tormented her? From the husband who neglected her? Hadn't she already made those irreversible decisions herself?

Mendez said nothing. If he had his own questions about my role in Sylvie's death, he didn't say. We sat at the curb in front of the house on Blaine Street. His eyes widened in surprise as I pulled him close, ran my hands up under his shirt to feel his strong back, and licked his ear. I needed him. He filled the emptiness inside me for a moment. We made love in the backseat of the El Dorado. My eyes stayed open.

$\triangledown$

28

WADE'S INDEPENDENCE DAY. Even though it was the fifth of July—not the fourth—it still made me smile. So did the nearly flat, placid waters of Flathead Lake, the cool breeze that cut through the mountain sunshine, tossing the mule's ears' bright yellow-daisy flower heads to and fro. A day to be free, that it was.

And Wade was free. Hondo had driven us up late in the morning as soon as the paperwork had been filed for dropping the charges. Melina and I had gathered Wade up, gotten in the old red boat of a Cadillac and driven to the west shore of the lake. We had spent an hour filling Wade in on the events of the last few days. The sun had warmed us as we finished eating dill pickles and ham sandwiches that Melina had packed.

Wade moved up on one elbow from his prone position on the blanket. He was thinner but happier than I had seen him in a long time. He stroked his beard thoughtfully. "So what did this Charlotte Vardis have to do with Tilden?"

"She got hooked up with the cult somehow. I guess she found out about the bluejay pictograph and got fixated on owning it," I said, shading my eyes to look at him. The bright daylight seemed to be melting the bad memories out of my brain. "She found the best way to get to Tilden was in the sack. But he still wouldn't give it to her, I guess."

"So she went home to Oklahoma," Mel said, "then came back this spring?"

"She spent some time up here last summer communing

under the full moon with the bluejay shaman. Maybe she tried to forget about it but couldn't. At any rate she came back about the time that Shiloh got murdered."

"That was just coincidence?"

"I guess. Tilden said she called him earlier in June and wanted to meet him as soon as he got back from Seattle. Which was not the date he told the cops."

"Why did he lie about that?" Wade asked.

"He came back early to meet Charlotte. Sylvie got wind of it and followed. But she thought it was Shiloh he was with and so killed her. Tilden had been with Shiloh but not that particular weekend."

"I'd like to see his date book," Wade grinned. Melina gave him a playful kick. I was happy to see them together again at last. It made me wonder about what would happen this fall when Melina was to start her doctoral program back East. "So then what happened to Charlotte?"

"She must have found out about Sylvie's doings. That's what I think. She offered to help Sylvie if Sylvie would help her get the bluejay pictograph. Charlotte didn't know that Shiloh had it at this point."

"How did Shiloh get it?"

"She stole it from Tilden. At least that's what he says."

Melina held up her hands. "Wait a minute. What did Charlotte do to help Sylvie?"

"She called me, sending me on a wild goose chase because I was nosing around."

"But then Sylvie figured out it was Charlotte who was making whoopee with her husband," Melina said. I bobbed my head, still feeling the exhilaration of the pieces falling into place and giving myself over to that feeling. It was better than guilt.

Wade rose slowly, sighing as he got to his feet. He went to the back of the Cadillac, made a fist, and banged the trunk in a certain spot that caused it to pop open. Mel smiled at me. What a guy.

I lay back down on the blanket and felt the breeze off the

lake tickle my face. My eyes could close now fairly safely, without more than an iota of memory flashing up. Steeling myself, I closed them, feeling the heat of the sun on my lids. I pulled the hat over my eyes.

"Got something for you, Alix." Wade's figure blotted out the sun. He held a large parcel wrapped in brown paper, lumpy but flat, in both hands. Carefully he set it on the blanket in front of me and sat down. "Open it."

"What is it?" I asked, fingering the taped edges but hesitating.

"When did you have time to buy her a present?" Melina wanted to know. I wanted to know too.

"Just open it!" Wade said, waving his hands over it eagerly.

I did as I was told. Inside the brown paper was a newspaper. Inside that was an old towel. Inside that was a square hunk of rock, smooth and red, hacked away at the edges to make it square. On the face of it was the bluejay shaman, legs up in dance, a blue crest and tail on the stick-figure man.

My jaw dropped. I had begun to believe it didn't even exist, that these people had wanted to believe in it so badly that they had made it up. But here it was. I drew my fingers lightly over the painted lines of the birdman. This was what two people had died for?

"Where did you find it?" demanded Melina.

"The cops had it all the time. It must have been in my trunk. When they gave me back all my stuff this was with it."

"But how?" Mel continued. I was still dumbstruck, feeling the stone with all fingers to make sure it was real.

"Shiloh," Wade said. "That's what I figure. The day I was at their camp, remember? We had that argument. But before that I was there a long time talking to Tin-Tin. Shiloh must have been worried about the rock getting into the wrong hands or something. She wanted it donated to the university, right? So she stashes it in my trunk. And at the same time—"

"She gets your knife," I said.

"Right. She was nervous, uptight. Maybe Sylvie had taken a swipe at her before."

"She was supposed to have all her things moved into storage that day," I said. "But somebody canceled it for her."

"Somebody who must have thought the pictograph was there," Mel said. "But why didn't Sylvie just break in and get it?"

"Because by then she was terrified because she'd killed Shiloh," I said. "She didn't want to be associated with Shiloh at all. Remember how strange she was at the memorial service? Detached? I don't think she meant to kill her. Otherwise she would have brought the gun. Maybe Shiloh pulled the knife on her, they struggled, and that's when Sylvie killed her."

I had been rubbing the stone painting unconsciously while we talked. As I looked down now I was horrified to see that some of the paint was now on my fingertips, flaked off at my touch. "Oh, my God," I gasped.

"Alix!" Melina cried.

To our amazement, Wade, the passionate professor, keeper of the native flame, friend to Indians across the prairie, only laughed. I had defaced a native icon, a spiritual symbol of an ancient people—and he laughed! I stared at him, awestruck.

He held up his hands helplessly. "I'm sorry. I didn't set you up. But it took me only one look at this to know it was a fake."

"A fake?" I touched it again, bending closer to the stone. "It looks so old."

"Oh, it's old," he explained. "About 1930, I'd say. No older than that. See this blue paint?" He pointed at the crest and tail of the birdman. "Tribes didn't have any natural blue dyes until they traded with the whites. All their natural colors were black, red, white, a little yellow, like that. No blue. At least no blue that would last in the weather for decades and not fade." He pointed at the crest of the figure. "And the work itself. It just doesn't look Salish. It's not something they would do."

"So who did this?" Melina asked.

"Probably old Seymour Smith, I'd guess," Wade said. "But nobody believed him with all his credential problems underway."

"So he stashed this away somewhere in the anthropology department," I said.

"And Tilden found it, anointed himself bluejay shaman, and began dancing the two-step." He shook his head. "Was Tilden the one responsible for the vandalism too?"

I nodded. "He had the women do some of it. He wanted to wake up the tribe, he said. Make them realize their native religion. Drive out the Catholics. I think Sylvie was responsible for the last of it with the spray paint. And that was just to implicate me."

"He's so—" Wade sputtered, his face reddening. "He never could see that meddling into their religion the way he persists in doing is just as bad as the Jesuits! He wants to change their history. Go back in time before the priests, before any whites."

Melina whispered: "You can't go back."

As the afternoon sun traveled the western sky we agreed that Marcus Tilden was a sorry excuse for an anthropology professor or human being. Melina was convinced that he drove Sylvie mad with his philandering. Wade was kind enough not to bring up that flirtation of years past but I felt it hovering in the air anyway.

Wade traced Tilden's break with reality to his long-time fascination with pagan religious practices. He apparently had been a member of the Native American Church in the sixties and ingested more than his share of peyote buttons. He tried everything, and when that didn't satisfy his craving for spiritual enlightenment, he made up his own religion.

As for me, I say he broke her heart. Sylvie couldn't reach into his world as much as she tried. No amount of marriage counseling or dream therapy or crystal-balling would let her touch that private part of him that needed so much nurturing. She saw that it did. But he wouldn't let her in. And it destroyed her.

$\triangledown$

Epilogue

MENDEZ MADE A last appearance before I left. I was packing the Saab Sister, thinking about him and what I would say to him, when he drove up in the El Dorado. The weather had turned beastly hot again. All I could think about was my cool mountains, my Tetons, wetting a line in a trickling glacial stream.

He was wearing his jogging clothes, shorts and a tank top that showed off his physique. My resolve for a clean break with him melted in the afternoon sun. We lived too far apart, my reasoning went. Send me a Christmas card and we'll call it even.

Fifteen minutes later I had squirted him with the new sprinkler Wade had turned on to rejuvenate the lawn and we had made plans to go backpacking in August in the Tetons. If Wade hadn't come out on the porch with a thermos of coffee for me I probably would have had Carl in the backseat of my car, licking the sweat from every inch of his body.

As for Wade and Melina, they seemed to be starting over. Wade took leave for the fall quarter and will go back East with Melina while she begins her program. He promised to at least consider a position back there somewhere while she is getting her doctorate. This, to Melina, was a huge victory, more than she had ever hoped for. She positively glowed, making her plans.

The prospects for Tilden weren't so cheery. The scandal, with all its juicy details of sex, moonlit ritual, and religion, hit the Montana papers with a splash reserved for really hot